Books by Spider Robinson:

*TELEMPATH
CALLAHAN'S CROSSTIME SALOON
*STARDANCE (with Jeanne Robinson)
ANTINOMY
THE BEST OF ALL POSSIBLE WORLDS
TIME TRAVELERS STRICTLY CASH
MINDKILLER
MELANCHOLY ELEPHANTS
*NIGHT OF POWER
CALLAHAN'S SECRET
CALLAHAN AND COMPANY (omnibus)
TIME PRESSURE
*CALLAHAN'S LADY
COPYRIGHT VIOLATION
TRUE MINDS
*STARSEED (with Jeanne Robinson)
KILL THE EDITOR
*LADY SLINGS THE BOOZE
THE CALLAHAN TOUCH
*STARMIND (with Jeanne Robinson)
OFF THE WALL AT CALLAHAN'S
CALLAHAN'S LEGACY
*DEATHKILLER (omnibus)
*LIFEHOUSE
THE CALLAHAN CHRONICALS (omnibus)
*THE STAR DANCERS (with Jeanne Robinson)
*USER FRIENDLY
*BY ANY OTHER NAME
THE FREE LUNCH
CALLAHAN'S KEY
GOD IS AN IRON and other stories
CALLAHAN'S CON
*VERY BAD DEATHS
VARIABLE STAR (with Robert A. Heinlein)

* Baen Books

VERY HARD CHOICES

BY

SPIDER ROBINSON

BAEN

VERY HARD CHOICES

Copyright © 2008 by Spider Robinson.

A Baen Books Original

Baen Publishing Enterprises
P.O. Box 1403
Riverdale, NY 10471
www.baen.com

ISBN 10: 1-4165-5556-0
ISBN 13: 978-1-4165-5556-8

Cover art by Stephen Hickman

First printing, June 2008

Distributed by Simon & Schuster
1230 Avenue of the Americas
New York, NY 10020

Library of Congress Cataloging-in-Publication Data

Robinson, Spider.
  Very hard choices / by Spider Robinson.
      p. cm.
  "A Baen Books original"--T.p. verso.
  ISBN 1-4165-5556-0
  1. Widowers--Fiction. 2. Psychics--Fiction. 3.
Police--British Columbia--Fiction. 4. British
Columbia--Fiction. I. Title.

  PS3568.O3156V48 2008
  813'.54--dc22

2008005951

Printed in the United States of America

10 9 8 7 6 5 4 3 2 1

Dedication:

For Jim Baen, David Crosby,
and John Barnstead:
wise, kind and generous men.

ADVISORY:

This program contains scenes of violence, nudity, sexuality, adult themes, casual drug use, committed drug use, incorrect politics, coarse language, fine language, extensive use of fixed, nonmoving cameras, and numerous shots lasting longer than three seconds. Viewer discretion is definitely NOT advised: tell all your friends.

1.

Saturday, June 23, 2007
Vancouver, British Columbia, Canada

This is how it was for him—not a reconstruction or guesswork. I have it on reliable authority.

Charles Haden had expected the border to be a joke, but it was barely even a sitcom punchline. He needn't have wasted one of his few remaining genuine passports. (But then, if this trip paid off, that worry would join all his others.) Length of stay, Mr. Haden? One week. Purpose of trip? I'm retired now and I always heard Vancouver was the most beautiful city on earth. Big smile and a pass.

No wonder his own government said terrorists streamed across this border at will into America: it was one of the few things his government claimed to believe nowadays that made sense. That not one terrorist had actually done so since the War of 1812 was a striking testament to the monumental stupidity of terrorists as a class. Drug dealers were smarter. Even poor Mexicans were beginning to figure out how cheap a ticket to Vancouver or Calgary was, and how much easier and more pleasant the northern border crossing. Any day now, al-Qaeda were going to wise up. It reminded Haden how important this operation was, how mortal the stakes—a reminder he did not need, as he had thought of little else for decades.

The half hour drive up to Vancouver calmed his nerves. Driving

1

is combat with rules, and Canadians had more of them and obeyed them *all*. By American standards the highest ranking male he encountered on that highway would have rated no higher than gamma or delta. He found himself thinking that he *usually* felt like a wolf loose among unsuspecting sheep, but here the sheep were drugged, hobbled and blindfolded. Just as well; he reminded himself it had been a long time since he'd done one of these insertions.

Halfway there, the observation was underlined. A breakdown in the right lane forced two lanes to merge into one. And the strangest thing happened: the two lanes merged into one. Every single driver in the left lane slowed, deliberately allowed a car from the right lane to pull in front of him . . . and no more than one car at a time ever took advantage of his weakness. The two lines of traffic meshed like a zipper, as if their behavior were rational. Haden found it irritating.

He saw large exit signs for a place with the implausible name of Tsawwassen. His GPS told him it was a very large ferry terminus servicing gigantic Vancouver Island, which was roughly the size of Maine and began thirty-odd miles offshore. That was the last feature of even that much interest on that highway for a long time. For most of the trip there was nothing at all visible in any direction. Endless fields of indistinguishable green growing crap, with and without smelly animals grazing on it. A zillion trees. Hills. A ton of distant mountains. Nothing at all. Postcards.

A few miles—no, kilometers—later, they went through a rather long tunnel underneath something called the Fraser River, and he noticed there was not a single camera in the tunnel. Yet each car stayed in its lane as requested, even when the other lane was moving faster.

Just short of the city he left the highway and deked west to the airport. He entered the long-term parking lot, idled around until he saw a woman park and walk away with a vast amount of luggage suggesting a lengthy trip, and swapped license plates with her. It took so little time the attendant let him leave without paying.

Shortly he went over a structure that his GPS absurdly insisted was both the Oak Street Bridge and the Arthur Laing Bridge, which spanned the same damn Fraser River he'd already passed beneath earlier. It got Haden thinking about the unreliability of names, and being high above water it was a fine place to scale a driver's license and passport out the window. By the time he reached the city limits of Vancouver, he had completed an ID dump, both the supporting documents and the persona itself.

Thomas McKinnon felt a little better once he was surrounded by tall piles of steel and stone and glass again. Other drivers started to act a bit more sensibly. The first chance he got he pulled over to the curb, opened his laptop, stole access and googled the lot where towed vehicles are stored by the Vancouver police. It was at 1410 Granville Street, which turned out to somehow be located underneath the Granville Street Bridge.

Even in Canada, traffic-impound lots are reasonably well-secured. But even in the paranoid States they're secured in only one direction, because nobody but cops and tow-finks ever drive one the other way. McKinnon's timing was good. After a single reconaissance spin around the block, he was able to drive right in, remove both his stolen license plates and put them in his travel bag, abandon the rest of the car, and walk right out without being seen. Everyone would assume someone else had screwed up the paperwork, and the car might stay there for weeks or even months. He only needed days. The identity that had rented it, far away in another country, no longer existed. He carried everything he was likely to need in a bag small enough to fit under an airline seat.

Almost everything.

He let his walking instincts take over, and within an hour he had located a place to buy a gun and a set of ID good enough to last a week. It was one block from police headquarters, but that did not alarm, amuse, or even interest him. He knew cities in which police headquarters would have been where to buy a gun. He loitered, watched a boatload of drugs being sold, had a few oblique conversations, and in under two hours he exchanged a fat sheaf of genuine U.S. currency for passable documents identifying him as "Thomas McKinnon," a Glock in reasonably good condition, a small-of-the-back holster, and four magazines. It was the "woman's model" Glock, with "only" 17 bullets instead of the 19 or 22 cops used, but he felt when you put 17 slugs in a man you've done enough for him. If he got himself into a fix that many rounds couldn't get him out of, two more wouldn't help.

Once he was armed and papered, McKinnon went shopping for another car. He settled on a Toyota Camry just too old to have a GPS locator in it, had it open and started in seconds, and drove it around until he found a spot where he felt comfortable dumping its license plates down a sewer drain and replacing them with the ones he'd stolen from the airport. Fifteen minutes, start to finish.

He was in a foreign nation, undocumented, with adequate ID that led absolutely nowhere, adequately armed and funded and wheeled. In one day. Not bad for a man his age, out of practice.

Afternoon rush hour was beginning to get under way by then, but McKinnon didn't fight it because he believed he had lots of time. And he was indeed right back where he had started, a block from police headquarters, just as the day shift must be ending. But after half an hour it was clear there was a problem of some kind; no gathering of black-clad crows was apparent.

He spotted a pedestrian who looked snotty, rolled down his window and asked if this was where the police officers came off shift. Sure enough, the man could not resist explaining to him how stupid he was.

Shortly he had to agree: he should have realized that if a city's police headquarters is situated one block from an enormous open-air drug bazaar like something out of Dante or Dali, that city will almost inevitably pretend police headquarters is somewhere else. The nominal headquarters, including the lockers and parking lot for all four of Vancouver's patrol team districts, turned out to be located miles away. And underneath a bridge, just like the traffic-impound lot—only this time it was on Cambie Street . . . underneath the Cambie Street Bridge.

(He wondered idly if all Canadian bridges were Möbius strips, the same at top and bottom. If he had driven beneath the one that was called *both* Oak Street Bridge and Arthur Laing Bridge, would he have found a second Oak Street, with a man named Arthur laying in it, perhaps?)

He finally found the place—and wasted yet another hour before conceding that he had reached it just *after* shift-change. For some reason they changed shifts *during rush hour* here. He controlled his irritation and had the GPS direct him to the target's address of record. In a sense, he got lucky then. The reason his target had moved and the new address wasn't in the system anywhere yet was that the listed address, an apartment building, had been badly enough damaged by a recent fire to be condemned. So he did not have to waste several hours staking the place out, before admitting to himself there was nothing more he could do until morning. If police shift changed at 6:00 PM, the next change would come at 2:00 AM, and the one he wanted at 10:00 AM. He got himself a meal and a room, and was alone in bed well before prime time ended and the news came on.

As usual these days, sleep came hard to him. It was the worst part of aging, worse than the aches. Each time he woke he used every relaxation technique he knew, but a little after four in the morning he knew he had slept all he was going to. Room service had not, so he showered, dressed in the clothes he'd worn the day before, and took the Camry out to look for an all-night restaurant. That took so long that a sense of stubborn professionalism made him decide to swing by the fake police headquarters first: four hours early was a good time to look it over.

A *very* good time: somehow he had badly misjudged the time of shift change, and it was unmistakably in progress *now*, at—Jesus, at 7:00 AM.

The same huge edifice also housed the headquarters of ICBC, the primary auto insurance company in the province of British Columbia, so naturally there was no possibility of a civilian vehicle parking or standing legally anywhere within blocks of the building. Accident victims who've just hobbled several blocks on their crutches or walkers are much easier to negotiate with. But fortunately for him, there was a combination of bad signage and diabolically placed one-way streets that made it almost impossible *not* to circle the building half a dozen times seeking escape from the loop. On his fourth go-round an infuriated McKinnon spotted his target emerging from the Stalinesque structure in his rearview mirror, in a crowd of other officers all carrying laptops under their arms like some nightmare of Steve Jobs's and walking north toward the parking lot.

He pulled over just past it and pretended to consult an imaginary map until the target drove past him, in a private vehicle. He noted the make, model and plate number, and let two other cars go by before pulling out. Tailing a police officer by oneself can be tricky, but again he encountered no problems he could not cope with. Within half a mile or so—no, he reminded himself for the last time, within a kilometer or so—he let the traffic cause him to start closing the distance.

When he saw a chance, he pulled into the right lane and made as if he intended to pass illegally on the right. Just as he entered the other driver's blind spot, he powered his window down, took something that looked just like a laundry marker from an inside pocket of his suit jacket, and used it to fire a GPS-snitch the size of an AAA battery at the rear bumper of the other car.

He *loved* using that sort of James Bond junk, always had, but his luck so far had been so unreasonably good he almost expected this to fail. He couldn't help grinning when it worked just fine, stuck fast on contact and began reconfiguring itself. A second later he sensed he was moving into the target's peripheral vision, and elaborately mimed a man suddenly realizing he's about to illegally pass a police officer and reconsidering his plan. He slowed drastically, dropped behind, and took the first right he could. From that point on, he never again came within two blocks of his target's field of vision, or needed to.

He was an old fart, no mistake about it, but he hadn't lost a step. Not yet, by God. And the prize he had sought for half a century as passionately and monomaniacally as Sidney Greenstreet had pursued the black bird was almost in his grasp at last, only weeks after he had finally begun to despair. Time enough for coffee and breakfast later. Life was good.

He had no idea that his target had made him even before she had driven past his parked car that first time, back under the Cambie Street Bridge.

2.

Saturday, June 23, 2007
Heron Island, British Columbia, Canada

Horsefeathers the cat purred in ecstasy as Jesse's fingernails found the right spot behind his ears. I stopped short of the screen door with the tray of drinks in my hands and stood silently a few moments, for the pleasure of watching my son unobserved, out there on the sun deck.

I got all too few chances. I'd had that deck built partly in hopes of getting him to come out to B.C. and spend some time sitting out there on it with me. Son on sun deck. Bright sun deck produces bright son. An effective magical pun.

Gee, I found myself thinking, too bad I don't have a magic *wife* deck, too. That'd get him for sure.

I swept that all away, and used all those precious seconds to study my only child, hungrily, as if trying to map him so well that I'd be able to recreate him with available atoms some day, like a transporter beam. Almost thirty years younger than me . . . three inches taller, three inches broader, and twenty pounds heavier, not boney like me . . . fit and strong, not a semi-invalid like me . . . buzzcut and cleanshaven, straight-looking even to a normal contemporary, let alone to his "old-school" hippie dad . . . beyond doubt the most expensively and tastefully dressed young man on Heron Island, and possibly in the Lower Mainland of British Columbia as well. I found

7

myself looking for any feature or other visible characteristic we shared—or for that matter, any trait of his mother's that manifested in him—and came up empty. I wanted to understand him, who he was, so well that one day I might risk telling him who I was and some of the things I had done. And I had high hopes that today might be the day we at least began that process, reopened the lines of communication, made a start. He was thirty, I was nearly sixty; if not now, when? God knew it had been long enough coming.

The heart-stopping beauty of the place where I live was surely on my side. I'd managed to rid myself of more than one stubborn grudge sitting out there on that sunporch; raw nature is nothing but object lessons, really. Try explaining to a crow that you have reason to feel sour, or making a passing dragonfly see that it's all about you. Tell a hundred-foot-tall pine how far behind schedule you are. Even a City Mouse like Jesse had to be feeling it, or at least starting to by now: peace. Give it a chance, I thought.

I smiled, slid the screen door open, and stepped out onto my magic sun deck with the tray of refreshments.

"Christ, Dad, how can you stand it out here?" my son asked. Horsefeathers jumped down off his lap and went off to find his friend Fraidy, the half-mad feral cat who grudgingly permits me to feed her.

I glanced around. "Too many bugs? Let's go in."

"Not out *here*. I mean *out here*—in the middle of nowhere on a tiny island at the ass end of the universe. A week here and I'd go out of my mind."

I sighed, and set the tray down on the table. "What would be so bad about that? *Two* weeks, and you might go back into it again." I went back and slid the screen door closed again. "And find it improved by your absence."

"What if you have one of your lung collapses out here? A bad one?"

I shrugged. "If I do, I'm an hour or two from a good hospital. And since I live in a civilized country instead of America, my medical care is covered."

He gave me The Look, said, "Dada," and shook his head. It was the way he said it that made my heart suddenly heavy in my chest.

※ ※ ※ ※

Jesse first started calling me that in precocious early adolescence, a pun on his very first word intended to indicate that he found me surreal. Fair enough: many do. It had started out a friendly enough insult, became contemptuous briefly during the worst of *late* adolescence, then reverted to a mere family joke again for nearly a decade . . . but ever since his mother was diagnosed it had been an epithet, the kind intended to be fighting words. This was the first glimpse of the blade concealed in the scabbard. He had been scrupulously polite since his arrival—but now, after less than half an hour in my home, my son just had to confirm that he still hated me and everything I stood for, hated the place I stood itself.

I told myself not to panic. He was all I had left of his mother; he *could not* be lost to me for good. She would not like it, so I must not permit it. Failure was not an option. A probability, maybe, but not an option.

I took a seat across the round table from him, passed him the beer he'd asked for, and used the ritual of constructing myself an Irish coffee to get some thinking done.

All right, then. If you must make the deal, and you can't make the deal, the problem has to be that you have failed to correctly see through the other party's eyes.

So I tried as hard as I could to look through Jesse's eyes. First at our surroundings, which to me were so surpassingly, transcendently idyllic.

I lived in a shithole, in Nowheresville.

Oh, there was indoor plumbing. It was a real house, nowhere near as rustic and primitive as some of the hippie shacks in which I'd spent my own early adulthood, over on the far side of the continent— Jesse had heard about those, even if he didn't remember them, and had seen photos. This place had electricity, lights, hot water, central heat, cable TV, highspeed internet access . . . well, it had all those things as long as it had the first one, anyway. And the power seldom went out more than once a month or so, unless it did, or for more than a day or so, unless it was longer. Even then the place stayed warm and tight in winter for as long as the firewood held out: it was a real, professionally built and properly maintained house, not something thrown together by hippies out of scrap lumber like the shack in which he had been conceived and nursed.

But to a New York public relations man, the distinction must be barely noticeable. It was a cheap little prefab cottage surrounded by completely unimproved wilderness in an out-of-the way corner of a relatively undeveloped island forty horrendously inconvenient minutes by ferry from the mainland and another hour's drive from anything worth doing or going to. The deck on which we sat was solid, honestly made and recently painted—but it was cheap, simple carpentry done with inexpensive materials. Even though I'd swept it thoroughly that morning, it was already lightly covered with crap that had blown down from the thirty-meter-tall trees all around, and I could already see at least a dozen new spiderwebs established at various right angles. Around deck and house were no garden, no flowers, no hedges or plantings, just raw nature, northern rainforest variety. Bugs, big and small. Other unknown small fauna. Paved road was a couple of hundred meters of deeply rutted driveway away, invisible through the trees. And all it led to was an island so small and undeveloped it had no bank branch, no taxi, no gas station, no hospital, no hotel, a single block with sidewalks and streetlights, one pub, and three restaurants. He did not yet know that one of the restaurants was excellent and another superb.

And of course since it was in Canada the island must be a frozen wasteland in winter, just like Nova Scotia. I had told him about B.C. weather, repeatedly, but I could tell he didn't believe me. In any case, it was in Canada—where they let queers get married and the money was worth doodly and the government took most of it in taxes and the socialized medicine system didn't work and everyone smoked pot and civil war was imminent and nobody could play football for shit and Arab terrorists crossed over into America all the time.

Only the first of those is actually true, but try telling an American. A straight one, anyway.

All this in the time it took to pour hot water out of my mug, dip the wet rim in the sugar bowl, turn it rightside up again, pour Tanzanian coffee into it, and add the Jameson's.

So much for the surroundings.

Next, I turned my son's merciless eye on *me*.

Old fart, just for a start. I had been calling myself a middle-aged fart for years now, but who was I kidding? I was eight years past the middle of my life even if I was going to get a century like my grandfather had, which I doubted.

Stir the sugar in; smell the coffee and whiskey getting acquainted. See your reflection recoalesce in the surface.

Worse than an old fart: a loser. Long scraggly hippie hair I had washed but probably forgotten to brush. Beard and mustache I could tell I had forgotten to trim. Dressed in drip dry mail order plaid shirt and unpressed jeans, generic socks, and superbly comfortable but undeniably ratty slippers, all of these finely coated with the hairs of my one and a half cats. My watch was the cheapest Timex sold. I wore old-fashioned eyeglasses with clip-on shades against the summer sunlight, instead of the self-polarizing contact lenses he had. The stud in his left earlobe was worth more than everything I was wearing, and his shoes cost more than my monthly mortgage payment. I could not have loitered in his neighborhood for more than a few minutes before being asked to state my business. Not even on a dark night: one of my pockets held marijuana so transcendently pungent that even I was aware of it, and to him I must have reeked.

And what has he got to compare to all this? I asked myself as I added an extra dollop of whipped cream to my Irish coffee. *A luxury apartment with parking, maid service and a view of Central Park, a job that brings in a hundred thousand U.S. a year, the respect of the powerful and privileged, a never-ending supply of beautiful intelligent women, the cultural, commercial and culinary attractions of New York . . . hell, who* wouldn't *dump all that in a hot minute to move here?*

Well, it's *good* to drink your Irish coffee in big gulps, before it has time to cool off.

"Do you remember when we moved from Halifax to Toronto?" I asked him.

"Sure. I was nearly seven."

"What did you think of the place? Can you still remember?"

He shrugged. "I hated it, and I see where you're going. I came to like it, yes. Eventually I found compensations for its immediately obvious drawbacks. I guess if I had to live here long enough, I'd find the compensations here, too. Thank God I don't."

"New York has no drawbacks."

He shook his head. "None I've ever noticed."

The caffeine and ethanol were playing tug of war with my brain, stimulant versus depressant. Isometric intoxication. "Stepping over the bodies on the sidewalk doesn't bother you?"

"There aren't any on my block."

"And you don't mind what it costs to live on that block."

He smiled. "I can afford it."

Only because you work for Mordor, I thought, but I couldn't say it, because if I did we were done now. I finished my Irish coffee instead.

Okay. Time to . . . what was the military euphemism? . . . to retire to a previously prepared position. It sounds so much nicer than "retreat."

"You certainly can. I respect that. I hope you know how proud of you I am, Jess. How's your work these days?"

"Intense but incredibly well paid."

I forced a smile. "I was thinking more along the lines of information I didn't have already."

"What would that be, exactly? You're a journalist."

I sighed. "I've told you before, I'm *not*. I'm a columnist."

"That's just a journalist who's allowed to make it up."

Exasperating young man. Exasperatingly smart: he was essentially correct. "I know who you work for. I know in general what you do there. I'm not asking for classified information, I'm not soliciting a leak or planning an exposé."

"Just making small talk."

"I'm trying to express an interest in your life. I'll ask about your sex life if you prefer. But you're always telling me you're all about the work. So fine: tell me whatever you can about that. Broad outlines. What's a typical day like?"

He didn't answer right away. And when he did, his voice was less antagonistic. "Actually, Pop, it probably isn't all that much different from a typical day of yours, in essence. I go to an office very near my home . . . I read a lot of news . . . I surf the net . . . I talk to people by phone, e-mail or webcam . . . I stare into space for a long time . . . and after a while, I start to type. You do it for the *Globe and Mail*, I do it for Burston-Marseller, that's all."

There's a damned big difference, I thought, *between a national newspaper and a planetary public relations empire.* But it was the friendliest thing he'd said since his arrival. Never criticize an olive branch. "It must be nice to get paid twenty times as much for it."

"Yes," he agreed, "but then you have to work twenty times as hard to keep it out of the hands of the tax man. Or else accept the blame for what they'll do with it. Hard, these days."

He was definitely trying to meet me halfway. The first encouraging sign since he'd arrived. "Actually, here in C—excuse me a second." I held up a hand for silence, and listened hard, frowning.

A car had just pulled into my driveway. And I recognized it by the sound—even though I had not heard it in a couple of years.

What the hell was *she* doing here? Now?

How come you can never seem to not-find a cop when you don't need one?

Detective Constable Nika Mandiç was an officer of the Vancouver Police Department whom I had not seen since we'd concealed the body of a homicide victim on my property together two years earlier. It had been the right thing to do, but neither of us much cared to remember it. And as far as I knew, we had nothing else to talk about.

Sure enough, her scabby old '89 Honda Accord came into view through the trees. I'd owned one exactly as horrible when I met her; you remember the sound.

"Who's that?" Jesse asked.

I got up, and gestured for him to keep his own seat. "Someone I used to work with. I haven't seen her in years. Wait here a second, will you, while I find out what she wants."

As far as I know, Nika's alert when she sleeps, not that I'll ever find out. She saw me coming, saw instantly that I'd left a guest behind me on the sundeck, and coasted by without slowing, parking much farther down the rutted drive than she needed to. It let us meet well out of the guest's earshot, which suited me just fine. She was out of the car by the time I reached it.

As always, she looked like a teenage boy's fantasy of a Lesbian, butch but incredibly beautiful. Like every Lesbian I've ever seen on television or in the movies, now I think about it, and few I've ever known I happened to know she was not gay, but I'd never seen her with anyone and had great difficulty imagining the hairy-knuckled, flashlight-dicked alpha male who'd have the confidence to take a crack at her. She looked, as always, fit enough to beat up a kangaroo. And agitated enough.

"Who's that?" she greeted me.

"Nice to see you again too, Nika. Those are the same words my son just used."

She frowned, moved closer and lowered her voice. "What did you answer?"

"I told him you were D.C. Nika Mandić, a Vancouver police officer with whom I had once criminally conspired to trap, murder and bury a wealthy citizen we could not have convicted of *anything*, against whom we did not have enough evidence to get a search warrant for his home, purely because a hermit we know, who'd never met or seen him, assured us the guy was a once-in-a-generation monster, getting ready to rape and butcher an entire family as a work of art. I talk fast. Don't worry, though, your *secret*'s safe: I didn't have time to tell him you used to drive the Jailer-Trailer . . . excuse me, the Community Services Mobile Unit."

"If I applaud, will you give me a straight answer?"

"Sure," I agreed. I never said a true one. "I told him I was getting you high. So he'd give us some room." I took the joint from my shirt pocket, lit it, and offered it to her.

She smiled hugely for Jesse's benefit, said "God damn it, Russell," through her clenched teeth, took the doobie and pretended to toke. Then she crossed her eyes staring at it. "Jesus, what *is* this shit?"

I took it back. "Kootenay Thunderfuck, they call it."

She lost the imaginary toke she'd been holding, and glared at me.

"That's what they call it. Now give *me* a straight answer: what are you doing here?"

She leaned in to take the joint back, and locked eyes with me. "Tell me the truth. Have you said *anything*? To *anybody*? Have you *hinted*?"

Those eyes were incredible. I wasn't sure if I could have lied to her. Happily I had no need to. "Of course not."

She wouldn't let go of my eyes. "Have you made any attempt

whatsoever to learn more about . . . him? Or to look for possible associates? Any attempt at *all*? Online, in the library?"

"Everything I've learned about Campbell since we last saw him, you told me. Well before that, I knew way more than I wanted to know about him or ever will. I've been trying real hard to forget I ever heard of him."

Still not done. Any moment her pupils would begin to spiral. "Have you had any further communication at all with . . . with Smelly? Or tried to research him in any way?"

"No, and no. Why?"

She let my eyes go, looked down at once and pretended to examine the joint. "I think we may be in trouble. Really serious trouble. If we are, I put us there. I'm sorry."

"*How* really serious?"

"I think I put my favorite cousin in serious danger. Maybe worse. If I did, I'm probably next. And then you and Smelly. Take this damn thing back, I'm getting high just holding it."

I opened my mouth, but nothing came out. So I put the joint in it.

"Can I have a hit of that?" my son asked from a few meters behind me.

Talk about mixed emotions!

One of my greatest regrets, in a life by no means undersupplied with them, is that despite diligent effort I never succeeded in turning my own father on. He had not been unwilling in theory; he was not afraid of the drug and admitted to me more than once that he was quite intrigued by my descriptions of its effects.

Unfortunately, the first time I ever discussed the matter with him was the day after he and my mother had driven several hundred miles at night in the middle of a snowstorm to bail me out on a felony charge of conspiracy to distribute the stuff, collect my belongings from the dorm I no longer lived in, and drive me back home to Long Island. Dad knew the charge was just barely a felony, a Class E, and furthermore a total utter crock, but you can see how it undermined my arguments for asking him to get high with me. As you know—

—but maybe you don't. If you're under thirty, there's probably no way you can imagine just how paranoid 1968 was. Trust me, then: it seemed reasonable in those times to believe that for the next year or so, our home would be under constant surveillance, visual and electronic, by government forces—and that I would probably be tailed when I left it, for months to come. Even I was smart enough to understand that it would be suicidally stupid to bring so much as a roach into my parents' home before the trial.

So although I am ashamed to confess I called my father a coward at the time, I knew perfectly well then and I admitted to him later that his answer to my request was eminently reasonable, under the circumstances, and better than most arrested college students could have expected. His answer was, "The day they legalize it, you and I will get blasted together."

I called him a coward then because *I* was one. Because I needed someone to be angry at, and I was afraid to be angry at either the cops or those who had delivered me to them. Being arrested and arraigned and kicked out of school are all humiliating; having to leave behind the person who doesn't mind you calling her your old lady is heartbreaking; having prison over your head when you're a skinny weakling with long hair is terrifying; I badly wanted one of those I'd disappointed most to agree with me that pot was worth all that trouble, to understand that I had not put him and Mom through all this for frivolous reasons, to empathize. One joint, and he would grok in fullness. I did not so much ask it as demand it.

But his point was inarguable. Bad enough to have maybe gotten his phone tapped; getting him (and Mom!) busted too was unthinkable. I yearned to turn him on—but wanting to turn people on was exactly what had gotten me busted in the first place. And anyway— here again I must ask you to believe this made perfect sense in 1968—anyway it could hardly be more than a few more years before grass was going to be legal, so what was the hurry?

A year later a genie waved his hands and the felony charge went away, *poof!*, so thoroughly away that I can legally answer "No" to the question "Have you ever been arrested for a felony?" It ended up being like getting a Heidelberg scar—unpleasant for a while at first, but not really dangerous, and then you get bragging rights for life. But even after the shadow was past, I remained reluctant to bring risk to my parents, even though I was starting to lose faith in the imminent legalization of pot by then.

Except for Apollo 11, 1968-9 was not a great period for hope.

Dr. King is shot by the FBI. Hersh breaks the story of the My Lai Massacre. Nixon bombs Cambodia. Ho Chi Minh dies; so do Ike and Allen Dulles, and Yuri Gagarin. Ted Kennedy and Mary Jo Kopechne drive off a bridge together and only one makes it to shore. Judge Hoffman tries the Chicago Seven, has Bobby Seale gagged and manacled in his chair. The Weathermen start setting off bombs, sometimes intentionally.

Québecois separatists kidnap Commissioner Cross, so Premier Trudeau invokes the War Measures Act authorizing the government to do anything it likes; 450 bystanders are arrested; Cross is soon found dead in a car trunk. Gay men riot in a Greenwich Village dive called the Stonewall Inn, and the planet tilts on its axis. *The Godfather* spends sixty-seven weeks on the *Times* list, and sells twenty-one million copies. Woodstock happens . . . but then so does Altamont. The first 10,000 heroin addicts are converted to methadone addicts, to protect them from drugs. The Manson Family do their thing.

Mind you, during the same period a booming U.S. economy employs a record number of workers, unemployment falls to its lowest level in 15 years, the prime interest rate is 7 percent, the dollar is strong in world money markets, and Wall Street's Dow Jones Industrial Average rises above 1,000 for the first time in history. But none of us hippies gave a damn about any of that—or much of anything. We already sensed somehow that the Beatles had broken up. John and Paul were both married, and the wives couldn't stand each other: it was only a matter of time. The dream was over.

By next May Paul had confirmed the news, and the *Let It Be* film publicly autopsied the corpse.

Things got steadily shittier for quite a spell, then. It became gradually clear that the Apollo Program was *over*, and that there was nothing of any consequence after it. A race had been won, and space flight was over, before anything was *done* with it. It would take more than thirty-five years before men would again have the sense and guts to venture more than a cheesey couple of hundred miles from the ground. The Vietnam War finally ended . . . in shame and disgrace, and as clumsily as we could manage. As for politics, let's not even discuss the Nixon Era. It was he who gutted NASA, at the moment of its greatest triumph, for being a Democrat's idea.

Hell, look at music. The Great Folk Scare finally blew over, rock and roll anarchy was finally tamed and lamed, and the industry proudly brought us disco instead. Who wouldn't have been depressed?

Maybe it's no wonder people moved away from smoking Happy Weed . . . or for that matter, tripping on acid, mescaline and peyote . . . and started to honk harsh powders that sometimes contained a few molecules of cocaine up their bleeding noses, or set their faces on fire freebasing, or spike speed, or even smack. When you cut your hair, shave, put on a suit, and get a job with a dental plan, you may discover that's what you need, just to get over. Joy would get in the way, cost you your edge. We only had fifteen years to convert ourselves from people who cheered for Captain America in *Easy Rider* to people who would cheer for Gordon Gekko in *Wall Street*, and coke and speed and skag helped.

I will never inject a drug for pleasure; I snorted cocaine six times in my life and never cared for it; I never stopped smoking pot myself, or enjoying it. But I stopped trying to talk my father into getting stoned with me. I came to think of it less as a sacrament and more as an analgesic, an anodyne.

Until the day Dad called with a funny little story, I wish I could quote it exactly for you, about the cosmic particle that had left a far-distant star eons ago, and traveled countless light-years for innumerable centuries before passing through his pancreas and the rest of his planet without even noticing, one unfortunate side effect being that he was going to be dead of pancreatic cancer in an absolute maximum of three months. Then pot became more of a sacrament to me again.

One I failed to share with him, try as I might.

I was then living over a thousand miles away, newly married. Jesse was six months old, and not a healthy baby. His mom was basically still recovering from a thirty-hour labor followed by Caesarian section, serious infection, and several long bouts of mastitis. I was trying to get my journalism career started, and had already used those excuses too many times to my obligatory crusty editor. I managed to carve out four days, arranged temporary support and backup for wife and child, and flew home.

Where I found it all but impossible to get two consecutive minutes alone with Dad in his hospital room. It is possible to get high in a hospital room without getting caught, if you know what you're doing; I had learned the knack on the second job I ever had, porter in a hospital, at eighteen, and used it in two subsequent long hospital stays of my own. But even when I finally came up with an errand that got Mom out of the room for a few moments, and worked up the nerve to propose the idea to Dad, he turned it down. I pressed him. "I can sneak back in after Visiting Hours, I know how hospitals work, Pop. It would really mean a lot to me."

He did hesitate. But then he shook his head. "Not at the end of my life," he said. "It would only confuse me, and I need my attention for dying now. I want to get it over with. Thanks, Son; too bad we didn't get to it sooner."

I didn't even get to respond; Mom came back that quickly.

So when my own son turned eighteen, I'd asked him to get high with me. He turned me down flat, then, and the next half dozen times I proposed it—with something eerily close to the same thinly veiled contempt I had given my own father when he offered to get drunk with me on my own eighteenth birthday. And for the same reason: he said he'd grown up seeing me use that drug, and wanted no part of it.

Of course, I had come to find use for alcohol later on—and I did, I'm happy to say, get pie-faced with Pop one glorious night—and I did in later years smell unmistakable evidence that my son was at least a social pot smoker. But I had never gotten him to share a joint or a pipe with me. "Can I have a hit of that?" were words I'd wanted to hear him say for a long time—and for him to say them now, here, was the best possible sign for my hopes of a reconciliation between us.

Add in as a bonus the fact that if Jesse became part of the circle, Nika would have to stop pretending and actually take a few tokes— and I found that I wanted very much to get her stoned, to find out what her robocop brain was like when it was wrecked. It would actually help calm her down, which it was clear she needed right now.

But damn it all to hell and back again, I did *not* want her getting stoned anywhere within a kilometer of my son. She was a neophyte, and among the most common effects on the beginner are a tendency to babble and a conviction that absolutely everything in the world is hilarious. I could easily picture Nika, in an explosive burst of laughter and smoke, telling Jesse how little he knew about his father, recounting for him the altogether side-splitting story of my old college roomie, Smelly the telepath, and how old Smelly had led her and me to conceal a body down by the stream that ran through my property, one ugly morning a few years before. Nobody who's been smoking dope for more than a couple of weeks actually behaves like that, except in folklore, but new users sometimes do.

So:

"A hit of what?" I asked, and made the joint disappear. "Have I introduced Detective Constable Nika Mandiç?"

It was ridiculous. The scent of Kootenay Thunderfuck cannot possibly be mistaken for anything else, and noses were probably opening appreciatively as much as half a kilometer downwind by now. Vagrant wisps of heavy smoke still stood in the air between Nika and me. I croaked it more than said it, and exhaled hugely afterwards.

But he had heard me say Nika was a cop, and he could see she was mortally embarrassed. He decided to let it go.

Let the drug go, anyway. "A hit of the conversation, of course," he said after a barely perceptible pause. "Hi, I'm his son Jesse, and you're Nika. So you're in law enforcement."

"Hello, Jesse. That's right, I'm a VPD officer."

"Well, I for one feel safer already," he said, and showed her how good his dental work was, all the way to the back teeth.

My God, he was *hitting on her.*

Even she could tell. She dimpled and said, "Thank you, Jesse. And what do you do that's dangerous?"

Holy shit, she was hitting back!

I stood there and gaped. All I kept thinking was, I really wish I could keep smoking that joint.

And I'm not even sure I can satisfactorily explain why I was so dismayed. My son and my collaborator in felony were of about the same age, both healthy and single. The pairing even made a certain sense, from some perspectives: they both had a stick up their ass, for one thing. So why did I keep trying to think of reasons why they'd make a bad pair? It wasn't all that hard—she arrested people for not telling her the truth, he lied for a living—she lived on a cop's salary, he was on the lower rungs of rich, with a good grip and strong arms—she was a Canadian, he was an American—but what the hell did I care? They were both adults, barely.

Okay, it's stupid. I'm closing in on sixty years old, and I get enough reminders of that every day to keep me popping acetaminophen. And other pills. But in my head, I'm still my son's age. In my silly secret heart, I had always thought of Nika as a possibility untried, always felt that if things had gone another way . . . well, they might have gone another way.

Right. I was still the star of my own movie, sure, maybe even the main character . . . but I was no longer the romantic lead, that was clear. The male ingenue had taken the set. My choices now were to become kindly old dad and give benevolent wise advice to the young couple, or fuck off.

When I thought about it, by all the standard criteria that matter to normal people, my son was a better man than I was. I happened to know his penis was bigger. So was his IQ. So was his bank balance. And she was a normal person. For a cop, anyway.

Five minutes later, on the sundeck, drinking the Irish coffee I had intended as my second cup, Nika remembered that she had a matter of life and death urgency to discuss with me in extreme privacy.

By then things had become even more uncomfortable for me, and if you're wondering how that could be, just think about it. That's right—they had started talking politics. Do I need to say he turned out to be a big fan of our current sissyphobe prime minister, Stephen Harper? Or that she was an ardent and annoyingly well-informed supporter of Resident Bush? Or that my teeth nearly met through my tongue within the first five minutes, from biting back brilliant rejoinders? Is there anything more frustrating than an argument you could win with your head in a bag . . . that you can't let yourself win? Probably, and it's frustrating that I can't think of it just now.

"No one's ever going to give up Osama, no matter how high a reward is offered, or what kind of torture is used," he was saying, and I was not saying *Of course not you silly shit, the dude's been deader than Dubya's dick for years now*, and then he went on, "If they want to find him, it'll take dumb luck or a mind reader."

Her eyeballs seemed to swap sockets and back again. "Oh. Um . . . Jesse, can I ask you to give me a few minutes in private with your dad? I just remembered the reason I drove out here, and I'm afraid it mustn't wait. We won't be long."

We walked to her car together, stopped short of it—and found that he had followed us. It startled me. His manners were better than that.

"I just wanted to say—" he began, and stopped.

"Jesse," Nika said, "you're a serious man. You've obviously done some government work. You're not cleared to hear . . . are you listening to me?"

He wasn't. He was looking past her, at something on or near ground-level. In a moment he caught up with what she'd said, and spoke to both of us. "You have some idea of the kind of resources and influence I can summon. Are you sure you don't want me to sit in on this discussion?"

Burston-Marseller was at that time the undisputed biggest and best public relations firm in the world. There probably wasn't a lot they *couldn't* fix if they wanted. I almost thought about it. "Thanks, Jess," I said. "But I'd rather not involve you."

"He's right, Jesse," Nika said softly.

"I think it's a little late for that," he said just as softly. "Whatever's going on, I'm already involved."

We exchanged a glance. "How do you figure that?" she asked him.

"I know that's not standard equipment on a Honda," he said, pointing. "I happen to know what it is. As a matter of fact, I think I could quote the suggested list price."

We spun to look where he was pointing. It took both of us seconds to see it, seconds more to grasp what we were seeing. At first I saw . . . dirt. My rutted driveway. Mud. Random puddles.

Then I saw a reflection in one. Something small and shiny, under Nika's rear bumper. *Moving* slowly. Size and color of a nail-clipper.

Seconds after I focused on it, it stopped moving. I tried to blink away floaters, failed as usual, and stooped for a closer look. Nika, *far* more effortlessly, went down on one knee and peered directly up at the thing, clinging to the underside of the bumper. It was motionless now.

It looked to me like a tiny toy robot lizard, with a horn sticking up out of its snout—just the right size to go in a box of Cracker Jacks. (Do they still sell them? How? Do kids with game boxes and video iPods want little plastic toys?)

I turned to Nika and the blood had drained from her face.

"I *don't* happen to know what it is," I said. "Do you?"

"I've heard about them," she said slowly, getting to her feet. "Seen a sketch that turns out to be accurate. It's a GPS snitch. It is the tracking device of the gods. Almost literally." She turned to look at Jesse. "I have no idea what it lists for. I think it may be a federal felony to recognize it. In America, anyway; I doubt our government has any, so it may not be proscribed here yet. Not that it matters."

"Not that it matters," my son agreed. "I think I've *been* involved since you drove up this driveway. That thing picks up audio extremely well."

I straightened up, almost. "Jesus Christ in a trenchcoat!"

"Russell, I'm sorry. He's right. I'm very sorry."

"You *think*?" I bellowed. "You don't know the meaning of the fucking *word*."

"As a matter of fact, I do," she said, just loud enough to be heard. "Don't you tell me I don't."

"Dad, how could she have known that was there? Now why don't you tell me what you're sorry I'm involved in, so I can decide whether I agree?"

I turned to Nika. "We have to tell him."

"We do now," she agreed sourly.

I propped an elbow on a fist, covered my face with a hand. "You sorry enough to take a crack at it?" I muttered.

She sighed. "We might as well sit back down."

We resumed our seats on the deck. But before we could say anything, Jesse held up his hand for silence. He took from his shirt pocket the hot new superphone he had been so quietly proud to show off when he'd first arrived; it wasn't even supposed to be on sale for another few days yet, and then only in America. He poked at the screen for a moment, and set it down on the table.

It began to play back—at plausible conversational volume— everything he and I had said on that deck since his arrival, with pauses longer than a few seconds edited out.

I wondered why he had recorded our conversation. I wanted to believe it indicated that mending our fences was as important to him as it was to me. Or did he just keep the phone doing that all the time, a kind of audio diary, and dump it to hard disk each night? I was too busy to ask.

Its volume was impressive for so small a device, making both me and Nika start at first. He made an adjustment with a forefinger, and the speed of playback dropped just perceptibly, not enough to distort our voices. Then he pointed the same finger in the air and made a circular motion to indicate that the recording was on a loop, and would repeat. Nika and I exchanged a glance, then both nodded that we got it. All three of us rose as silently as we could—me least of all, damn it—and I zipped the screen door open in its track as quietly as I could, and we all slipped into the house, pulling the solid wooden door closed behind us.

"You really think that thing picks up *audio*?" she asked as soon as it shut.

He shrugged. "It wouldn't add much to the cost."

She looked around, seeing the room for the first time since the night a man had died in it while she watched and thanked her lucky stars, and I knew from her body language it was all coming back for her. Jesse let her pick her seat first. She chose the near end of the couch, beside the end table where a reading lamp stood, and I took the daddy chair on the other end that I knew she was avoiding. He pulled the old rocking chair at an angle to face both of us across the coffee table, and waited while she finished her drink. So did I. I found I was curious to hear how she would say it.

"A long time ago, back when he was in college, your father had a roommate nobody else on the whole campus was willing to share a room with, for two semesters."

"Excessive tolerance has been one of his flaws as long as I've known him. What was this dude's offense?"

"He didn't bathe. Ever."

I could hear him inhale. "My God, I think I remember my mother *mentioning* that goofball, once. Stinky, they all called him, right?"

I put my hands down and took a deep breath. "Smelly," I said. "We called him Smelly."

3.
Tuesday, February 14, 1967
St. William Joseph College
Olympia, New York, USA

"Slim, I don't care *how* much grass you can get away with smoking in your room." Slinky John said to me. "I still don't see how you can keep from killing him. No mosquito has ever been thirsty enough to even circle *that* fat son of a bitch! Flies have died trying—upwind. Worms won't go near him when he dies, until a year later when he starts to smell a little better."

The other card players, kibitzers and paralyzed drunks gathered in the end hall lounge of Nalligan Three all growled loud agreement, even though it was three AM and the door to the hall was open. Even one or two of the studiers present half-woke up to add their voices.

How long ago was this? "Ruby Tuesday" by the Rolling Stones was Number One, followed by the Buckinghams' "Kind of a Drag," and "Georgy Girl" by the Seekers—does that help? Crosby, Stills and Nash had not formed yet. Roger Chaffee, Gus Grissom and Edward White would have been taking off that very day in Apollo 1, if it had not killed them on the ground a few weeks earlier. We had been sending combat troops to Vietnam in large numbers for two years, and would have soldiers there for another five years to come.

Slinky John's point was not only popular but well taken, and his descriptions if anything charitable. I had often wondered myself how I could stand to room with Zandor Zudenigo, and knew I was not about to come up with an answer for Slinks now, at three o'clock in the morning in the midst of a marathon poker session. But pretending to think about it was good cover for any expression that might have flickered across my face as I discovered that he had just dealt me a nine, a ten, and three royals, all five wearing diamonds. "Slinks, I've told you a hundred trillion times to avoid absurd hyperbole. The guy reeks, no possible argument. But any smell wears off; after a while you just stop noticing, as with your extreme physical ugliness. It can be endured."

"Okay, but *why*? It has to be easier to kill him. Hell, you might even end up making friends. Wouldn't that be a nice change?"

There was a lot of money in the pot, so I thought harder than usual about his question. "What's the hardest thing to do in a dormitory?"

"Jerk off in privacy," Matt Mee said at once. He peered at his hand and called, and so did Jim Clooney.

He had me there. "Okay, what's the second hardest?"

"Getting any God damned studying done," Bill Doane said, raising a hundred bucks. "Noise, water fights, hall parties, room-jobbing, assholes knocking on the door with something more interesting to do. Card games in the end-hall lounge."

"Exactly," I said. Bill seemed to have been using more words than he needed to, so I just called instead of raising back, to sucker him in further. "It's real peaceful in my room. Nobody comes near it. I was on academic pro last year . . . this semester, I've got a shot at Dean's List."

"You've been on *his* shit list for a *long* time," Slinks said, raising fifty.

"No, seriously. B's and up, man. If that stinks, so be it."

Matt folded, got up and went down the hall to the can. "When Slim's right, he's right, Slinks," Bill said. "I myself derive a similar though lesser benefit from the healthy respect our own neighbors hold for your foul personality, psychotic instability, and known interest in explosives." He raised Slinks five hundred bucks.

"Okay, but I don't *stink*."

"At what?" I asked happily. Verbosity and confidence—just what

I liked to see in Bill when I was planning to skin him first. I raised him a thousand dollars even.

Silence. The kibitzers leaned closer, and one of the studiers opened an eye. Far away down the hall somewhere, someone cried out in disgust. Someone else joined him, and then a third voice imitated a girl screaming in a horror movie. Nobody around the table even glanced up.

Slinky John stared at me intently. "You're full of shit," he decided, but he closed up his hand anyway and gestured with it to indicate he was folding, then reopened it and fanned himself with it.

Bill regarded me balefully from under a forest canopy of red curls, and stroked his vast beard. He was smarter than I was, but he looked like a guy Conan the Barbarian would try to bribe before fighting. I dropped my head and swung it from side to side to crack my neck. "You always do that when you're bluffing," he said. "Raise you a grand right back."

I grinned at my chest. That was indeed a pattern I'd been establishing for weeks against just such a moment. "And back at you," I said, putting a quaver in it.

"And five thousand more," he boomed triumphantly.

Oh God, if only we'd been playing for real money! "Ten thousand," I said, and looked up grinning.

His face fell.

Mike Linkman and Frank Vezina burst into the room. "Holy fucking Jesus Christ," they shouted in unison, as if it were an act they had rehearsed well. Then they said it again, sloppier this time. Then they turned to each other and nailed, "It *can't* be!" After that, they went into counterpoint, with one saying "Of course," while the other said "I don't believe it," and then "It explains *everything*," dueting with "How could he possibly *not*?" and like that.

Bill rose from the table like a time-lapse movie of a redwood growing, grabbed their collars, and gently whacked their heads together. "Stop that," he suggested.

They didn't, so he did it again, less gently. "Serious matters are at stake, here. I'm being screwed with my pants on."

"Forget it," Frank said. "Listen to this."

Bill regarded him thoughtfully, starting to become interested. In order to make Frank's and Mike's skulls meet, he'd had to lift Frank more than a foot off the floor, and was holding him at arm's length. "Okay," he said, set Frank down and released Matt too.

Given the floor, they passed it silently back and forth like a hot potato for a few seconds.

Frank started. "We see him plain as day, okay? You know how bright the light is down at that end?"

"They're not gonna believe us," Matt told him.

"Shit, I don't believe us," Frank said. "But I'm gonna tell it anyway. While I still don't believe it."

Matt frowned. "Yeah. You are."

"Everybody knows we got the can back today, right?"

Slinky John had the grace to blush slightly, and fan himself a bit harder with his dead hand of cards. Nalligan Three's big common washroom had only just reopened, after an unreasonably lengthy closure necessitated by someone's scientific curiosity—admirable, really, considered objectively—as to whether or not it was really possible to lift a whole commode entirely off the floor using hypergolic chemicals alone. The answer is yes, but not just *one*. The long trudge down to Nalligan Two's washroom had become onerous for us, the territorial resentment and mockery there tiresome; we were all glad to finally have our own crapper back.

"As it happens," Bill said, "we were discussing that very problem earlier."

"Huh? How could you?" Frank asked, baffled.

"What problem are *you* talking about?" Matt asked.

"The difficulty of jerking off in privacy in a dorm. That is where you're going with this, right?"

"I wish!" Frank said fervently.

Something even *more* embarrassing! We all were starting to get interested now, even the studiers. "Just tell it," I suggested.

Frank started to, then thought of one more thing we needed to know first. "We're in our socks, right?" He gestured to his and Matt's feet, and they were indeed wearing only double pairs of socks on their feet. So was I; it was a popular choice. The dorm floors were quite warm enough even in February— on the upper floors, at least—and so heavily overwaxed by generations of dirt-despising Marianite Brothers and their minions that a man in socks could learn to skate on them quite efficiently, if the alternative were studying.

"But we're not zipping, just walking," he went on.

"Not talking, because it's late, we don't want our asses kicked," Matt added.

"And we just turn the corner, and there he is."

"Right there," Matt agreed.

Bill cleared his throat. "Where who is?"

They looked at him, blinking.

Bill closed his own eyes. "Whom did you see?" he inquired with massive patience. "And what was his location at the time?" His voice sounded like a locomotive idling a few floors below.

"Him," Frank almost explained.

"Right there," Matt unamplified.

Bill's expression did not change, but his complexion began to approach the color of his shoulderblade-length hair and nipple-length beard.

I jumped in to try and save their lives. "Say his name," I suggested, in the tone of voice one uses to say "Fetch the stick."

"I can't," Frank said. Matty too shook his head.

Which direction to take now? Ask why not? Say yes you can? Just let Bill crack their skulls, since there was nothing to leak out? Hadn't I been *doing* something important a minute ago? Oh, right—

Frank picked then to qualify his statement, and intersected glancingly with coherence. "I can't *pronounce* it," he said, managing to actually explain, so effectively that his added, "Zibba Zabba-zooba," was redundant.

Bill's eyes opened and we exchanged a glance. "Smelly," we said at the same time.

"Yeah, but that's not his *name*," Frank said. "I can *pronounce* that."

"Not without a tongue," Bill said dreamily.

"What?"

"A momentary pleasure you could regret for hours," I told him soothingly. "Allow me. Frank, Matt, you rounded the corner and saw Zan—" Lost cause. "—my roommate Smelly, coming out of the bog, is that right?"

They both shook their heads and said "No no no," emphatically, "That's just what we *didn't*." (Frank.) "Didn't see him doing." (Matt.)

"Going into it, then."

Even louder no no no's. "That's *exactly* what he didn't do." (Matt.) "That's what he *doesn't*." (Frank.) "Exactly." (Both.)

No civilians had hand guns in 1967 except lone-gunman assassins, if there actually were any. When I had first come to St. Billy Joe I had thought it silly that they actually bothered to put a no-gun clause in the dormitory residence manual. But not for long. I wished I had one now. "Where was Smelly when you saw him?"

Could I possibly have projected more menace with my voice than big Bill Doane had? I guess, because Frank just started spilling—at last. "He's coming toward us, halfway down the hall, but he isn't *coming* toward us. Frozen in his tracks, I'm saying. Deer in the headlights. One foot in the air, no shit."

"Already," Matt added.

"Right, that's what I'm saying: we come around the corner and he's already frozen, before he heard us or saw us. And he's standing directly under the good light, holding it right there by the top like a, like a, a—Jesus—you know: the thing with the fucking incense in it at fucking High Mass—"

"Censer," Bill said.

Frank blinked at him. "Sorry. Like the thing with the incense in it at High Mass, he's holding it like that. One of those Mason-Dixon jars, the biggest one they make, I guess. Big enough the first thing I'm thinking is, that's enough sausage there for all three of us."

"Jesus, me too!" Matt agreed, shuddering.

"Then I'm thinking, no, that's gotta be pickles: if it was sausage, there'd be something else solid in the soup with it, onions or *something*. Only by then I'm starting to notice his face, in spite of myself. I mean, you know, that's not a face you need to look at once it stops being funny."

"Right on," Slinky John agreed, and others chimed in. If Sir Winston Churchill had been shaved bald, he and the cartoon character Baby Huey and Smelly could all have passed for brothers, and Smelly would have been considered the ugly one.

"But he's got this expression like . . . I don't know what. I never saw anybody with that expression before. Matt?"

"Maybe this kid in high school shop who cut a couple of his fingers off."

"Okay. Anyway, I see this expression on his face, and right then, don't ask me how, I know what he's got in the jar. And I take a closer look, and it is."

"I didn't get it until you yelled," Matt told him. "Well, I did, but I didn't want to believe I got it until somebody else did first."

"Yeah." They nodded at each other in shared understanding.

The sound of Bill inhaling was clearly audible, and went on for what seemed a long time.

"It was a jar of shit," Frank and Matt said in slow unison.

Bill stopped inhaling. Pretty much everyone else started.

"A jar of shit and piss," Matt said.

"His own shit and piss," Frank repeated.

Everyone started talking at once, at the top of their lungs. Nice arrangement.

Bill rode on top of the chorus by sheer lungpower. "Holy Christ on keyboards, it almost makes sense."

His roommate stared at him. "Fuck you, it does."

"Well, all right, no—but it almost makes *sick* sense, like deconstructionism."

"Derrida versus da reader," Slinks couldn't help saying.

"Exactly. Think about it—all of you, think hard. Did you ever see Smelly in the can? Going in the can? Going out of the can? Ever?"

We combed our memories, with difficulty. It wasn't the kind of record one tends to store retrievably. I couldn't seem to bring a specific instance to mind myself, but surely someone would. It would only take one of us—

Nobody. A lot of glances, shrugs, grimaces, not one retrieved memory of Smelly in the washroom.

Bill turned to me. "He drinks coffee?"

"Tea. A lot if he's pulling an all-nighter."

"Ever see him get up and go piss?"

I frowned. "No." This was silly . . .

"I still don't get it," Frank said.

"He's terrified that if anybody ever catches him in the john, that close to soap and water, a posse will spontaneously form, and toss him in the goddam shower and scrub him down with a toilet brush and a gallon of Mr. Clean."

"At last, a plan," Slinky John growled.

Bill spun on him. "Yeah? *You* go get him. Get close enough to put your hands on him—" Slinks was paling. "—and stay that close long enough to drag him down the hall and into the can."

"I take your point."

"Guys, guys," I said, "this is crazy. How would he make it through the weekend?"

"Huh?"

"A guy Smelly's size could fill the biggest Mason jar they make at least once a day. At least. I've seen him eat. So what about weekends?"

"Huh."

"On a school night, sure, you can be guaranteed at least a couple of hours of peace, to skulk down to the can. But Friday night? Saturday? Sunday, even? Forget it. No way."

That won me a few supporter skeptics.

Bill was frowning. "More than one j—"

I shook my head. "In a room *that* size? I'd've noticed."

"Out the—"

"My bed's directly under the window, remember?"

"The answer is right under your noses," Slinky John said.

Bill glared at him. "Well? Out with it."

"He holds on to it," Slinks said. "And it comes out his pores."

There was a cry of general outrage, and pretty much everybody threw whatever was closest to hand at him. Unfortunately, I did too, and even more unfortunately, so did all the other card players, so the pot was void.

Nobody ever came up with a better explanation than Slinky John's, though extravagant attempts were made. None of us—least of all I, his roommate—ever got up the nerve to raise with Smelly the question, why do you shit and piss in a jar, much less, how do you manage the logistics. The entire incident served mostly to solidify a long-standing tendency on the part of everyone to think about Smelly just as seldom as humanly possible.

Maybe I'm editing memory, making myself smarter than I actually am. I do that sometimes. But I do think, I do, that it was a little later that night, sitting alone in the room I shared with Smelly at the end of the hall, that it consciously entered my head for the very first time—purely as a joke—that my roommate Zandor Zudenigo might be a telepath. If he were, went the thought, what spot on earth could possibly be more terrifying than the place where dozens of male college students went to masturbate?

It was more than thirty-five years later that I learned I'd stumbled on the truth.

4.
Saturday, June 23, 2007
West Vancouver, British Columbia, Canada

He was given plenty of signage warning that the road was about to bifurcate, the right fork continuing to be the Sea to Sky Highway, and the left fork coming to a stop at a ferry terminal in a village called Horseshoe Bay. And his GPS snitch was more than good enough to tell him which fork he wanted: the left. So he continued to follow just out of sight, slowing from highway speed at the same rate as his target did.

It was the *size* of the ferry terminal that took him by surprise: not as big as the monster he'd driven past at Tsawwassen, but not the one-boat commuter-pooter he'd expected either. By the time he grasped how many different options there were, he was very nearly too late to see which one his quarry had chosen. Irritatingly, it was the one he would have to cross the most lanes of traffic to reach; he barely managed it without causing horns to be honked. And at once he had to deal with an attendant who, by his standards, took forever to do a simple credit card swipe and issue him a ticket. To someplace with the uncouth name "Heron Island."

Hell.

He knew it would be the smallest destination served, because all the others had at least two booths. Therefore he was about to park *just* behind his quarry, and sit there motionless for an indeterminate time, and there would probably be hardly anyone else around for her to look at whom she didn't already know.

"Lane One," the attendant said and gave him an unwanted receipt.

"Can I get a newspaper somewhere nearby?"

"As soon as you're underneath," the attendant agreed.

Underneath? This kept getting better.

All lanes of traffic past the ticket booths funneled leftward into a single lane—God knew why—and again, the Canadians all queued up politely and waited their turn. After a bit of winding, it just as inexplicably opened out again into a dozen or so lanes, and Lane One was the one he was already in. Everybody else got out of his way and let him make a little speed. This cheered him until he hit the first speed bump. It was a serious speed bump, and turned out to be the least serious of the series.

Lane One took him, very slowly, past long lines of stopped cars waiting for their ferry to arrive. His was empty. When he got to the front of it, there was a midget imitation of the ticket booth. He stopped by it. Without glancing up, a uniformed attendant inside pointed diagonally to the right. He followed the finger, and sure enough there was an unblocked entrance to a roofed-over area. He drove in cautiously, as slow as he dared.

Four lanes were full of cars, two on either side of a concrete walkway lined with pillars that held the roof up. No, five lanes: a fifth had just started up to the left of the rest, with one or two cars in it. He saw his quarry at once, at the end of the lane furthest from him. It was nearly but not quite full.

He thought fast. Take the lane farthest from her, and he was in front of her, in full view. Way in front, okay, but suppose they boarded the right lanes first, and she drove past him at three fucking kilometers per hour? Being what she was, how would she *not* notice him?

He parked right behind her, in the last space in that row. To examine him she would have to either turn around, or use one of her three mirrors, and in all those cases he'd at least see it and know she was checking him out.

He could see the newspaper vending-boxes the attendant had mentioned. Up at the head of the line; forget it. Fortunately she was engrossed in a newspaper of her own.

Time now to consider whether he should board this ferry with her. Or develop engine trouble at some point before he reached the head of the line.

An island meant fewer witnesses. It also probably meant they all *knew* each other, and would be likely to notice and remember him. On the other hand, *all* islands are tourist destinations; solvent-looking strangers his age and apparent status would probably be so familiar as to go unseen.

And this might be *it*. This might be the location of the ultimate target, the end of the quest. It would make sense in many ways. He *had* to at least get a GPS fix on wherever she was going, even if he didn't dare go for a visual.

Yes. It was worth the risk.

He leaned forward, crossed his forearms on the steering wheel, rested his forehead on them, closed his eyes, and was asleep nearly at once. He woke when he heard engines starting.

The ferry ride was forty minutes of total boredom. But he soon saw that only regulars, islanders, were bored. First-timers such as him found the scenery orgasmic. So he had to. Irritating. There was a whole lot of calm water, a big sissified sea. Rock stuck up out of it randomly in various directions, at varying distances, in assorted shapes. Some were green, some just grey. The sky was as big as a sky, and fully as skylike as every one he'd ever seen. The sun was on today. So what? Why did the view give so much pleasure? And why *only* to those who'd never seen it before?

It amused him to reflect that he might actually be on the verge of understanding those questions, and countless others like them, after so many years. An unimportant consequence, surely . . . but amusing.

Of *course* there was a place to park within a hundred meters of the end of the ferry ramp in (God help us all) Bug Cove, if you didn't mind paying an arm and a leg per hour or portion thereof. Unfortunately it was on the left, and the ferry debarked two at a time, with him in the right lane. To avoid drawing attention he took the first right he possibly could instead, and found himself in the parking lot of what looked like an old-timey train station whose tracks had been stolen, but was in fact the Heron Island Public

Library. He paused before choosing a space, and a voice came in his open window. "Library parking only, mate. They're serious about it, eh?"

He turned to see Colorful Coot standing beside him. "I can see how they'd have to be," he agreed in his best imitation of Canadian manners. "I'm just waiting until I can get through the traffic to the pay lot across the street." He must have got it right because Coot bought it, nodded and walked away and never looked back.

He turned around, waited a couple of minutes while the ferry finished emptying. But his access to the lot was still blocked by cars waiting to board the ferry for the trip back to the mainland—and although the two immediately in the way saw his problem and tried to maneuver to make him a hole, they were unable to. Everything had to wait while the foot-passengers walked aboard first . . . or limped, or shuffled, or lurched on their walkers. Only then did the cars board, and they did so for nearly five full minutes.

Finally the way was clear; he zipped across the street and into the lot, where he found the only empty spaces were as long a walk as possible from the automatic kiosk where you had to buy your parking permits. The kiosk took only Canadian coins; he had just enough. He made himself consider the bright side. Most of the lot serviced a small but fully occupied and surprisingly unseedy marina operation. He was almost invisible way down at the end, and facing out at all the water just as yokels were expected to. He checked his GPS snitch's readout the moment he was back in the car, and saw that his target had gone to ground. The unit had automatically recorded the coordinates. He checked all his mirrors without seeming to, rolled all his windows up, and activated the GPS snitch's audio circuit in time to hear:

"*—worry, though, your* secret's *safe: I didn't have time to tell him you used to drive the Jailer-Trailer . . . excuse me, the Police Community Services Mobile Unit.*"

"*If I applaud, will you give me a straight answer?*"

"*Sure. I told him I was getting you high.*'"

Ah, he thought. Now we're getting somewhere. Leverage . . .

Unfortunately, the cop dropped out of the conversation nearly at once. The strong silent type. Okay, that was information, too.

Now, who were these other two assholes she was listening to?

He accessed the net with his phone and was only slightly surprised to learn GPS alone could not get him an address for that location. He could wait until business hours in the morning and inquire at the municipality's office. Or he could go there tonight and look at the street sign and the number on the door.

5.
Saturday, June 23, 2007
Heron Island, British Columbia, Canada

"What does this guy look like?" Jesse interrupted Nika.

"The Michelin Tire Man with Baby Huey's face," I said.

"I don't know who they are."

"Neither do I," said Nika. "Think of a totally bald Tony Soprano—who's never been angry in his life."

"Got it," Jesse agreed.

Nika resumed her account. "So I agreed to meet your father—"

"Could we call me Russell? Or just Gramps?"

"—to meet Russell down at Spanish Banks Beach in the middle of the night. That's by—"

"I know where it is,' Jesse said. "Dad sent me a photo of Vancouver once that said on the back it was taken from there."

"Well, Zandor was just offshore, in a small boat. I couldn't reach him, and he could regulate his distance from me. He came within range. Then he spoke to me on a cell phone, and he . . . " She glanced away for a moment. "He told me things, that . . . well, he proved to me that he could read my mind. Deep."

"Okay," Jesse said.

She shook her head. "No. Not like you're thinking, like a carnie act, where he asked leading questions and I told him how to hook me."

"Okay," Jesse said.

She shook her head again. "You have to really *get* this. He told me when, where and how I'd lost my virginity, which only the other party knew, and he told me how I'd felt about it, which *nobody* knew." Her cheeks darkened.

"Okay," Jesse said again, blushing slightly himself. "I buy the premise. My father knows a telepath. Please believe I'm not being flippant when I say I'm not terribly surprised. He would if anyone ever did. We can move on. This Sandor—"

"Zandor. Zandor Zudenigo. It's Serbian."

"This guy proved to you he was a telepath. But you say it hurts him to do it."

"Horribly. And there's no off switch. He's a hermit by choice. Your fa—Russell is one of the few people he can stand to be near."

Jesse nodded. "Because he doesn't judge people. I get that. Except for me."

"Beg pardon?"

"Skip it. Zandor proved all this to you. Told an armed police officer he knew all her secrets. Why?"

"He had unwillingly read the mind of . . . a monster."

"A Bundy?"

She shook her head. "Much worse."

He blinked. "A Dahmer?"

"Much worse."

"We're not talking about Picton? The pig farmer slash prostitute killer they're trying right now, supposed to have taken out a couple of dozen women?"

"Much worse."

He paled slightly. "Not just . . . worse."

Again she shook her head. "Much worse. I've never heard or read of anybody as bad. In history. At the time that Zudie . . . I'm sorry, I should call him Zandor, but he looks *so* much like a cartoon character or a bald Tony Soprano, it's hard not to think of him as Zudie. At the time Zudie read him, Allen was planning to kidnap and rape and degrade and torture to death as perfectly blameless a family of four as he'd been able to find in Vancouver. Over a period of days. With great ingenuity and with true scientific brilliance and without a morsel of mercy. As a work of art. He created and enhanced agony as others make music or dance or paint." She broke off.

"And he was an Armstrong," I said. "A Baryshnikov. A Salvador Dali. In his *spare* time he became a cybermillionaire, a respected code warrior."

Jesse was finally beginning to boggle a bit, and I could see it irritated him. He wanted to believe anything Nika said to him, even if I agreed with it, but this was getting thick. He soldiered on. "So Zudie gave you evidence that would—"

I took it. He was used to being skeptical of me. "All Zudie had to give us was what happened to be passing through Allen's head during maybe fifteen to thirty seconds—during which time he believed he was just about to crash his plane into Howe Sound and die. He spent most of that time regretting the ghoulish masterpiece he wasn't going to get to complete, savoring the ones he had, and gleefully telling God to go fuck Himself. Then his engine caught again, and he flew out of Zudie's range. We had *just* enough clues to start hunting him. And no choice in the world."

"And absolutely *nothing* on him in any legal sense," Nika clarified. "I couldn't have gotten a warrant to tap his phone, even if I'd known his last name. I didn't have reasonable grounds to stop him on the sidewalk and *ask* him his name."

"All we had was his first name, and that his private playground, his outdoor art studio, was somewhere along the Sea To Sky Highway," I went on.

"Jesus Christ," Jesse said. "That's like saying, somewhere along the New England Thruway, isn't it?"

I nodded. "Except it's ninety-eight percent empty forest. Handy for a man who doesn't *want* them gagged."

Jesse closed his eyes for a moment. "So what did you do?"

"We started driving the Sea To Sky, pointing a camcorder out the window as we went."

He opened them again. "Hoping *what*, exactly?"

"That when we got home, Zudie might spot, somewhere in several hours of video, the unmarked turnoff he'd seen beside the highway in Allen's mind's eye. The trail that led to Painland."

He started to look interested. "I see. How'd it work out?"

"Badly," Nika said, "He was much smarter than we were."

"With much better video gear," I said. "It filmed license plates of anything that so much as slowed down near his special turnoff. A live feed, back to his home near the city. He damn near beat us here."

"Which turned out to be good," Nika said. "He was taken by surprise, busy torturing us, when Zandor showed up."

We both fell silent. Jesse waited a reasonable time, then a little more, and finally burst out, "And did what?"

I looked at Nika. Nika looked at me. She shrugged *you try it*.

Okay. I turned back to my son. "Zandor ate his mind and his body died. Right about where you're sitting."

I heard Nika draw breath, but if she had any correction or amplification to offer, she thought better of it.

I watched Jesse decide to believe us, and start thinking it through, and waited for him to ask what we'd done with the body. He did not, then or ever. If you want to say that's appalling, I won't argue. If I say it made me proud, you'd better not either.

Nika and I let him sit with it until he was ready to proceed. "So," he said, "you now figure a partner, or apprentice, or acolyte or admirer or art-lover or whatever, has connected you with this rich man's disappearance, and put an ultra-high-tech GPS snitch on your car? Why the hell did you come out here in the first place? Have you got Zudie out there in the woods, somewhere, getting ready to eat this guy's mind too?"

"We can't reach Zudie," I said. "He stopped talking to us."

"To you," Nika said.

"To either of us. To anybody. He jumped in a hole and pulled it in after him."

"Why?" Jesse asked patiently.

I gestured vaguely with my hands. "He ate a guy's mind."

"He had to."

I nodded. "Apparently that doesn't help enough."

He closed his eyes and began massaging one eyebrow. It is a mannerism I have myself, one that my wife used to gently mock me for. "I think I'm actually relieved to know that," he decided.

Neither of us responded. I know part of me felt the same way, strongly. But the question was complicated. What Zandor had done that night had saved my life, and Nika's, just for openers. It unquestionably also saved the four other innocent lives we knew Allen already planned to take, at the very least. Arguably it *also* saved all the countless *other* lives Allen would have gone on to take in the course of pursuing his Muse. And "lives" is only part of it, and not even the worst. Allen didn't just take lives, he took souls, He cultivated agony like orchids, cut despair like diamond. Many of his victims never bled at all, but each one hemorrhaged every single drop of hope they had in them before he let them go.

And *still*, what Zudie had done—had been forced to do—creeped me out a little. I guess because it creeped him out a lot.

Jesse shook his head and rebooted. "Okay, this is all history. Let's get back to: how did you realize there was a new problem to come talk over with Russell, before you knew there was a bug on your car?"

Nika took a deep breath. "My cousin Vasco . . . " She started over. "My cousin Vasco does computer stuff for CSIS in Toronto. That's our—" She saw that he knew what CSIS is. "Deep stuff. They caught him hacking into their system when he was a kid, and recruited him. We were best friends growing up, so I think he talked about what he does there to me more than to anyone else— and he told me hardly anything. Just hints, and not many of those. Once, he said if I ever needed to know everything there was to know about some person badly enough, I could have it all within an hour. *Everything.* Every penny he ever spent, every e-mail he ever sent, every webpage he ever looked at. *Anybody.* The chief of police. The premier. Anybody not in the intelligence community, was how he put it."

"So you asked him to very quietly and very anonymously find out who Allen might have swapped jpg's and videos with?" Jesse guessed.

She winced. "I didn't have the courage. Allen was *so* smart, I was terrified of anybody he'd trust that much. And . . . look, I was not going to give my cousin, a fellow officer, the name of a man I helped murder and ask him to run it. Okay?"

He nodded. "So then—?"

"I asked as a hypothetical what could he do with somebody who'd been dead thirty-five years, since before computers? How much information could he turn up now? He said that was *much* tougher, could take as long as a couple of days to run, unless there was something special about him, and I said he was considered a math genius in his day, and—"

My ears started to ring. I sat bolt upright. "Oh my God, no!"

"Russell, I never so much as hinted or implied that he *hasn't* been dead for thirty-five years. I just—"

"Nika, he *told* me the fucking *CIA* almost got him, once! That's *why* he's supposed to be dead."

"He never told *me* that, and neither did you!" she said angrily.

I had no reply. I never had, now that I thought of it. I had simply assumed that Zudie would.

"And even so, I warned Vasco to be careful, that there might have been a time when three-letter-agencies were interested in Zudie, back in the day. I didn't tell him why I wanted to know about this dead guy—but I *did* stress that it was not important enough to be worth any risk at all, that he should back away if he sniffed anything bad. He laughed at me."

"How did you—" I started to ask, and she guessed where I was going.

"We used to exchange holiday e-mails and phone calls like everybody, but for real communication we always used a goofy system he came up with when we were kids together, that was totally secure."

Jesse looked politely dubious. "I've been told there's no such thing," he said.

She shrugged. "You tell me how to beat it. He got one of those free e-mail accounts, under a name that was just a string of meaningless letters, and gave me the password to it verbally. Any time one of us wanted to write the other privately, we'd open that account, type our message, without addressing it to anyone . . . then put it in the Drafts folder, and quit."

"My god, that's *beautiful*," Jesse said at once.

It took me a little longer to grasp it, but once I did I had to agree: it was breathtaking. God himself couldn't intercept the transmission . . . if no transmission ever took place. As far as the system was concerned, the message never *went* anywhere: it merely got contemplated by two different computers. Nika's cousin was *smart*.

Because she was frowning Jesse felt he could, so now we were all frowning. Time to find out why. "What happened, Nika?"

"I get a call from my sergeant passing on a phone message. My cousin in Toronto had called to say goodbye, he was being transferred overseas."

"Jesus Christ," I said involuntarily.

"What did you do?" Jesse asked gently.

"Sat still and thought hard for a long time. Then I got hold of a laptop that couldn't be traced to me, pirated wireless from a café, and checked our Drafts folder. No message. Three days in a row I tried. I was trying to make myself believe that a little thing like being paralyzed would be enough to keep my cousin Vasco offline . . . when he called. On the telephone."

She stopped talking. We gave her time.

She attempted a smile unsuccessfully. "He said he'd been promoted to a better position in CSIS's Albanian office, as if that made sense. It was hard to say how long he'd be there. He had a plausible-sounding story about why they were sending him there, and what he would do there, and I think he convinced whoever was monitoring the call that he had convinced me. I did my best to help. But we both knew he was reading a script. He made no mention of my data-search, and cut me off at the first syllable when I started to. I forgot to ask him for his phone number, had to get it from Call Identify after he hung up. It took me ten minutes to think of it."

"Jesus." It was Jesse who said it this time.

"Look, we should get back outside," she said. "Even if whoever owns that bug isn't paying close attention, they're bound to notice eventually that I hardly ever say anything."

"Damn it, we're not even close to done here," I said.

"For now we are," she said, and got up.

"She's right," my son said inevitably, and headed for the door with her. "Look how late it's getting: it's nearly dark."

"Don't be silly," I said. "It's only—"

"Oh shit," Nika said, and opened the door just in time for a wave of thunder to roll in. At once it began to *pour*.

"Where the hell did *that* come from?" Jesse asked indignantly. "It was sunny just a while ago."

I wedged past her and Jesse, sprinted to the porch table, grabbed the recorder and scampered back to the house, a total of fourteen steps. When I got back inside I was as wet as if I'd stood in the shower for twice that long. I stopped on the doorway rug that kept pine needles from being tracked into the house, and wrung out my shirt and hair and stepped out of my sodden shoes. Jesse watched me with wide eyes. "That's not rain," he said with awe. "That's a fucking waterfall."

"What, that little drizzle?" Nika and I both said at the same time, looked at each other in surprise, and then both added, "It rains more in Seattle than it does here," and looked at each other again.

Jesse shook his head. "Vancouver people, no shit. It rains more in Seattle than it does in *Nairobi* in monsoon season."

I excused myself, went to my bedroom, and changed into dry clothes as quickly as I could. I gave my hair a quick toweling and hasty brushing but didn't feel I had time for the hair dryer.

Nika felt the urgency even more than I did. "It strikes me," she said as I returned to the living room, "that now would be a good time to get out of here."

Jesse and I both turned to look at her.

"Russell, I'm very sorry," she said to me. "I checked my car for bugs myself before I left for work this morning. I spotted some asshole staking me out this morning after parade, but I was *sure* I'd lost him. It just never occurred to me anyone could manage to bug a car parked outside the police station. I made damn sure nobody tailed me after I got off the ferry. I thought I had taken adequate precautions to protect you. I fucked up. I've burned this location. It's time to be someplace else while we figure out our next move. The rain will cover the sound of us leaving."

"To go where?" Jesse asked. "And in what? SCUBA gear?"

I knew she was exasperated, and he probably did too, but she kept it out of her voice. "To anyplace at all where we're sure nobody else knows we're there. We need to break the tail. If that means walking through the wood in a downpour, then hot-wiring somebody's car and getting off-island on the next ferry, that's what we'll do. We have to lose this jerk and buy time to figure out what to do."

"I see that." I agreed reluctantly, and took a deep breath. "Okay, let me get some water bottles from the fridge to take along."

"I *don't* see that," Jesse said. "There are three of us. Nika, you're a cop. None of us has done anything wrong. Why don't we just go out to your car and in loud voices invite the jerk in for coffee?"

She shook her head, the exasperation beginning to show. "Jesse, being a cop doesn't give me the kind of weight to deal with somebody who uses gear like that bug. It makes me *more* vulnerable, because there are handles on me, that people like that know how to use. Nobody I know has the weight to help me. Maybe nobody has that much weight."

"I know people who might," Jesse said. "I work for the largest PR firm on the planet."

"And they probably *work* for the CIA," I said bitterly. "No, thanks."

Jesse shut up, looking stubborn.

Nika said, "I need more information and some advice before I confront him, and I only know one place on earth where I might get either one, but I don't dare go there or even attempt to until and unless I am absolutely certain I'm not leading this asshole there."

"To Zudie," he said.

"To Zudie," I agreed. "If Mr. X still remembers Zudie after all these years, it's a good bet Zudie will remember him too. And he got clear of him once already, and stayed clear more than thirty years. Maybe with us to help, he could . . . " I trailed off.

"What?" Nika said, her voice harsh. "Maybe he could *what*?"

I dodged. "Maybe we could discuss this in the rain? For all we know Mr. X on his way here right now. I've got two spare pairs of boots and one spare umbrella—let me get my cellphone—"

"Got a coat and hat I can borrow?" Nika asked. "I don't want to get mine from my car."

"Whoa," Jesse interrupted us. "Nika, I know my father has incipient Alzheimer's—but you're a cop."

"Yeah?"

"Look at me. I come from New York to visit my father on a remote island. Am I going to depend on him to drive me around? Or rent a car at the airport?"

"So where is it? Oh! You wouldn't take a rental down this drive-way. It's the one I saw out there by the mailboxes."

Not far from the mouth of my driveway is what I call the Mailbox Box: a blocky green metal box which contains the mailboxes for sixty-four different rural dwellings that are all arguably within walking distance. It's how we spare Canada Post the onerous chore of actually delivering our mail, as if we were real humans, living on the mainland. For tolerably obvious reasons there are parking verges to either side of it, and Jesse was parked on the nearer one.

"That's right," he said. "You might have taken it for Dad's car."

"I did when I saw it," she agreed. "Didn't even notice the rental plates. By the time I saw his out there in the driveway. I'd stopped thinking about it."

Jesse happened to have chosen the same car to rent that I had bought a few years earlier, a Toyota Echo—the same year and color as mine, right down to the bumpers, generic black rather than color coordinated. The amount of delight I'd taken in that simple coincidence was a sign of how nervous I'd been about Jesse's visit, after an estrangement of so many years. (Maybe you can explain to me why the majority of people who buy Echos—a cheap car designed to run just as cheaply as possible—pay extra to have expendable bumpers painted the same color as the car. Do they have their galoshes painted to match their suits, too?)

I tossed Nika a hoodie from the front hall closet, set out an umbrella on the bench just inside the front door, and collected my phone, a flashlight, and three one-liter bottles of cold water while they both suited up for rain. While getting water I noticed the open catfood can plastic-bagged in the fridge and was reminded to put some out for Horsefeathers, adding another dish of the paté kind he hates for Fraidy; then I propped the laundry room door open enough for them both to get in and out. When I got back Nika had found my own boots and was holding open my jacket for me; as I turned around from putting it on, she was holding open the door for us.

I held up a hand. "Hold on. I go first. I live here. You two don't show yourselves until I whistle. If I start singing instead, go out the back door fast and low, head straight into the woods until you hit the stream, then follow it uphill."

"Uphill?" Nika said.

"Harder going, but very soon you come to a footbridge and a path that'll take you to the road and Jesse's car. I'll meet you there if I can. If I'm not there, bug out, go to ground someplace, and find me a good lawyer."

"No such thing," she said automatically.

Jesse's eyes were wide. "Dad—"

"Text me, son. I gotta go," I said, and stepped out the door, closing it behind me.

No one immediately apparent. Rain so thunderous there could be a platoon a hundred meters away counting cadence without being immediately apparent.

Behave naturally. Do not stare in all directions. Act like you're walking to the Mailbox Box to get the mail, which come to think of it you haven't done yet today. Natural to reach into pants pocket for mailbox key. Inspiration: pretend you can't find it. Slow, stop, turn back toward house, excuse to scrutinize everything to your left. Palm keys, remove them from pants pocket, pantomime finding them in jacket pocket—just in time to make it seem natural to convert a 180 turn into a 360, excuse to scrutinize everything to your right. Call me Chingachcook.

No one immediately apparent. No official-looking vehicle visible. It is certainly possible to enter my property and find the house without using the driveway, but I did not believe any city men could or would do so in this rain without extensive preparation. If they were that good, we were screwed. I continued walking up the driveway until I reached the road. No vehicles visible in either direction except Jesse's Echo on the right. A driveway was visible in either direction, and for all I knew squad cars or tanks could be parked fifty meters up either or both of them. The woods could be full of commandos. The rain made it easy to believe there were choppers somewhere nearby.

The hell with it. I walked a few dozen steps back down the driveway, and gave the two-fingered stevedore's whistle my bus-driver father taught me, which can be heard in a hurricane or Manhattan rush hour. At once came the sounds of the front door being opened and closed firmly, and footsteps on my creaky porch, so I turned and finished walking to the mailbox. No mail. I walked back the few steps to Jesse's car and waited there. Externally it looked just like mine.

Jesse and Nika appeared at the mouth of the driveway. I was standing beside the passenger side front door, but Nika walked past me and stood right beside me at the same door, until I got it, and moved to the back door. *Okay . . .*

Inside, the Echo was quite different from mine. Clean, for a start.

No inch-thick layer of forest detritus on the floors. No CDs or MP3 discs in either of the compartments to either side of the car stereo. No ice-scraper in the door boot. No smell of fine marijuana. Worse: it had been sprayed with fake new-car scent recently. It started more easily for Jesse than mine did for me, too, and I knew why: he was starting it *correctly*, by just turning the key. I cannot for the life of me seem to unlearn the habit of stamping on the accelerator once, first, to set the choke—which today is not only unnecessary but counter-productive. "Have you ever heard of starter fluid?" I asked my son out of curiosity.

"For charcoal briquettes? I use propane. Someone please tell me where we're going."

Nika turned in her seat so she could see both of us. "Russell, is there a place on the island we can use as a base for a day or two while we take turns mounting watch to see who shows up here to get his bug back?"

I thought hard. Or tried to. "Yes, but what's your job situation?"

"Shit." She bit her lip. "I have to get back and book off at 6:00. But I can be back again by, say, 8:00—"

"You'll never make the 7:00 ferry from downtown," I said with certainty. "You'll have to wait for the 8:30, and be back here about 9:15 at the earliest. Just as the last ferry back to the mainland is leaving: you'll be staying the night."

She nodded. "Okay. But after that I have four free days."

Jesse said, "It sounded like you just said you have four days off."

"I do. VPD officers all work four days off, four days on, and today is Day Four for me."

"Sweet."

She shrugged. "Uniform officers work eleven-hour shifts. Investigative section can run longer. We need a longer weekend than most."

"And they shoot about five percent as many people each year as NYPD," I put in. "Even though the GVRD has about a third of New York's population."

Jesse was scowling, but not from the implied insult to his beloved Big Apple. "I hate this plan. Dad, what other ways are there to get to the mainland, other than ferry? Could we rent a boat? Borrow one? Steal one?"

"What's your thought?"

"Where is Mr. X?"

I spread my hands. "Maybe on his way here right now."

"Exactly. We don't know. What we're fairly sure of is that he is not around *now*, because he couldn't have heard us discussing coming up the driveway but he wasn't here when we did. Even a man unfamiliar with the island should've found this place by now, with GPS. If he hasn't come here yet—*why would he*?"

"The rain cutting off his audio could have just made him decide to close in." It doesn't take any effort to argue with my son; I could do it in my sleep.

"Only if he was trying to follow the conversation," Nika said. "And if he was, he'd have closed in earlier, when that tape started to repeat. He'd be here by now."

Two against one. "Okay, fine," I said. "Where are you going with this, Jesse?"

"If he's not here or on the way here, where is he?"

"*Oh.*" The penny dropped. He was right. "Very close to the ferry."

"You think?" Nika said. "Wouldn't he stand out?"

"He stands out less there than anywhere else," I told her.

Jesse nodded. "He draws minimal attention, and we can't get on the ferry without him seeing us."

"I can disguise—" Nika began.

"Are you confident you can fool a professional?" Jesse interrupted. "A ferry line is a slow conveyor belt. He could have a camera and face-recognition software on his laptop."

"In the rain? I think I could. Or one of you could drive me, while I lay on the floor in the back—"

"—and blink up at him, standing there on the sidewalk as you go by at five per—"

"*Okay*—the trunk, then, all right? Unless you think he'll have radar on his laptop." It wasn't just me: Nika was picking up the knack of arguing with him, too.

"I don't know *what* he's got," Jesse insisted, "except for a bug so expensive, assuming the worst is not a bad policy. What I do know is, when all the cows line up and start moving forward slowly, you don't want to be there."

She rummaged for a comeback, and finally sighed. "I know what a choke-point is. Okay. When you're right, you're right." Damn. Agreeing with him. I'd never tried that. She turned to me. "Well? What have you got?"

A splitting headache. "I can get us a couple of boats."

"Why two?"

"You and Jesse need to get to the mainland before six. I need to get somewhere else fast."

"Why both of us?" Jesse asked.

"Because you're not welcome where I'm going."

"I shouldn't go *anywhere*," Jesse said. "I stay here and surveil this place. If someone does come, we have to be watching: it may be our only chance to learn anything."

"Don't be silly, Son," I said. "You're a stranger here."

"Which makes him the only one of us Mr. X can't know anything about," Nika said. Arguing with *me* came naturally to her.

Jesse nodded eagerly. "I haven't even used my credit card since I left New York, Dad. My car was pre-rented, and the company paid for it. Unless he checked every airline flight for the last few days to see if by any chance any of your relatives is in town, I'm invisible. Would any of your immediate neighbors put me up for a night without asking too many questions?"

In spite of myself I saw where he was going. "Doug's barn is close to the driveway, and it's warm and dry inside. He won't mind, he's off shooting Harrison Ford."

"Beg pardon?"

"He's a cinematographer. Ford's in town this week."

"I'll see if he left an infrared camera behind."

"*Don't take any chances*," I said, at the same instant that Nika said "*Don't get* near *this guy*." Our combined volume, in a tiny car *called* Echo, was enough to make all of us jump.

"I won't," Jesse assured us both, suppressing a natural impulse to smile in order to show us how serious he was. "Where is this barn?"

Reluctantly I pointed behind us. "The driveway just before mine on the same side."

"Even better," he said. "He has to go past me to reach your driveway; I'll definitely hear him."

"And you'll be approaching on the opposite side of Russell's house from him," Nika said. "Time's short. Let's go."

They both opened their doors and got out. Only Nika got back in, on the driver's side this time. Jesse was already on his way in the rain. She buckled up.

"Wait—" I began.

"Wish I could," she said, and put it in drive. We turned around in old Milt's driveway, and I just had time to roll down my window and call, "Be careful, Jesse," before we were by him. I wished I'd had the hairs to add, "I love you." I turned to see him out the rear window, and he was gone. It was unsettling, but impressive.

6.

I told myself he'd be fine. The barn would be unlocked because it was on Heron Island. Even if a neighbor happened to see him, he'd think nothing of it because this was Heron Island. It wasn't freezing. Jesse was smart enough to keep his head down. He seemed to know about high-tech surveillance stuff—again, unsettling but impressive. After a while, I turned around and faced forward again.

A five-minute drive will take you to anywhere on the island that isn't closer. The one I directed Nika on now took us to the home of The Young Salt, as I usually insisted on calling him. Keith Salt's father Sam had definitely been The Old Salt until his recent death, and Keith has managed to inherit both his love of the sea and his seamanship without also acquiring the old man's sour personality, his deeply pessimistic conservatism, or his allergy to pleasure. Keith and his wife Lina live in a beautiful house of their own right down on the water, with a small dock for their boat, which they call the *Asclepeadean* and everybody else on the island calls the *Encyclopedia*. She's a 27-foot Erickson sloop, if that conveys anything to you—to me it sounds like a kind of fuzzy bug. As we parked in their turnaround and got out, I hoped they were both home. If so, there was no question they'd both agree to be Samaritans on a rainy night with a minimum of questions, whether they were happy about it or not, because it was Heron Island. If you want to live in a place where you can depend on others, live where they all have to depend on you too. Then don't fuck up.

Lina had the door open by the time we reached it, having heard us arrive. I waved Nika in ahead of me and followed on her heels. A huge amount of white noise went away when the door shut, as if a poorly tuned radio station had suddenly been dialed in properly. (If you're old enough to remember when radio stations could be tuned poorly. Back in ancient times, when "sky the color of TV tuned to a dead channel" did not mean "blue sky.")

"Hi, Russell," Lina said as we were dealing with wet things in the alcove. "Who's your friend?"

"Lina, this is Nika," I said. "AKA Constable Nika Mand—I do beg your pardon, *Detective* Constable Nika Mandiç, Vancouver Police. I forgot the terminology's been changed."

"Hello, Mrs. Salt," Nika said.

"Lina. Out of the bag already, at your age, huh?" Lina said. "Way to go, hon."

Nika looked at her with more respect. "Thanks. I got lucky. Sorry to crash in on you without phoning like this, but our hand was forced."

Lina had been about to usher us into the parlor; now she stopped. "What do you need?"

I already knew Keith wasn't home, because he wasn't either here or bellowing greetings from the interior, but hopeably he was at least nearby. "Is himself around?" I asked hopefully.

She shook her head. "Sorry. On the mainland for the night, helping a friend move."

Shit. "Just what *we* need, too. Unfortunately, we need to move in two different directions at once. Very soon."

"Okay, we can—"

"And neither of them can involve the ferry, or anything in the marina."

"I see," she lied politely. "Well, I can solve half your problem."

"Know anybody who can solve the other?"

She closed her eyes and thought for a full second before she said, "No," so I didn't ask if she was sure. She knew all the other boat people, and all the seaplane types, and the guy with the chopper pad.

Shit. That was bad. Nika *had* to go first, or draw unwelcome attention from her sergeant, who would surely ask why she was booking off late, and would surely have an excellent bullshit detector. But that left me with nothing effective whatsoever to *do*—for hours—except wonder if my son was all right. Hell, until morning! Lina would get back no earlier than ten o'clock, and way too tired for me to ask her to go right back out with me. I wouldn't be—

"—except you, anyway," Lina finished.

"Beg pardon? I don't . . . oh. Oh dear God, I do understand." It was actually the ideal solution, really: I saw that at once. As quickly as my stomach began to protest. She was paying me an enormous compliment *and* doing me a serious favor at risk to herself, so I couldn't even be mad at her. There was nothing else to convert my fear into, nothing to do but suck it up.

"How far do you have to go?"

"To Coveney and back."

"Not far. You'll be okay if it doesn't get any uglier out than this," she said.

"You trust me that much? In bad weather?"

"I figure you'll just fall overboard and drown. I can live with that. If you sink her, I'll never speak to you again."

I wanted to find that touching, but was already getting seasick. "Thank you too much. No, just enough."

"Chicken. You'll be fine. Anyway, the boat will. Just don't sink her."

I smiled broadly. I looked at Nika, still smiling. "What's wrong?" she asked.

"I'm calculating." Let it go.

She had to ask. "Calculating what?"

Precisely how much I'd care if you got killed by some CIA spook. "Don't ask."

Her eyes flicked to Lina and she let it go. Quick on the uptake.

Yeah, damn it, I'd care.

The *Encyclopedia* was equipped with a little-outboard powered inflatable job (that's hyphenated correctly: it was powered by a little outboard) that Keith called the Fiendish Dinghy, and Lina called the Killer Zodiac. It was a great little conveyance, if you didn't mind bailing a lot and getting wet anyway—and assuming you never had engine trouble someplace where you'd need to paddle it more than a few meters, downstream, with the wind.

It would suck if Nika bought it.

I'm not a big fan of boats. I'm not even a tiny fan of *tiny* boats. If the tiny boat is basically a truck-tire inner tube with a floor—a rippling, inch-thick floor—and a propellor sticking out the back, I become a microfan at best.

Okay, it would suck a lot.

I'm gonna be the only one in the truck tire? Toward sunset, in the rain? Heading for a destination that's likely to kill me on arrival? Now I'm in the nanofan range.

I looked at her, looking back at me.

Detective Constable Nika Mandič, not only *not* a friend, but my spiritual and psychological and emotional antipod, had once—almost the last time I'd seen her, I was ashamed to admit to myself—knowingly risked rape, torture, maiming, dismemberment, personality disintegration, soul extinction and, after what would surely have been far too long for it to be any mercy, death, for no better reason than to save me from the same fate. Well, and a family of four, also strangers. And dozens if not hundreds after that. But *that night* she could have just turned around and left. Gone home and made a plan, come back with reinforcements, confident that I'd be alive next morning, if not necessarily still salvageable. Nobody else on the planet suspected I had a problem, or that she knew a thing about it, or even that we'd ever met . . . save one person, who couldn't talk to *anyone* but me. Total available backup on the island was two RCMP officers, and the sober one was a fuckup legendary throughout the whole Lower Mainland.

She had gone through the door. Alone. Up against that *creature* with nothing but a handgun, not one of its slugs cast from silver. For her trouble she'd ended up sprawled across my couch with her own handcuffs on her wrists and his on her ankles, bleeding from one ear and waiting for a brilliant, very bad death to begin.

Face it, Russell: if she got taken out by some government golem— just because she was lucky enough to meet you, once—it would suck one holy jumping fuckofalot. Not as bad as losing Jess, not as bad as losing Susan was . . . but in that band of the spectrum.

"Well?" Lina prompted. She'd waited more than a polite interval.

Still meeting Nika's eyes, I felt my smile become smaller . . . but now it was genuine. She saw it at once. "I already knew the answer. It's just better if I check my math. Let's roll."

If you've sailed, or even read a magazine with pictures of boats in it, you can probably skip the next part. The rest of you . . . this is the part Travis McGee glosses over, when he makes *The Busted Flush* sound like fun.

Damn, it's tough to pull out, when the lines are all wet and tied in knots you've never seen before, and the engine's not that happy to start, and the wind is insistently advising you to re*main!* right *here!* up a*gainst!* this *SLIP!* Where you're **SAFE!**, and even the wheel is saturated, and it's not looking to get better anytime soon.

Sure, you're wearing borrowed slick yellow overalls, jacket and comedy hat that probably don't *really* weigh twenty kilos, and most of the water is rolling off. But while man can make a suit that will keep out Ebola virus, keep him breathing in vacuum or cool in a furnace, it is apparently fundamentally impossible to fashion a garment that will keep out more than ninety-eight percent of a British Columbia rain, which leaves about a pint a minute unaccounted for. God knows why, it seems to seek the neck area. And for some reason, sailors have not yet evolved as far as divers in intelligence: *their* rubber suit is way too loose for wet-suit effect to provide any warmth.

If you've got any sense, you've changed out of the runners that have been your only footgear for over a decade now into nine-league boots. But you hate clumping around a small sailboat in boots, and you see yourself putting a booted foot through the floor (deck?) of the rubber truck tire, and if you had any sense you wouldn't be here. So each shoe holds another pint. Socks and Stanfields make great wicks: moisture is approaching your crotch from both above and below, before you've even sat on anything.

Lina coaxes the engine into surly life, and then it all starts to happen fast. You and Nika each spring to untie one of the spring-lines (a little sailing humor, there). Then Nika springs to untie your springline too, while Lina curses in Greek. You don't waste seconds being mortified—there'll be *plenty* of time later—but spring to untie the stern line. There's just time to break a fingernail and see a half-full film-container of Kootenay Thunderfuck fall from your shirt pocket into the drink before Nika frees the bow line and comes to untie yours, apparently with a gesture, while Lina curses in *classical* Greek. Nika mimes: *push it away from the slip and jump aboard real fast.* You mime: *are you fucking* kidding *me?* Nika glares: *idiot, it's not our boat—HURRY!* You nod, turn to push and discover as you leave vertical that by now the boat has done *fine* on its own. Instantly you compute distance—as far as you can jump with a running start—form the theory that sufficient desperation is just as helpful, and decide to test it, since you're leaving the dock one way or another anyway. Total effort. Belated realization that half of effort merely pushed dock away from you. Joyous realization in midair that you *will* nonetheless reach the boat, just like in the—

—then things happen *very* fast as you land on the rail on your groin and fold and your face hits both of your fists just as they hit the deck just as both knees hit the hull just as Lina *guns* it in reverse and you roll left which makes your body half-close and fly wide-open again like a dropped laptop so now the *back* of your face and groin both hurt too but there's enough rebound so that it's easy to get your elbows under you and try to sit and start sliding off the rail feetfirst toward an *astonishing* quantity of water and hook both forearms under the rail and find out what a great idea *that* was and your eyes open wide and refocus on Nika standing at the edge of the dock already a mile away just in time to see her crouch all of ten centimeters and step across the water and pass over your head—

—and then things slow rapidly, so that by the time she's hauled you back aboard, you're reassuring yourself the extensive inventory of Places You Hurt does *not* seem to include either of your collapsible lungs.

Lina bellows, "Leave the rubbers on," or something like it, from up at the wheel of the boat.

Pause. "I'm not wearing them," you yell back with your test chestful of air.

Pause. "Don't, take, the fucking, rubber, *off* yet!"

I looked down at my groin. I hate admitting that. But I may as well—Nika caught me at it, and *must* have told people by now. She made a noise like swallowing something horrid she'd snorted, touched my relocating shoulder and pointed just as that sneaky dock came *racing* at us without warning and whacked us square in . . . the *rubber* bumpers hanging over the side. She was pointing with one hand, and keeping me from tumbling headfirst back onto the dock with the other, so I assume she held onto the boat with her butt-cheeks.

We waited until Lina had put her in drive and pulled away, and then a minute more, before hauling the rubbers in and stowing them. There was being not-laughed-at by Nika, and then there was being laughed at by Lina, and if you ask me which was harder to take, I'm going to need more time. I was distracted by how hard to take wet clothes are. In the movies, boats are nearly always adequately equipped with spare dry clothing for all, in some unseen storage space. Unless the wet person is a woman with attractive breasts—and sure enough, Lina, a woman with attractive breasts, had no clothes aboard at all. Except for an orange life vest I was glad to put on, even though it made me look like a gay Imperial Storm Trooper, and a pair of boat shoes that looked even flimsier than mine but had better traction.

"Good weather," Lina said.

We stared.

"It is," she insisted. "Nothing hard about sailing in the rain. Rain accompanied by high wind and waves is bad. Your timing's good, too: you'll be heading *into* what wind and current there is on your way to Coveney."

"Super."

"Would you rather they were against you on your way *back*, when you're tired?"

We booted it straight out from the Salts' dock for half a klick or so, then Lina turned right, or in nautical terms, hung a right, and we began circling Heron Island. Left would have been a shorter route both for me and for Nika as the crow swims, but right, while longer, was better for me. Lina explained the wind, tide and current reasons why this was so, even drawing little caligraphic objects she believed illuminated things; I bought it, but didn't get it or bother to retain it. In only a few minutes we were rounding the point by the west-facing beach imaginatively named Sunset Beach. I went back topside. The wind picked up a little, and the rain eased off a little, and Coveney Island came into view in the declining light of late afternoon. It looked like something it would take an Apollo Program to reach.

"Not that far," Nika said behind me. She actually sounded confident I'd have no problem.

Maybe it wouldn't suck *that* much. "No."

Strong hand on my right shoulder. "Good luck, Russell." Squeeze. "I'm really sorry."

I tried to shrug without shrugging off the hand, and succeeded. "You and I were going to have to do something about Zudie sooner or later anyway." *And each other.*

"Should have a long time ago."

The rain let up some more. "All we needed was the faintest clue what to do."

She snorted. "See? We didn't actually need that after all."

"Speak for yourself."

She cleared her throat. "Look, I'm probably going to have to send Lina home without me, and find my own transport when I can. Booking off is going to be more complicated than usual tonight, and I don't know how long it will take."

"The new chief?" Two days before, the mayor had appointed a new chief of police—Jim Chu, the first Chinese-Canadian ever to hold that job, in a city whose ethnic Chinese population approaches twenty percent. The transition period was bound to be a complicated time for cops.

"Exactly. I don't know how fast I'll be able to get back out here tonight, but I promise you it'll be as fast as I can make it." Her hand squeezed my shoulder again. "I'll watch out for him."

I was touched. And relieved. And slightly jealous. "Thank you, Nika."

"You remember my cell number?"

"Christ, no." I patted my hip pocket. "But mine has it and Jesse's in memory."

The rain slacked way off, to the condition I've always called smutch, a random floating dampness like being underneath one of God's sneezes. I looked up, began to offer thanks, decided not to risk calling attention to myself, realized I was worried about a God I had not believed in for half a century, and wondered if I should be allowed out without a keeper.

The engines slowed, then died. Lina went below, as we sailors call downstairs, and came up out of the hole thing carrying a big duffle bag. "Time to make sail. Russ, you're underfoot: why don't you jump overboard?"

"Of course." Together we all got the inflatable over the side of the *Encyclopedia* without either sinking or losing it. (I wonder why boats stop being "her" when they get real small.)

"The *Fiendish Dinghy*," I said admiringly.

"The *Killer Zodiac*," Lina said automatically.

"I devoutly hope not."

"Don't be silly. I told you all you really need to know."

"Tell me again."

"Don't let the waves hit you from the side. Keep 'em dead ahead or dead astern. That's basically it. Long as you don't run out of gas, you'll be fine. And you won't: I checked."

"What if a big gas leak just started now?"

"Row." She pointed. I hoped for oars, and saw paddles.

"How's it handle?" Nika asked.

Lina shrugged. "Like a kid's swimming pool."

Nika turned to me. "Have you done much rowing?"

Politely phrased. I don't tell a lot of people about the annoying tendency of my lungs to collapse; how was she to know Lina was one of the ones I had told? I said what I always used to say when my late wife Susan asked me if a given task was within my acceptable range: "Oh, sure. No sweat." I wasn't going to have to row anyway, Lina said so.

Unlike Susan, Nika bought it. "Good luck, then." Lina echoed her.

I thanked them both. With their help, I managed to get into the *Dinghy* without soaking myself much further, learning in the process why Keith called it "Fiendish." I'd assumed it was a Beatles reference. "Where's the handle?" I yelled back up to Lina, looking the motor over for a pull-cord to yank.

Pause. "Just under your ribs on either side," she yelled back, pointing to the ignition key.

Pause. "I knew that!"

I turned the key and it started up *much* faster and smoother than the *Encyclopedia*'s main engine had. I heard Lina yell what must have been "We never doubted you," then figured out the throttle and went away from there.

Somehow it took only seconds to be all alone. And no time at all to be lonesome.

The first half of the voyage wasn't too bad. The seating was comfortable enough, once I got the damn cellphone out of my hip pocket and into my shirt pocket. Despite the overcast and the smutch there was enough light left to see where I was going. Although Lina had been right about the wind and tide, the *Dinghy*'s little motor was up to them. It sounded like a sewing machine having hysterics, but it performed more like a big chainsaw. The direction of the waves was such that by diverging only slightly from a head-on course I could approach Coveney Island. I thought at the time I was miserable, but in retrospect I was just uncomfortable, apprehensive, and heartsick.

If I'd been miserable, I wouldn't have had attention to spare to beat myself up for having somehow dragged my son, my only remaining piece of Susan, into deadly peril. I'd awakened that morning hoping today would be the day I'd finally manage to bury the hatchet with Jesse, so Susan could finally get on with the resting-in-peace part of her afterlife. Instead we both had a fair chance of joining her—thanks to an old mess of mine I'd failed to clean up. Good one, Dad. Fortunately, after perhaps half an hour of that I was distracted by the rapid onset of mortal terror, followed almost at once by incredible peril.

It began with the idle observation that the rain seemed to be picking back up again. Rather . . . no, very fast.

Then the wind did too. Hard.

Then the waves did too. Big.

That quickly, I was in Hell. It was dark and windy and cold and noisy and *active* out there. The rain came down so hard it felt like a vibrator was strapped to my skull. It became a good idea to do a bit of bailing, now and again, with the hand I wasn't using to steer. Never in my life have I been more grateful that I don't get seasick. (I grew up riding subways and the Coney Island roller coaster.)

Then the damn water began to *cheat*. The direction of the waves *changed*: to keep making for Coveney, I had to go at an ever-increasing angle from perpendicular to them. A point was going to come when I'd have to steer away from my destination to keep from being flipped, swamped, or both. After hard thought I decided when that point came, my move was to turn counterintuitively, in what felt like the wrong direction but somehow looked right. I'd be moving *away* from Coveney, then . . . but at least I wouldn't drift *past* the bastard. Past it was nothing but a whole lot of the Strait of Georgia; I could just make out the lights of Nanaimo on the horizon, but the bulk of Vancouver Island itself was too far to make out in this light. Each time I ran the problem, I got the same answer. As the angle changed, I began to get a stiff neck from keeping both my eye on the prize and my hand on the tiller.

The decision point came. I squinted at my cards one last time, put my money on the table, hauled on the tiller and waited to see what Nature had.

I came about fast and was once again perpendicular to the waves. I stopped approaching Coveney . . . but I stopped sliding past it, too. I started to gain ground, a little. *I hadn't fucked up.* I began to envision a point at which I would be able to do a quick one-eighty, and almost coast to Coveney. Call me Ishmael. Predecessor of email.

That raised the question I'd been postponing: just exactly what the hell I was going to do when I got there?

The first reason little Coveney Island is a terrific place for a man in Zudie's predicament to live is, there's no good place to land. The second reason is, there aren't even any mediocre ones. There are only one or two even *rotten* ones charted, with warnings in boldface. Ugly rocks, laid out like a Driver-Ed obstacle course. Completely invisible rocks in no pattern at all. Crashing surf, with an occasional geyser like a sounding whale. Whirlpools. Randomly reversing currents. Enough rusting pieces of ex-ships to qualify as Davy Jones's Dumpster. Even horny teenagers on drugs don't try to land on Coveney. (There are better places closer.) I think Keith could have done it. Lina would probably never have tried.

I told myself I'd think of something, once I got a closer look. Hell, I'd figured out that I needed to go the wrong way, hadn't I? There'd been a time when Columbus was the only guy on earth that smart.

How hard could it be to *park*? No wonder the boat was barking like an applauding seal and shaking my hand. It was—

Barking like a seal?

—I spun around. A similar sound can be made by inhaling sharply while saying the word "We!" repeatedly. What was producing it now was the motor mount tearing itself free of the *Fiendish Dinghy*. No, the *Killer Zodiac*. All rubber breaks down if you leave it out in the sun for enough years, and the first warning is usually failure. A visible gap widened with each "We!" as the motor tried to deny our inevitable parting.

It wasn't because I'm stupid—really. It was because I'm so much faster than a normal human being that I tried to hold onto the motor. Even as my hands touched it I was thinking *it's going to be loads of fun, rowing with ten burned fingers*, so you can see I really was alert. It just didn't help.

Neither did my sacrifice. "We!" became "WE!" and then with one terminal "*WHEEEE! Pah-**LOOT**!!!*," the motor left me. Followed a moment later, with the exquisite subtlety of a Chuck Jones punchline, by the barely audible "wish-*poop*" of my cellphone leaving my shirt pocket and chasing the motor.

It was suddenly much quieter. Just the white noise of the rain, and the oscillating signal of the wind. I waited for the overgrown inner-tube to start hissing, go soft, and sink, but Fate's sense of humor was subtler than that.

Lina was going to kill me. Worse: Keith was going to break my balls for the next twenty years.

It wasn't fair: all she'd said was *don't sink my boat*. Once the motor left the boat, it wasn't *my* responsibility. If it had asked me first, I'd have told it to stay.

If you're going to burn all your fingers, it is useful to do so in a swimming pool with a decimeter or two of ice water in it. They didn't hurt too bad at all until I picked the paddles up. Then they *did*. It was hard getting the paddles into those oarlock things; when I finally succeeded I told myself I was an Oarlock Warlock, smart as Sherlock. Myself said it was sheer luck, so I called it a Person From Porlock. A split personality, suffering from share-lack. *When in danger, when in doubt: run in circles, scream and shout!*

Look where you are. Look where you're going . . .

No: rowing is better. In straight lines. Check position. Assess wind and current. Plot course, and:
Row, row, row your boat, gently down the stream
Merrily, merrily, merrily, merrily, life is but a dream
Row, row, row your boat, gently down the stream
Screw merrily. Too many syllables.
Row, row, row your boat
Row, row, row your boat
Fuck, fuck, fuck this boat—
—for about as many iterations as you used to be able to stand singing "Ninety-Nine Bottles Of Beer" on the schoolbus, before your chest starts to hurt.

Right side, low in back. Rest, get breath back. Pain fades reassuringly. Just a pulled muscle, this time. Lift head, assess position and course . . . yikes . . . so much for resting, pick up paddles in sore hands and:
Row your boat
Row your boat
Row your boat
Row your boat
Blow me, boat
Row your boat—
—chest pain comes much sooner this time, high and on the side. Sharp, too, but that's the good news: it's only one of the braces the surgeons left in there, shifting around a bit, pinching some nerve. No biggie—usually. Work the right shoulder around and it starts to back right off. Longer pause for recovery this time before you dare lift your head up, check position and course, and:
Row!
Row!
Row!
Row!
Row!
Row!
Row!
Row!
—mild pain now, but it's dull and intimate. This summons some of the scariest memories you own; even resting doesn't give you much of

your breath back. One of the little bubbles you were born with on the bald tire that is your lung is officially threatening to let go. You remind yourself that sometimes the little bubbles are bluffing. And sometimes they pop and they're just minicollapses, of no consequence, a day or two in bed moving carefully. The Charter of Rights and Freedoms must surely set some statutory upper limit on the amount of bad luck a man is allowed to have in any given day. Unclench teeth, open eyes, and holy Jesus it's not too much further, let's:

Row, row, row, row, row, row, row, row, row—

Okay: *row . . . row . . . row . . . row . . . row . . . row . . .*

All right, dammit!

Row . . . row . . . row . . . row . . . row . . . row . . . row . . . row . . .

I had wondered all my life what the word "landlubber" was all about. I got it, now. It came from a guy who was trying to tell the universe he was a land lover, and drowned before he could finish.

. . . row . . . row . . . row . . . row . . . row . . .

Some tasks you can't ever complete, no matter how hard you try—but you have to keep on trying anyway, die trying if that's what it takes. You know what that's about, eh, Russell?

Everything melted away—the pain, the fear, the boat, the sea and sky themselves—and I paddled through memory instead. Some of my least favorite memories, but I no longer had the strength to push them back.

I was with Susan, on one of her last good days. Don't ask how far our definition of "good" had contracted by that point, and don't even think about the days that came after that and redefined "bad" just as drastically.

Lying beside my beloved wife in our last living room, on the foldout couch my friends and I had converted to her deathbed. Her head on my chest, her left arm across my belly, carefully placed to avoid dislodging the IV. Talking quietly to me about some of the problems I would have to deal with after she died, advising me one last time. I've done very few intelligent things in my entire life that weren't based on Susan's advice.

She saved Jesse for last.

"Forget it, Russell!"

"He's got a perfectly good brain. There has to be *some* way—"

She shook her head against my chest. "Spice, listen to me. I'm not saying you won't be able to do it. I'm saying it isn't going to be doable, by you or the best shrink in the world or *anybody*."

"But it's so *stupid*."

"That's not a word that applies in this context. It's like saying apples are awkward."

"But—"

"It's sad, yes. That won't be easy to take. *But it's nobody's fault.* Not yours; not his. It's just the way it is. Who Jesse is. The age he happens to be now. Who *you* are. How he relates to you, and to me, and . . .and to *this*. All the history between all of us so far."

"Suppose I—"

"No matter what you say or do, no matter how rational he is on most other subjects, Jesse is going to hold you responsible for me being gone. He is going to believe—no, he's going to know for a fact—that you could have talked me out of it if you really wanted to, that your voice added to his would unquestionably have turned the tide. Ergo, you must not have really wanted to; ergo, you are evil. You are merciless, indifferent, selfish . . . you are the cancer itself. It will take him *years* to get past that; it's just who he is, and who he imagines you are."

I didn't answer. I knew she was probably right.

"That's a shame, because you don't deserve his anger, and trust me, he's going to feel like a major jerk about it one day. But I can live with . . . no, I can *die* with . . . the thought of him hating his dad's guts for a few years. He'll move as far away from you as possible—don't be surprised if he actually picks New York, just to spite you—and that'll actually be a good thing. I think you both need to be alone for a while, to heal separately before you try to heal together. Does that make any sense?"

"I guess. I'm not sure."

"But what I *can't* die with is the thought of you hating him back. Of you doing just what he's doing: being mad at him for something he can't help. You're supposed to be smarter than a twenty-one-year-old. If you let yourself stay pissed off at him, together you're both going to dig yourselves a hole you'll be too stubborn to climb out of even when you finally figure out you should."

I sighed. "Damn it, babe, I've *been* letting him be pissed off at me since he was sixteen."

"Sure: that comes with the job. That's the point: he's about to become ten times as pissed off as ever, and you're his customary whipping-man."

"Terrific. What am I supposed to do with my own rage against the universe for stealing you?"

She reached up, being careful of the IV, and touched my face. "Put it to good use. Sit down at your keyboard and aim it at all the sons of bitches and bitches in the world. 'Right livelihood,' the Buddhists call it. Cut 'em all a new one for me."

Pain, with its reminder of mortality, brought me back to myself.

I learned a long time ago that I can die; being reminded wasn't even interesting. I was absolutely unsurprised to be unready again, this time. I kept rowing because now it was easier to keep going than to stop, somehow.

. . . row . . . row . . . row . . . row . . . row . . .

Maybe not.

. . . row . . . row . . . row . . . row . . . row . . .

Noise asserted itself. Noises. Ugly noises. Death-rattle thunder. Giant turds falling into a bowl from a great height. Whiplashes. Lions roaring. Birds shrieking. God trying to shush them all. This was some *very* groovy acid. Maybe I should stop a minute and dig it. Smell the fish. Open my eyes, the visuals might be even better . . .

Holy shit!

I was nearly there.

Now what?

I had a very short list of contingency plans for this. Always go with your best hope first. At least it didn't call for physical exertion. I closed my eyes again, and thought as hard as I could, so hard that I saw bursts of acid-colours again, saw them shape the words I was thinking in shimmering blossoms of fire, heard my voice chant them in my head louder than all the Gyuto Monks in Dharamsala:

HELP ME, ZUDIE!

HELP ME, ZUDIE!

HELP ME, ZUDIE!

It's a hell of a note when your best hope is something you don't think is going to work.

Zandor Zudenigo had told me a few years ago—the first night I'd seen him since we'd been college roommates back in the sixties—that these days, he had to stay at least a hundred meters away from people, or it was "agony." (If you're an American baffled by the metric system—nobody else is—a meter is about a yard.) From anyone but me, anyway: apparently I don't think as loud as most people or something. That was my sole data point for his current telepathic sensitivity. With absolutely nothing to go on but intuition, always a poor guide in novel circumstances, it felt to me like if a hundred meters was safe range, anything over five hundred meters would be out of range altogether. I was a good three hundred from the catastrophe zone where sea and land met snarling, itself a good hundred meters across, and beyond that were fifty meters of horrible rocky rising shore before you came even to the edge of the twisted, deformed, but quite thick woods. God alone knew whether Zudie's home even lay on this side of the island. There was no guarantee he had not gone to the mainland for a quart of milk today. There was no guarantee he was even still alive, if it came to that. Hermiting is a risky profession. It had been more than six months since the last time I'd come out here to try calling him again, and as always gotten not an answer . . . but at least the sense that one was still being withheld.

HELP ME, ZUDIE!
HELP ME, ZUDIE!
ZANDOR*, PLEASE *SAVE MY ASS—AGAIN—

Okay, no problem: go to Plan B. Close my eyes, cross my fingers, arms, and legs . . . head straight in . . . and pray to all the gods I didn't believe in that—

Coming across the rocks of the shore like a ghost walrus: the cartoon character Baby Huey, or Tony Soprano if you prefer, bigger than life and stark naked. Holy shit. Reaching the surfline, beckoning me toward him with exaggerated gestures, indicating, "This way— this way—right here, straight toward me—this way—"

Well, hell. That had been *my* plan. THANKS, *MAN—HERE I COME—*

More gestures, all unmistakable: "NOT SO LOUD! That's better— keep coming—"

Sorry! I started paddling with all I had left.

"—keep coming—keep coming—that's it, straight in—"

He had me heading into a rock funnel toward an unbroken line of exploding foam. *Are you SURE? It really looks—*

"—STRAIGHT IN—"

Giant ragged boulders went by on either side. I was committed now, and everything ahead was ghastly. *I trust you with my life, Zudie, but ARE YOU SURE?*

"STRAIGHT IN!"

One last huge black stone went by on my left, like the spine of a submerged whale, or a submarine with no conning tower. *Okay, but listen: some CIA or NSA spook is after you—Nika's cousin was—*

Suddenly he was gesturing even more frantically than I was paddling: "GO LEFT! GO LEFT! DO IT NOW! GO LEFT—"

I went left, saw no point, kept going left, he gestured even harder, I gave it everything I had left, and all at once saw a clear open channel to a tiny sand beach maybe six or seven meters wide, two or three long even when the waves came all the way in, quite invisible to anyone who had not committed himself to certain death and then been directed just as I had.

THANK YOU, ZUDIE!!!

Row, row, row, row, rowrowrowrowrowrowrow . . .

He came out waist-deep to meet me. Helped me beach the *Killer Zodiac.* Helped me out of it. Helped me climb up onto and stretch out on a flattish bit of rock which was very hard and very cold . . . but not wet, and not moving in any direction at all. Dragged the *Killer* completely out of the water and up onto rock that would not gut her. Came and sat beside me.

Familiar voice. The voice of the little Martian who keeps threatening Bugs with his Illudium Q-36 Explosive Space Modulator. "You're okay now, Russell."

I felt like a crumb. "I'm sorry, man."

He shrugged. "I know what I look like naked."

"How close behind is he?

"Oh. Hell, for a minute there, I thought there was a problem or something.

"Yeah, you too.

"Well, give her mine, too.

"Because this is my shower; you caught me bathing. Not *that* cold.

"I don't drink it, remember? No, not even tea. Yes—dry, and warmer than this."

Talking with Zandor can be unsettling for someone who doesn't smoke marijuana, but one compensation is, it doesn't matter a bit if you're out of breath. You don't *have* to condense your own side of the conversation to the fewest possible gasped syllables, and then take forever to get them out.

7.

Saturday, June 23, 2007
Bug Cove, Heron Island, British Columbia, Canada

McKinnon's state of the art, top of the line GPS receiver had a bad earphone jack.

So even though he was very hungry for breakfast by now, and wanted coffee very much indeed, he had to stay in the car if he wanted to keep on monitoring the conversation taking place. It never occurred to him not to; in similar situations in the past he had gone hungry for days, gone without peeing for a day, remained motionless in the sun for hours. Years ago. He concentrated hard . . . on what turned out to be nothing much, which is a classic first step to the hypnotic state. The conversation started out with an interesting sentence or two. But nearly at once it wandered off into nothing but meandering meaningless chatter between the two males, which his target seemed prepared to let go on forever. Could Canada really be such a sissy place that even female police officers were too self-effacing to interrupt men talking? Or was she simply too busy smoking the pot they'd mentioned? The men's voices were remarkably alike, and they were so far from the mike he had to strain to make out what they were saying, and when he did it never turned out to be worth the trouble, and he didn't even realize he had fallen asleep until the first crack of thunder and avalanche of rain arrived together.

When they did his first thought was that he'd had a stroke. The truth made him little happier. He had *never* fallen asleep on stakeout before. It rattled him—might have frightened him a little if it'd had time.

First things first. The conversation was over; obviously they had gone inside to wait out the rain. The GPS snitch said it had not moved a centimeter from its last known position. He could probably expect them to stay inside until the rain at least moderated . . . so he would have time to play back the conversation he'd just dozed through.

Once he had dealt with *second* things. Now he was *starving* for breakfast, and *desperate* for coffee, and his bladder was about to *burst*.

The last problem was easiest to deal with, thanks to the heaviness of the rain. Anyone still outdoors would have better things to do than gawk at cars in a parking lot. He opened his door, swiveled on his seat and planted both shoes on the ground as if he intended to get out, and urinated between his feet.

By the time he was as close to done as he felt he absolutely needed to be, and could swing back inside and slam the door, he was soaking wet from the knees down, and both his shoes were *overflowing*. He removed them, tipped water out of each, removed his socks, and wrung them out. He did his best to wring out his pant legs, but was not willing to remove them to do a proper job because he had seen too many comedies use that set-up to introduce a policeman. He started the car, forced himself to wait patiently while the engine warmed, then set heat and fan to max, and arranged all the fan grilles he could to aim at either his ice cold calves or his sodden shoes and socks. It gave him plenty of time to consider his other problems.

He could carry the GPS receiver around with him as long as he kept it dry, and it didn't need headphones to work as an alarm. It was smaller than an iPod. He could set it so that if the target's vehicle started up, or another started nearby, or there was loud conversation, the receiver would imitate the sound of a ringing cell. No one thought anything of it if you shut the phone off inside your pocket without bothering to take it out.

So it was safe to go find caffeine and food, in that order. And about time—dear God, it was nearly 5:00 PM! He had not fallen

asleep so much as passed out from hunger. He could not have artic-
ulated why that was less dismaying, but it was. He found a way to fit
his socks over two of the dashboard grilles and turn them into
warmwindsocks, held his shoes before two others. Waiting for everything to dry, for the first time he had spare attention to notice that he
had a vicious pulsing headache, so powerful it ran halfway to his
shoulder blades, as if yearning toward the duller but deeper ache
below, in the muscles of his lower back. *It serves me right, he thought
darkly, not only for passing out on a stakeout, but for not at least
admitting it to myself and putting the damn seat back first.*

By the time everything was dry enough to put back on, he was
speaking to his own blood sugar, telling it that it wasn't the boss of
him, and close to doing so aloud. He thought about accessing the net
with his phone and googling up a decent restaurant—then realized
he was being silly: there wouldn't be any. Nor any shortage of
mediocre ones near the ferry ramp and marina. He put his shoes and
socks back on, got his top on and over his head, popped the trunk,
got out into the rain and looked inside it, saw no umbrella, cursed the
car's owner, turned at once on his heel and set off uphill on what
appeared to be not only the village's main, but its only, street.

Nearly at once his luck took a sharp turn for the better.

The first business establishment he encountered, only a hundred
meters or so after leaving the marina lot, was a restaurant.

That at least was his first assessment. As he neared the door, a
number of subliminal signals caused him to revise it to "a very good
restaurant." Because an overhang kept him dry enough, he took a
moment to glance at the small discreet menu in the window, and
nearly at once knew that somehow, absurdly, he had stumbled onto
an *excellent* restaurant in the middle of nowhere. There were only
four main courses offered! He was nearly drooling as he entered.

He was nearly weeping as he left. Collinsia Verna's was not a
mere excellent restaurant—but one of only three genuinely *great*
ones he had ever been privileged to worship at. By polite inquiry he
learned that a culinary genius, chef at a Vancouver restaurant so
good McKinnon had heard of it, called Bishop's, had tired of the
urban rat race and decided to move to the country for a while
instead; her husband Stephen ran the restaurant with equal genius
while Carol cooked with a baby on her hip. Few on the island could

afford their prices—but those who could seldom ate anywhere else. And those who couldn't, McKinnon learned, could usually afford to buy prepared frozen dinners and microwave them at home, accepting or failing to notice that this reduced their quality from sublime to merely superb.

Sublime food is good for thinking. By the time he finished his appetizer, he realized his target might well be here for the night, in which case so was he. Ideal in several ways. He could take the target's own vehicle back to the mainland, and abandon it somewhere near the border. The question was, should he bother to stay here *above-radar*, in some motel or B&B, or was it better to just find a quiet place near his target to park unobserved until daybreak? The answer depended in part on whether such a quiet place existed.

He bought two frozen entrées for takeout without even thinking about it, a brisket of beef in mustard gravy with mashed and a butter chicken with rice, confident that he would be hungry again at least twice before either could spoil, and had an engine block for a stove. It took nearly all the American cash he had left on him—but he could not bear to stiff such an artist with a *fugazee* credit card.

An hour had passed by the time he got back to his car, so the ferry line was exactly as he had left it, just getting long enough to disappear around the curve at the distant top of the hill. The rain had not changed in intensity either. But the sun was nearly down now, and the streetlights came on as he set his frozen dinners on the passenger seat beside him. Thinking about his bogus credit card had reminded him that his identity might be melting already and surely would eventually; he lost no time in driving toward the location of the target's vehicle.

He lost a fair amount of time in finding it, however. A GPS fix is only as accurate as someone has paid to make it, and nobody with a big checkbook was interested in Heron Island. More than one road his locator confidently told him to take turned out not to exist; one was a fifty meter long driveway serving three small cottages. It was close to eight o'clock by the time he drove slowly past the driveway where his target's car was parked. He couldn't see it through the trees and brush—*this* driveway seemed to be *hundreds* of meters long—but his locator was sure. A rural postbox station just past it offered a convenient place and excuse to pull over and think the situation over.

So far he'd seen no good prospects for an overnight hideaway. Lots of tempting dirt roads . . . but any of them could lead to the cabin of some paranoid hermit, and if they went nowhere, kids probably used them at night for social purposes. He'd seen no municipal lots with buses or trucks to hide behind. Not even one big snowplow—wasn't this Canada? A chain motel seemed like his best choice; or failing that, a B&B. Apple Computer had recently stunned the world by releasing a breakthrough phone which was nearly as good as his own; he used it now to access the net. So it took him less time to learn that Heron Island had no motels, chain or otherwise, and only a single B&B with the sense to have a URL or a listing with Google, than it took him to marvel over the information. He phoned the B&B before he was quite finished, was able to make a reservation for that evening, and smiled when Mrs. Meade the owner cautioned him that he must be there to pick up his key before nine o'clock, when she went to bed. He agreed he would.

Well. He had just over an hour to reach a place at most fifteen minutes away. If he came back later, the rain might just stop, aiding reconnaisance. But if it did, the sound of his car would carry a long way, and would be an unusual sound after the last ferry of the day.

How would he explain to Mrs. Meade his being soaked to the skin on arrival?

Who said he had to?

God damn it. He shut the engine, restarted it in neutral with the parking brake engaged so that it would idle without lights, disabled the overhead light, and got out of the car. He looked longingly at the driveway . . . and entered the woods. It was still early enough that his target might decide to go get in line for the last ferry of the night at any time.

How was it, he wondered, that James Bond had never found himself in Africa in the rainy season, or in Bangladesh in monsoon season, or in the Pacific Northwest *ever*? He did have an umbrella, which he had seen carried into Collinsia Verna's by a man who had disrespected its food, but as he'd expected it provided minimal help in the trees. He was wet pretty much everywhere below the diaphragm by the time he saw the lights.

The way the terrain was laid out, he saw the two vehicles in the driveway before he had a good view of the house. The target's

Honda, all right, and a recent Toyota just past it. When he could see the house he knew it was candy. He could walk in anytime he liked and walk out with anything he wanted. A *kid* could. The same with the big toolshed or pottery studio or whatever the hell that adjacent outbuilding was. He couldn't understand people like that. Why have a house, if it wouldn't keep bad guys out? It was like keeping a dog that wouldn't bite, or feeding a cat.

—which, most unexpectedly, he did just then. A sudden shocking agony in his right ankle reached his attention simultaneously with the hallucinatory image of a light-coloured short-haired cat running away from him at full speed, backwards. Long training aided him in squelching a scream of pain and outrage; he was shocked to hear it anyway, and realized it was coming from the damned cat. As feral as himself, by the sound of it, and territorial. Damn it, here it came again—*sideways*, this time, but no less rapidly.

There was no question in his mind that he could kick its head off. That might draw attention from inside the house—the cat squalling must be a common sound, the cat dying not so much. The truth was he didn't want to. He identified. He temporized by slamming the umbrella against the ground just in time to make the cat abort its attack in panic. As it did, he saw that one of its eyes was solid white. That decided him; before it could regroup, he turned and bugged out. One of the features his phone lacked was a flashlight: he risked using his to avoid breaking an ankle or a leg. Or a hip, he reluctantly admitted to himself.

Back in the car, breathing hard for the first time in entirely too long, he imagined what the Major would have had to say about his performance. Routed by a cat! He staunched his bleeding with Kleenex from a box the previous Mr. McKinnon had tucked between the front seats, and found that he had lost about a quarter's worth of meat to the vicious little carnivore. Well, good for *it*. Pretty good for a critter that couldn't possibly have any depth perception. He glanced again at the Kleenex . . . checked the trunk and found that the same thoughtful previous incarnation of himself kept a first-aid kit there.

Okay. Temporary setback. Go check in at—he shuddered—the HereOnHeron B&B before the window closed, take a shower, dry his clothes, do a little websurfing without rain doing a drum roll just above his head. At midnight, park a reasonable distance away from this spot, hike here in stolen rain-gear nobody will have bothered to lock up, and walk down the center of that driveway bold as brass, prepared to meet any oncoming cat with a handful of butter chicken in the snoot. Drift in and out of that house without waking anyone, and *with* a lot of information and any weapons or computer hard drives he encountered. Possibly return once more before dawn, move in, and commence interrogations.

As he backed into the driveway to turn around and head back to the village, he caught himself humming the chorus of an old militant antiwar song by Graham Nash, and smirked as he remembered the words. "*We can change the world/rearrange the world/it's dying to get better.*"

It was good to have hope again.

The car did seem a bit too noisy as he pulled away, but it wasn't going to be his car much longer. And he did keep automatic watch for a tail, from force of long habit, all the way to his B&B. But it did not occur to him that there weren't that many roads *on* Heron. Or that after dark in such a rustic place, he could be tailed by sound alone, almost as well as if there were an expensive GPS bug on *his* bumper. Nor that it *is* possible to drive with the lights off in a modern car, if you don't mind replacing the fuse when you're done.

8.
Saturday, June 23, 2007
Coveney Island, British Columbia, Canada

The downside of talking with a telepath, of course, is that he knows when you've stopped being out of breath. Long before I wanted to be, I was on my feet and following Zandor Zudenigo home. I divided my attention between careful observation of where I was putting my feet, and equally careful assessment of the pain in my right upper chest. I was already pretty sure I was okay, but the bad news can arrive as much as half an hour after the trauma sometimes. (And once there *was* no cause: I reached for a cup of coffee and a lung went.)

Well, the division of my attention was not really fifty-fifty. More like forty-forty. A good twenty percent of my mind, despite everything I could do to censor it, insisted on marveling at Zudie's body. He was barefoot to his scalp, wearing only an oversized wristwatch on his left wrist.

When I'd roomed with him back in the late sixties, I had on rare occasions seen him without a shirt or without pants, though never entirely naked, and he'd basically been a pile of bread dough in the approximate size and shape of a walrus. A couple of years ago, when I'd seen him for the first time since those days, he'd been the same size and shape, so I had assumed the same body under his clothes. Wrong. It wasn't a matter of muscle definition: he was still padded

. . . but not with flab. He was in the same kind of shape Nika was, now. It was obvious from the way he moved and carried himself. I reminded myself he had been living alone in the wilderness for . . . an indeterminate number of years.

And although I was looking mostly at his back, I could still clearly see his chest and groin in my mind's eye. Third nipples are not *that* rare, but they almost always occur near one of standard ones; Zudie's was smack dab in the middle of his nearly hairless chest, just above an imaginary line connecting the other two. And he was hung like Rocco Siffredi.

Which started me thinking, for the first time in decades, of Oksana Besher.

And she was an extremely awkward thing to think about in the close vicinity of Zandor Zudenigo, for at least two reasons. Because I was fairly sure the memories must be hurting him, and because I knew for certain they were shaming me.

"Go ahead," he called back over his shoulder. "I let go of her long ago. And forgave you way before that."

Feeling my ears get hot, I let the memories return.

Smelly, as everyone called Zudie back then, put the administration of William Joseph College in a quandary. Complaints about his eye-watering reek, and world-class weirdness even in the context of the sixties, were continuous and angry from students, faculty and staff . . . but such was his reputation in the world of mathematics that he raised the school a whole couple of notches in international prestige all by himself, simply by attending an occasional class there, and choosing its professors and grad students to discuss his work with once in a while. Professors from other schools, and occasional students, would sometimes come long distances just to talk with someone who had talked with Smelly.

That at least was how I explained the administration's extraordinary tolerance level to myself at the time. It wasn't until later that I learned the Zudenigo family had given old Billy Joe U. a large enough endowment for a new gymnasium and a celebrity coach to run it . . . on the condition that young Zandor not be sent, or encouraged to go, home again for at least four years. The school was motivated to put up with a few problems.

I myself solved one of the administration's biggest problems for them by agreeing to room with Smelly. Down the road, their gratitude would have a lot to do with my being able to end my college career with a Bachelor's degree rather than a prison record.

He solved another problem for them by quietly agreeing to eat his meals after everyone else was done. Smelly could not be reasoned with on the subject of his monstrous body odor—he would not discuss it at all, rationally or otherwise—but he was willing to at least *listen* to reason when absolutely necessary. The cafeteria staff didn't mind remaining to serve him, because he actually got them home faster: almost nobody *else* ever loitered after their meal once Smelly arrived. Nor did he necessarily always eat alone. I frequently shared a meal with him simply because I was late to *everything*. A bare handful of others had the same quirk. And there were even one or two so fiercely committed to personal weird behavior of their own—this was the sixties, remember—that they felt obliged to pretend they didn't notice anything odd about Smelly.

So there were witnesses when Oksana Besher appeared across the cafeteria table from him one afternoon, cleared her throat, and asked if this seat were taken. He blushed and nodded; she sat; and they ate their lunches together in perfect silence. Then they got up and left together in silence, not touching, but side by side. The story was so good, one witness would have been enough: it was all over campus by dinnertime. Because they were perfect for each other.

"It's a Battle of The Giants, like Godzilla versus Rodan," as Slinky John put it. "Dueling Freaks." As a child, Oksana had dived into a lake somewhere and shattered her nose on an unseen rock. They rebuilt it, of course, but she had managed to destroy her sense of smell, and for that they could do nothing. She was perfect for Zudie.

It was impossible to say which was the more ridiculous. He looked and sounded like Baby Huey; her overpronounced overbite and lisp and absurdly thick finger- and toenails made her look and sound like Bugs Bunny with an earectomy. Zandor was tall, Oksana was short; he was wide, she was thin; he was as heavy as his smell, she as insubstantial as her self-opinion. Smelly could be detected approaching from a city block away; nobody but him was ever likely to get close enough to her to notice what, if anything, Oxy smelled like. Each was cursed with almost unmeasurably high IQ and a freak intellectual gift: mathematics in his case, poetry in hers. You tell me which had drawn the short straw there. He was a perfect and total social failure as a man, she as a woman: put them side by side and their individual weirdness was not doubled but squared. As a couple, they'd have made a cat laugh.

They didn't appear to notice the stifled grins. They began eating lunch together most days. Perhaps they felt the pressure of everyone else's amused expectations. Within a week or so they were observed to take walks together, and the gossip mill exploded in laughter and jeers.

I've worked hard to retain my chosen self-image as a Pretty Nice Guy, and I really did feel an almost painful degree of empathy with both of them, having been an outcast all my own life . . . and even *I* am profoundly ashamed of what I thought of them as a couple. I liked them both, wished them both well, and wanted to howl with laughter every time I saw them together. I don't even want to imagine what Zudie must have been picking up from everyone *else* he walked past. I just wish I could wash my own mind out with soap, retroactively. Somebody said once regret is the sharpest pain.

Oxy became part of our shared life as roommates with no discussion at all. I hardly ever saw them together, actually, and then usually from a distance. Whenever I did encounter her, with or without Zudie, she was friendly enough, but even less talkative than he was. I thought of offering to leave the room to them until curfew on Friday or Saturday nights, as some roommates did for one another . . . but I never actually worked up enough nerve to raise the subject, and Smelly never asked, so as far as I know Oxy never saw the inside of our room. If their relationship was ever consummated, it must have taken place off campus somewhere. So did my own all-too-rare consummations that year. Getting a Catholic girl to agree to sneak into your dorm room was hard enough; getting one to sneak into *that* room was out of the question.

(This all occurred during an historical period in which, for reasons I despair of explaining, university students—not just in Catholic colleges like Billy Joe but *everywhere*—lived in sexually segregated quarters with absolutely no parietal hours ever. I can still recall the day in my final year when our floor R.A. called a meeting to tell us the stunning news that the school was considering instituting co-ed visiting hours, "periodically." Slinky John brought the house down by calling out, "Yeah, I knew it. Every twenty-eight days.")

Everyone on campus of course assumed the Smelly/Oxy relationship had been consummated, and most had theories as to where, and exactly how. Some of them were quite imaginative, and a few were actually funny. Not until Michael Jackson married Lisa Marie Presley would I again hear any couple's sex life speculated on with such avid distaste. Apparently we never really do get much less cruel than we were in the playground. Not even in a Catholic college . . . less than six months before what would come to be known as The Summer Of Love.

I'm including myself in that judgment.

I had spent most of my life—pretty much right up until the day I left for college—getting my ass kicked on a regular basis, and being ridiculed in between. For being too smart, too skinny, too sensitive, too sarcastic, too scared, sometimes just for being handy. I knew what it was like to be an outcast, a figure of fun. But even I, who knew just how bad it felt, was not immune to the shameful human pleasure of making myself feel bigger by making someone else seem smaller.

Only in my mind, at least. I was quite sure I hid my secret amusement so well that neither suspected its existence. I took pains to treat Oxy the same way I took pains to treat Smelly: with the same respect I would anyone else, just as if I had it. But inside, I got a big kick out of them.

I tripped over a rock as I stumbled behind him through the Coveney Island undergrowth, banged my knee when I went down, and accepted the bright pain as long overdue penance. A Catholic upbringing is awfully—awfully—hard to shake.

Now, of course, I burned, knowing that back then Zudie had known perfectly well just what a hypocritical condescending smug arrogant jackass I really was inside. The same respect I had pretended to pay him, he had paid me by not busting me for it.

Zudie's arm, astonishingly strong, helped me to my feet. We were out of the wind and away from the shore by now; he didn't have to raise his voice to be heard. "There wasn't anything you could have done differently if you *had* known. You can't apologize for finding something funny. It isn't an act of the will. All you can do is be polite about it, and you were. I found just about everyone on that campus— yes, including you—hilarious to the point of heartbreak. I also found the majority of you horrifying to the point of hysteria. It wasn't easy to conceal either one, sometimes . . . even with the overwhelming advantage that you people could only see what was shown and hear what was said."

I thought about that, as the pain in my knee dropped back to bearability. "You did okay."

"I know. So did you, is my point. All things considered. You're welcome." He turned and continued on his way.

I felt a weight leave me. I followed him, my thoughts turning now to how it had all ended. I wished they wouldn't, but there was no point trying to stop them.

Smelly and Oxy never attended any school social events, either before or after they met. They were just seen around the campus together, usually in some out of the way corner, and then snickered about behind their backs. A couple of girls who knew Oksana privately asked me what Zudie was really like, and in return I tried to pump them for information about her, but we really didn't have a lot to trade, and nothing very interesting on either side.

Before her hookup with Smelly, Oxy had not been considered particularly eccentric, at least by the standards of sixties college students: just funny-looking. The word on her had been, brilliant poet, here on full scholarship, a little flakey. She was rumored to spend her summers at Duke University in North Carolina, being tested for some sort of mild ESP ability at the famous institute J.B. Rhine had founded there, but just what sort of ESP wasn't clear; it wasn't something she talked about. Not one of the interesting ones like reading minds or making things float, anyway. Remote seeing, maybe, or guessing the weather. Of far more interest, as far as I was concerned, was her poetry. Out of roughly one hundred English majors on campus willing to publicly express opinions about poetry, about ninety-five were willing to admit they found hers impenetrable, and five worshipped her to the point of awe so incoherent, they couldn't explain it to anyone else. I was among the former group, rather to my own surprise. I *liked* weird, exotic, avant garde stuff, prided myself on it, but hers was just . . . *out* there. Most often I simply couldn't grasp what she'd been trying to accomplish well enough to hazard a guess as to how well she'd succeeded.

I guess that's my prejudice with art. I don't care what set of rules the artist used . . . as long as I'm given a fighting chance to guess what they were. I like to feel I could tell if he made a mistake.

By the time that school year ended, I had probably had fewer than a dozen conversations with her, none of them long, none about anything of substance. The most personal thing I learned about her was that she could barely taste anything; it turns out the sense of smell is essential to the sense of taste. (Try telling strawberry ice cream from vanilla, blindfolded and holding your nose.) I always meant to ask her about her poetry, but never found a polite way to say, "I find your work impenetrable; can you get me started?" I meant to ask about the ESP stuff, but never found a polite way to ask, "Do you really believe in that crap?" I meant to ask her about her childhood in the Ukraine, but never found a polite way to ask, "So what was Mordor like?" Above all, from the moment she and Zudie first connected I wondered, just like everyone else on campus, how in the *hell* she could possibly stand to be near anyone who *stank* so, even if she herself couldn't detect it . . . but I doubt there is a polite way to ask that.

I remember that twice, before the end of that semester, I managed to get her alone, with the intention of working the conversation around to Zudie's unique personal hygiene standards. I wondered if she might be able to shed any light on exactly what his problem with bathing was. Each time, she reacted the same way: she didn't know what I was talking about. She seemed honestly unaware there was anything wrong with the way he smelled. The first time she thought I was making an odd joke; the second time she got mad and I had to apologize.

I didn't dislike her. But I didn't especially like her, either. I couldn't connect with her, didn't *get* her. I couldn't seem to find a topic of conversation we both cared about. Except Zudie, and she didn't like to talk about him. Most people I'd known who were in love could not be *stopped* from talking about their beloved, but I guessed maybe poets were different.

I take it back. There was one topic we did nearly discuss . . . until we realized how it was going to turn out, and backed away by mutual agreement. To keep the peace—which was ironic because the topic was war. She supported the war in Vietnam.

Reading accounts of the sixties today, it's easy to get the impression that after some initial confusion, my entire generation united in opposition to that war, and worked arm-in-arm to end it, chanting "Give Peace A Chance!" as one. That's revisionist horse shit. Less than ten percent of Billy Joe's student body opposed the war when I arrived in 1966, and I doubt the figure *ever* rose higher than thirty percent while I was there . . . until the U.S. pulled out and our numbers doubled overnight retroactively. They've been climbing ever since. Try looking today for someone my age who will admit that he supported the war, voted for Nixon, went short-haired and beardless, abstained from psychedelics, or cheered when antiwar protesters got the shit kicked out of them by right-wing thugs. I haven't found one in decades. All I can tell you is, back then they were in the overwhelming majority on my campus. Perhaps they all died. Of lameness.

But if I stand for anything at all, it's tolerance. So Oksana was not the only friend with whom I tacitly agreed not to discuss the war. A lot of my fellow hippies enjoyed arguing with the straights, because it was so easy. I was more the kind who believed I made my best contribution to the discussion by having better vibes than the pro-war people. And she seemed to believe in the same tactics on her side. There was never a trace of bad feeling between us. I just never warmed to her, or she to me. Our senses of humor didn't match; she always smiled when I made a joke, but clearly only from politeness, and when she made one I usually didn't notice she had until minutes or hours later. She had a knack for telling me things about myself I didn't want to know, and I couldn't even get irritated because she never did it in an aggressive way but merely offered all-too-astute observations. It was only partly because I never saw her without a science fiction paperback in her backpack (she wore a backpack) that I started thinking of her in my head as part Martian.

"I told her that," Zudie told me now. "It made her laugh hard."

I thought about it. "I'm glad to know I made her laugh hard. I used to try."

"You succeeded more often than you knew."

We had reached his home. A big heap of rock at the edge of the water, heavily overgrown with scrub vegetation and moss, over on the far side of the island where no sea landing was possible. He lifted his left hand, and a section of the rock face developed a vertical crack and swung out on hinges, vegetation and all. I keep forgetting that nowadays they can pretty much pack a full service computer, phone and remote control into a watch no bigger than the one he wore. It began to dawn on me that Zudie might be about as naked and defenseless as a cartoon superhero. Who knew what weapons were trained on me now?

"None," he said. "You're with me." He went inside.

To keep being with him, I did too.

I was half expecting to walk into a fully modern luxury apartment with hardwood floors, indirect lighting, all the latest high-tech appliances and entertainment dispensers, and a two-car Batcave in the basement. What I found was quite different . . . but I had to admit it was by far the best upholstered and appointed cave I'd ever seen. Not to mention the neatest bachelor's quarters I'd ever seen: mine were a disaster area by comparison.

He handed me a bath towel. "Give me your clothes; I'll rinse and dry them."

I nodded. I was dripping on his floor. And overdressed.

Temperature and humidity were not cavelike at all but ideal for naked humans. The floor was stone, but somehow warm enough for bare feet without feeling heated. Adequate lighting, with the new hyperefficient bulbs. Ceiling just a bit low for a man of my height, which despite advancing years is so far still 186 centimeters, or six foot one. I saw the room's heat sources, a pair of the same highly efficient Super brand electric/gas radiators that I used myself at home. The floor was stone. I could just barely smell his dinner, something with garlic, and nothing else.

We were in a large kitchen/dining room/living room space, and directly ahead of us was a corridor running the length of the place, with four doors off it. I guessed the total square footage of the place to be a little more than half that of my own cottage. There was a minimum of furniture in the living room area to my right, just two chairs and a coffee table made of a slab of rock, on which lay a Powerbook and an assortment of remotes. But before them were three very large flatscreen monitors, each with its own eight-core Mac Pro workstation, one of those Apple TV gadgets I'd been lusting for, and a couple of eight-speaker towers that looked capable of vaporizing us and sending our constituent molecules back through time. I didn't see any wires anywhere except a few power cords.

"Don't ask," he said, so I didn't. I remembered that Zudie had come from money. Evidently his family had found a way to leave some of it to a scion who did not legally exist.

That pretty much exhausted the high-tech in the place, though. The kitchen was simple, basic, no gourmet gear at all. Small electric two-burner stove with tiny oven, small microwave. Water pumped from a cistern, heated in a standard tank. To my horror I could see no coffee machine, or even a teapot, and I remembered that Zudie regarded caffeine as a poisonous substance. I'm a hardcore caffiend. At home I have a Jura Scala Vario I got thirdhand. Push a single button, and sixty seconds later you're drinking fresh-ground French Press-style coffee. Every few days you toss in a pound of beans and a few gallons of water, and empty the used-grounds hopper. I hoped I wouldn't be here too long.

"Relax," he said. "I have some, and means to make it." Without asking he went to the kitchen end and started a pot of water boiling. After some rummaging in one of the harder-to-reach cabinets, he located coffee, sugar, and one of those little red plastic cones designed to hold a one-cup coffee filter above a cup. "No cream."

"Fine."

As the water heated he said, "Okay, sit down over there and go over it again. Slowly this time. Visualize rather than summarize."

I sat in one of the chairs by the TV and reviewed in my mind everything that had happened from the moment Nika had pulled into my driveway until I had set to sea in the *Fiendish Dinghy*. He never interrupted. By the time I was done, I was drinking hot coffee. It was startlingly good, for already-ground coffee that was neither refrigerated nor vaccum-packed.

The first comment he made after I finished my mental recap surprised me. "Very impressive young man, your son," he said, sitting down across from me. "It tears you up inside, being hated by him."

"Almost as bad as her death itself," I agreed. "That, I'm getting past, slowly."

"You can't finish getting past it until he at least starts," he said.

I stared at him. Even back in college he'd had a way of doing that: speaking a single short sentence that didn't really say anything you didn't already know, exactly, but somehow got you looking at it from a fresh new angle. "And as long as he stays pissed at me he doesn't have to start," I said.

"It isn't you he's pissed at. You're just the one he can reach."

"Jesus." He'd done it again. "What should I do?"

He smiled a bitter smile. "You are asking *me* for advice on interpersonal relations?"

I looked him in the eye. "Yes," I said, and nodded. "Yes, Zudie, I am."

Slowly the bitterness leached out of the smile. "Thank you."

"Thank *you*. What should I do?"

He thought for a moment, and his smile broadened. "Punch him in the mouth."

I nearly choked on my last sip of coffee. "What?"

"Think about it awhile." His smile went away. "Another time. We're busy right now."

He was right. My problem with my son was chronic, Zudie's was acute. "Sorry," I said. "But you brought it up."

He nodded. "It's important."

"And now we move on. Okay." I stopped and tried to organize my thoughts. Suddenly I thought of a question I'd wanted to ask him ever since we'd met again a few years ago and he'd confessed to being a mind reader. "Zudie . . . can you ever *send* thoughts, instead of just receiving them? To someone receptive?"

He became a statue of himself.

Was I offending him by suggesting he was a mental voyeur? I tried to explain. "I need a lot of information from you, and it would save an awful lot of time if you could just give it to me in a data dump the way I just did to you. I . . . I'm just asking," I finished lamely.

The sudden transformation in him was horrifying. He was not seeing me anymore. He was not there anymore. Wherever he was, the best thing you could hope for was a week's vacation in Hell.

I closed my eyes and shouted with both voice and mind, "*I'M SORRY, ZUDIE!*"

Just as suddenly, he was back. "Not your fault. Perfectly reasonable question." All at once I found myself recalling that on the day I'd met Zudie, more than forty years ago, one of the very first thoughts that had gone through my head was, *this man can forgive* anything. "It just derailed a train of thought. Tesla resonance."

I nodded. "Happens."

He took a deep breath and let it out, then another. Then he rotated his head from side to side to crack his neck. I noticed for the first time his excellent posture.

"Okay," he said finally. "I'm going to tell you the story. I've only told it twice before, and not in years. And when I am done, you will understand why I am absolutely positive that I will *never* be able to directly touch another mind.

"But listen carefully, Russell: in order to make you understand that, I'm going to have to tell you the most terrible secret I know. One nobody else knows. Once I have, you'll be stuck with it, forever, just like I am." He locked eyes with me. "And it's really rotten. Are you willing to share that with me?"

"Absolutely." I never hesitated. This man had saved my life—and Nika's, and the lives of at least four strangers we never met—by killing a monster with his mind in my living room, in some way so ghastly it had cost him his self-respect and peace of mind for the past two years. If he needed to share a burden, I was there.

"Thank you," he said. His voice quivered just a bit.

So did mine. "You're welcome."

He got up and made me a second cup of coffee. He used the time to organize his thoughts, so I shut up too and used mine to look his place over a little more closely. He'd obviously been here for *years* before dropping in on me. Just ferrying all this gear out here was a lot of work, and apparently he'd managed it both singlehanded and undetected, a neat trick. Keeping the place supplied must be another neat trick. No wonder he was in such good shape.

I forced my mind away from both puzzles, for fear of distracting him with involuntary questions. The Powerbook on the coffee table went into its screensaver mode, and Zudie used the same one I did, Electric Sheep. It produces random visual effects *strikingly* like what

I used to see behind my eyelids while tripping on LSD-25 back in the sixties, bright and colorful and mathematically elegant and quite hypnotic. I was about to hear a story from the sixties: I stared at the screen and let the thought of tripping carry me back in memory—

—Zudie was handing me my clothes, still warm from the dryer, and a plastic container that held my belt, keys, lighter and other pocket junk. When I wondered about my wallet he gestured to where it and its contents were spread out on a counter to dry in the kitchen area. He was wearing grey Bermuda-type shorts himself, now, which I thought very gracious considering we were in his home.

"Wrong initials," I said as I dressed.

"Beg pardon?"

"They warned us about dreaded acid flashbacks. Remember? I've waited eagerly for one ever since, and I've never had one in my life, or met anyone who did. The dreaded flashbacks that *have* recurred over and over, roughly every decade, aren't LSD. They're KIA and MIA."

He sat back down. "And CIA."

"I thought that was where this was going."

He was silent for so long that I began to watch the Electric Sheep display again to silence my mind, lest I derail his train of thought again. Whether it helped I couldn't say.

Finally he spoke. "Russell, I think I have to tell you why I've been holed up here for so long, ignoring you. Why what I did to Allen nearly four years ago tore me up as badly as it has. You think you want to know . . . and you really do *need* to know. If I do, I think you'll agree that I needed to tell you. But you won't thank me. You'll wish I hadn't. Wish I hadn't *had* to.

"Now you have to make a very hard choice. Whether to let me."

I sat and thought about that awhile. "You're my friend," I said then, "and you know more about what's going on than I do. Do what you think you need to do."

9.

Saturday, June 23, 2007
Coveney Island, British Columbia, Canada

Those were the last words I spoke until Zudie had finished his story. It was quite obvious that telling it was hard for him. I didn't want to make it any harder. Whenever he stopped to search for words, I waited until he found them.

He said:

The last you saw of me and Oksana, at the end of that semester, we told you we were going to spend the summer together at ESP Camp: a remote retreat in the woods somewhere in Maryland, where we were going to be paid guinea pigs for a bunch of white coats from the psych department at Duke University. That's what we were told. Nobody mentioned any government involvement to us. The only initials we heard were ESP and PSI. We thought of it as a paid vacation in the country. And just possibly an approach to some way of learning to cope with . . . my predicament.

The last you heard of either of us was when you got back to William Joseph in September and we weren't there, and all you could find out was that Oksana had been killed in a tragic hunting accident, and nobody knew where I was. You tried very hard to learn more, thank you for that, but there wasn't any more to learn, and after awhile you came to the same conclusion everyone else had: that in my grief at losing her, I'd taken my own life.

That was pretty close to the truth. I didn't kill myself. But I did get Oxy killed. And then to stay alive, I had to kill my identity.

Right, getting ahead of myself.

Oksana was the one they were really interested in. They had been for years, since she'd been in high school. Her gift wasn't as dangerous as mine, so she'd never learned to hide it. They'd finally gotten her to sit down for a week of testing during Spring Break, and the data suggested that she seemed to have a limited ability to influence probability somehow. Only on a very small scale . . . but if she was in the right frame of mind, she could roll sevens for as long as you liked, with your dice. She made enough in roulette winnings to pay for an entire semester before the Atlantic City Benevolent Association asked her nicely to stop playing there. This was way before we decided to make up for our degradation of the noble Native Americans by letting them milk gambling-addicts: Atlantic City was pretty much it for the east coast, now that Havana was gone.

After a few disastrous incidents in my childhood, and a *long* talk with my grandmother, I'd never told anyone but her about my own ability, and I didn't plan to. I've always known how most people would react if they knew, and I didn't *want* to be feared. But I did want to spend the summer with Oksana, so I compromised: I used telepathy to fake just enough talent at guessing Rhine cards to make me an ESP suspect too. If it turned out that anyone there actually knew anything about telepathy that I didn't, I thought perhaps I might just consider slowly "coming out" to him or her.

I was at that age when hope doesn't take any effort at all.

It started out great. The place was beautiful, a lodge beside a lake in the middle of nowhere that we had all to ourselves. White birch and maple everyplace. Bullfrogs and a trillion crickets at night. Comfortable rooms, decent food. No TV. Great library. Everyone on the staff was a decent person in a lab coat: honest, earnest, academic. The other Specials—as we were encouraged to call ourselves—were a fascinating crew, ranging from utterly ordinary to crazy as a basketball bat. But we all got along well despite our sometimes wildly incompatible quirks, because for most of us it was the first time we'd ever been in a group where we were *not* considered weird. It was a novel and pleasant experience, not automatically being the strangest person in the room. The work was interesting and not onerous.

Then new directives came in from somewhere outside, and the direction of the research started changing subtly.

A guy with a talent for clairvoyance who'd been trying to predict stock market or sports results would be tasked with predicting the outcome of a specific military operation in Southeast Asia instead. A woman with telekinetic ability would find herself being asked not to make marbles roll uphill, but to try and cause a guinea pig's heart to stop beating. A road-company psychic like me would be asked not what card a man was looking at, but whether he was lying to me about it or not.

And then one day Oksana was asked by her tester whether she thought she might be able to influence the probability of an individual uranium atom fissioning—and if so, from how far away? Could she, hypothetically of course, prevent or discourage an atom bomb from going off? Or, say, encourage one far away to go off by itself, or fail to?

We talked quietly between ourselves that night, and we both began to have problems with our paranormal powers. Nothing as obvious as a strike . . . but our test scores started to trend downward. We also talked about sharing what we knew with the other Specials. A few of us were strongly in favor of the Vietnam War—I was myself, then—but not one of us was interested in learning to use our special talent to kill people. Especially not on a nuclear scale.

But we were both nervous about taking that overt a step. Once released, the demon could not be put back in the box: if it was a government operation and they knew we'd outed it, we could end up in very deep shit. We wanted to know how deep.

We'd all seen the nominal director of the place, listened to him address us from a stage, gotten memos from him—but he seemed a bit snobby, always kept his distance. I doubt anyone else remarked it, but he was the only person in the whole place who'd never come within fifty meters of me, or any of us. Well, I was the only one capable of getting within fifty meters of *him* without being stopped, and one day I did.

Then I ran all the way back to Oksana's room, and got her to take a walk with me to one of the places I now knew was not bugged, and we began planning our escape.

His mind was one of the scariest I'd ever encountered, then—very much like I'd always imagined Mengele's mind must have been. But what really terrified me was the mind of the man who terrified *him*, the master he served and hated. A CIA senior agent, who called himself Pitt and didn't offer a first name. If the director's mental picture of Agent Pitt was remotely accurate, I did not want to ever meet him.

At Pitt's insistence, the director had placed surveillance devices all around the perimeter of the place, not just at the access points but in the forest itself too, even though he privately considered it a stupid waste of money and technology. It was very good technology for the time, CIA technology: it could not have been defeated by anyone but its designers, the techs who monitored and serviced it, the director who'd had it installed, or someone who'd been reading his mind.

If you're privy to another man's secrets, if you're better informed than he thinks you are, it can give you the illusion that you're smarter than he is. You can get so used to everyone you meet considering your special talent to be unimaginable, when you finally encounter one of the rare minds that *is* capable of imagining it, it blindsides you. I forgot to be humble.

I paid dearly for it.

We gave it a few days. Let our test scores come back up to baseline, so we'd stop standing out. It must have made Pitt look even closer, realize we were getting ready to make our move.

Zudie stopped for so long that I started to think he'd reconsidered telling me the rest. And then enough longer that I started to wish he would, if it was really that bad. Then he went on.

Oksana was from a tiny little place in New York called Saranac Lake, so remote they had their own phone system. Her mom's phone number was LE-27; you had to ask an operator to connect you. Oksana knew about living in the woods. She filled backpacks with what we would need to survive in the open for as long as a week. Anything we didn't have, I stole to order. It got to be kind of fun. Adventure. Tom Sawyer and Becky Thatcher, outwitting Injun Joe.

Finally she said we were ready. That night, we went over the wall.

It was a piece of cake. Almost an anticlimax. After all, I knew all the security procedures.

Wrong. I knew all the security procedures the director knew about. All the ones Agent Pitt had told him about. But Pitt had no problem at all dealing with the concept of a telepathic opponent. A security system he had carefully *not* told the director about—a robot system with no mind for me to read—caught us just as we were becoming confident enough to talk to each other without whispering. She was leading, I think it read us as a single target. She said over her shoulder, "Zandor, it's going to be so—" and then it shot her. With a rubber bullet. Marketed as nonlethal. Agent Pitt didn't want to *waste* any assets, just stop them leaving. It was supposed to hit the target in the lower chest, knock the breath out of him. Oksana was very short. She took it in the larynx. She fell down on her back. I laid down with her, held her in my arms. She kicked her legs and died. Half a minute, maybe. That was very bad.

Then it got a whole lot worse.

Zudie got up abruptly.

He went to the kitchen end of the room and made more coffee. He moved slowly, deliberately, like a monk being mindful. When the cup was full he carefully dunked a shot glass into it, then set the full shot glass aside and replaced its contents in my cup with brandy. He brought me the cup and the bottle of brandy, kept the shot glass for himself. I'd never seen him drink caffeine before. He'd always treated it the way some unfortunates have to treat peanuts. He'd once turned down a cup of decaf Nika offered him, saying they didn't decaffeinate it *enough*. I set the bottle down on the coffee table and made a toasting gesture. He responded. *Clink*. We drank.

He said:

I'd never been near anyone when they died before. Rich family. Sheltered life.

In the movies, on TV, in books, everywhere, it's always the same. When people die, they die like a light going out. Or at worst like a TV getting turned off: *z-z-z-zip*, shrink down to a single pixel, *click!*, gone. It's pretty to think so. Maybe even necessary.

But it's not true.

Well . . . maybe it's true for those who die of sudden catastrophic brain trauma. I don't know. Maybe it's even true for those whose death is the culmination of of a slow natural process of dissolution. But not for those who are killed.

It wasn't for her, anyway.

I *know*. I was there.

Her breathing stopped. Her heart stopped. Her body died.

Consciousness persisted.

How much? Enough to feel pain. Know loss.

How long? A minute. An hour. A million years. Somewhere in that range.

Oksana had faith. That helped her. A little. For awhile.

I'd *never* really been religious. At age seven, I already knew what the Catholic Church was trying to do to me; I just kept my head down and my mouth shut.

But they got to her. Her parents were so overjoyed to get out of the Ukraine, they made sure she joined them in thanking God for the miracle. Like most good people, she took the good parts of her religion to heart, and tried her best to resolve the contradictions.

She called on that faith to sustain her, and it did help. Some. For awhile.

But Oxy wasn't an idiot. She felt herself going away into the darkness. Alone. Blind. Helpless. Terrified beyond all description. It was impossible not to wonder how, why, a loving God could leave one of his children in this state *for one second—*

Let alone a million years.

No atheists in foxholes? My ass.

No. No, you're wrong.

No, it wasn't like that either. Think about it. All the Near Death Experience stories you've ever read were, by definition, recounted by someone who *didn't* die. Maybe that's what you experience just *before* your brain starts to die, I don't know. The ones I've read sound a lot like anesthetic-dreams on an operating table. Bright light in your face, shadowy people all around you with benevolent intentions who look a little like your dead Uncle Phil.

Yes, maybe the Buddhists are right. Maybe she was just heading for one of the Bardos, a place between incarnations. How can I know? To me the Buddhist universe has always seemed cold, indifferent. Not much comfort in it. Life is suffering. Somehow they're okay with that. Oksana wasn't Buddhist.

She just saw extinction coming. And she was scared shitless. Jesus stopped being plausible. She missed me so much.

She cried out for me.

That's how I know, for absolute certain, that I can't send.

With my whole heart and brain and mind and soul, more than I wanted to keep living, I tried to shout back. I wanted to reach out and and tell her—

I'm here.

I'll always love you.

You made me so happy.

Let go now.

If it can be done, I'll find you again.

I tried harder than I ever had before to touch *her* mind, the way everyone touched mine. I gave it everything I had. More. Like a mother lifting an SUV off her child with one hand.

Total failure.

We were both screaming at the top of our minds. I heard her. She heard nothing. She started to crack—

Zudie lifted the shot glass to his mouth, moistened his lips from it. Sighed. Emptied it with a gulp, knocking it back like raw whiskey. Set the shot glass down on the table.

You've read Daniel Dennett's *Consciousness Explained*?

I know. Don't feel bad. His reasoning isn't hard to follow at all . . . it's just hard to wrap your mind around. Big surprise. I'll summarize as best I can— without writing another book longer than his, anyway.

Basically Dennett says the Buddhists have it right: the self is an illusion. Consciousness is just a cover story: there *is* no you, really, but your body finds it extremely useful to pretend there is. Its various systems—organs, glands, nerves, muscles, blood, gonads—are what the Buddhists call dependently co-arising. They all have to be there, working in concert, for any of them to exist at all. The illusion that there is a tiny little man sitting in a control room in the middle of your brain, coordinating things by looking at a monitor screen and deciding what should be done next, is *so* useful that not long after your birth your body comes to consider it utterly essential, and to depend on it.

Consciousness is your DNA and bloodstream and nerve cells and gut putting on a puppet show together, and they need a director so badly they create one out of thin air, the self, by the process that is the backwards of denial. If any part of the cast or crew loses the illusion of *self* for too long, all die. The same kind of reverse-denial on a societal scale can produce religion for similar reasons: without it, all die.

That's why meditation is never going to be really popular. Most people would rather die than stop thinking even for a few moments, because deep down they equate the two. When the ceaseless monkey chatter of the mind becomes oppressive, they just turn on the TV or play some mp3s to drown it out.

But basically the mind exists because all the various parts of the body believe it does.

That goes for both the conscious and the subconscious mind—and also for the "body-mind" even below that, the part that would remember what side you like to sleep on and how to play your favorite instrument and where your genitals are located even if the brain were removed. Okay?

Somehow . . . kneeling there in a forest in the dark with Oxy's head on my thighs, while my conscious mind was tearing itself apart trying to send solace to my Oksana, somehow . . . somehow my subconscious mind or my body-mind or both knew it wasn't going to work, and somehow they intuited the only thing that would, and knew there was no time to hesitate.

Yes, that's right. You remember what I said that night in your living room, standing over Allen Campbell's corpse. "I made his selves disbelieve in himself."

That's what I did to my Oksana. I can't tell you how: I don't know, and if I did there are no words. If it helps to think of it as pulling memory cores from Hal 9000, be my guest. In some manner I dispersed the communications between all those interlocking systems, dis-integrated them, made each doubt the existence of Oksana Besher, their self.

She ceased. She was gone in less than a second. I think.

It is possible to feel infinite regret and infinite relief in the same instant. To be grateful to the universe in the moment of despair. To be ashamed of being proud, and proud to be ashamed. Incredibly enough, it is even possible to experience those paradoxes while running full-tilt through the forest in the dark.

What I had done for Oksana was mercy . . . and at the same time it felt like ultimate obscenity. Perhaps even Original Sin: not to lust for forbidden knowledge, but to forbid knowing. Paradox generated more paradox. With all my heart I wanted to go directly to Hell and stay there; I felt I deserved to. And at the same time, I never stopped being aware that a demon from Hell was coming for me—specifically to take me to that very place, where I would spend my life being used for disgusting purposes by the man who had killed Oksana's body. I agreed I had that coming, but that didn't mean I accepted it. The moment the last particle of her essence departed from this plane of existence, I pushed her head off my lap like an old pair of gloves she wouldn't be needing anymore, took off her backpack and slung it over my shoulder, got to my feet, and started running.

If I had wasted as much as a whole minute mourning, I think Agent Pitt would have had me that night. It was that close. He must have had to come some distance—how could he know my range wasn't as long as a few miles?—but he came *fast*. When his alarms went off, he must have rolled out of bed and hit the ground running. What saved me was, he knew woodscraft, knew the area well and was extremely physically fit, and I was clueless and totally out of shape. He had trained to hunt other wolves, not cows. Nothing I did made sense to him.

He came close enough for me to read him. For maybe a minute.

I've spent every minute since running from him. Almost forty years, now.

Now I'm going to go out for a short walk, to check a few security arrangements, and let you process this.

I was grateful for his tact. There certainly seemed to be a lot to process, and it's easier to process stuff of that level of profundity without anyone looking over your shoulder. I sat there thinking a dozen thoughts at once, feeling a dozen emotions at once, while he got up and left. Some monitor component of my mind noted how the door was opened from the inside and stored the information. A minute or two later, my mouth—I think it was my mouth— caused me to get up and go make yet another cup of coffee. I was halfway to the kitchen end of the room when I stopped in my tracks.

That's how long it took for it to hit me, for the implications to sink in. For it to dawn on me why Zudie had thought I might need some time to process his story.

Nearly ten years earlier, at her request, I had helped my wife Susan end her life.

I had been with her, done what was necessary. When her body died, I felt it happen. And then I'd sat beside her for half an hour or so, taking what comfort I could from the knowledge that her suffering was over, telling myself that now it was finally all right for me to be selfish, and give in to self pity: go indulge in some exhilarating, stupid, self-destructive behavior for awhile.

And all the while, if Zudie was right, my beloved lay beside me— utterly helpless, totally terrified, absolutely alone. For an hour, or a hundred million years. In that range.

Thanks to me.

My son Jesse had never forgiven me for that act. I'd only really managed it myself in the last four years or so.

I dropped the coffee cup. It landed on my bare left foot, hurting so much I nearly noticed, and skittered crazily away across the floor. I turned around and went back to my chair and sat down and stared at Electric Fire on the laptop for half an hour or so without moving, until I had finished rewriting the story of my life to date in light of the new information I now had, in a way that would let me continue. I think I sang to myself from time to time, but don't remember what songs. Oddly, it never occurred to me to drink any of the brandy in the bottle sitting next to the computer.

The moment I had the ridiculous thought that perhaps I should go yell out the door that it was okay to come back now, Zudie came back in with an armload of firewood, opened a thigh-tall bin with a foot-pedal, dropped in the wood and lowered the lid again. I didn't see a woodstove anywhere, but did see several areas where one could be concealed. And when I thought about it, he'd have been a fool to depend on electricity here on Coveney, no matter how he was getting it—which I also didn't understand. Hell, on Heron Island we lived with blackouts for at least a dozen days out of every year, and often much longer. And B.C. Hydro was aware we were paying customers.

He brushed wood debris from his bare chest, got a pitcher of cold water and clean cups, brought them over and sat by me.

"Have you ever read Heinlein?" he asked me.

"Name rings a bell."

"Dead science fiction writer. Considered the First Grandmaster of that genre."

I nodded politely. "I'm colorblind in that range, sorry. 'Stranger' something?"

"*. . . In A Strange Land*,' Yes. Among many other achievements, some of his stories inspired the development of cryonics, freezing dead people in hope of future resurrection."

"To tell you the truth, I always kind of wished I had the kind of money it takes to make that bet," I said. "I mean, sure, it's lousy odds—but look at the payoff!"

He nodded . . . but oddly, as if I'd said something very sad. "Well, one of the first cryonics firms offered him a free freeze to thank him. Heinlein turned them down and wouldn't say why. Drove them crazy. After his death it turned out exactly one of his friends had had the nerve to ask him why he would reject even a long shot at extended life, when it was free."

"Okay, Mr. Bones, what did he say?" I said, trying to lighten things up.

Zudie's voice was as bleak as if he'd been delivering a death sentence. "He said, 'How do I know it wouldn't interfere with rebirth?'"

"Oh. *Oh.*" Suddenly I saw what he was driving at. "Oh, wow . . . "

He spoke with his head down, absurdly as if he were addressing his penis. "I have no opinion about what happens after death. Maybe we go to the Christian Heaven and, if we've been good, get to spend eternity in a drab white robe playing the harp without food or drink or sex, content to adore the guy who invented pain and aging. Maybe we go to the Muslim Paradise and spend eternity getting smashed with inexperienced lovers and adoring the same guy played by a different actor. Maybe we reincarnate Buddhist style, or Hindu style, or New Orleans style. Anybody who says he knows is lying or crazy."

Again I made a feeble attempt at levity. "Or dead."

He looked up. The pain in his eyes was shocking. "Whatever happens . . . how do I know I didn't fuck it up for Oxy?"

"Hey Zudie, man, come on—"

"I'm pretty sure what I did to her never happened to anyone before. Certainly not as often as people get hit by meteorites. There *can't* be a protocol for it in the system—"

"Come on, brother, what about the *most likely* answer, okay?"

"What's that?"

The question was exasperating. "That *nothing* happens. That we don't go anywhere when we die, we just *end*, and are *gone*, from everywhere but human memory anyway, and as James Taylor said, life goes on without us, all around us. That you fucked up *nothing*. That all you did was shorten a really horrible last moment for someone you love. You stupid fat bastard, *I* should only be so lucky as Oxy was. I wish to God you'd been there for Susan!"

He gaped at me, looking more than ever like Baby Huey.

"Jesus Christ," I said, "Nobody ever looks as hard for anything as a person looking for something to feel guilty about."

He got a quizzical look . . . and then his features began to relax. The pain started to leave his face. "Thank you, Russell," he said.

My own irritation was gone. "You're welcome."

"You really think that's the most likely answer?"

"Seems to be the one with the least amount of wishful thnking in it."

"Maybe so. I've always felt it was the *least* likely answer, myself. I mean, I see the flaws in all the other ones—I just have trouble persuading myself a) that random chance produced matter, music and Oksana's eyes, and b) that none of them *matters* at all."

"I know what you mean," I agreed. "Substitute Susan's eyes for Oxy's and I'm right with you. But see, I *want* those things to matter, with roughly equal intensity, so my opinion is suspect."

"Doesn't make it wrong."

"Makes it suspect."

He sighed. "I don't disagree."

"And I'll tell you the truth, in a way it's the answer I prefer. I mean, I don't think I want to spend eternity in Catholic Heaven even if Susan *is* there. Or learn to read the Koran in Arabic, or stop eating beef, or pork, or enter the Void, or any of that crap. Beautiful brief flickers in the darkness that the universe was too dumb to cherish . . . I can live with that."

"I hear you, my friend," he said. "But . . . isn't that a hell of a thing to be the outcome you prefer?"

He had me. "Yes, it is." I finished the water in my cup and replaced it with brandy. "I wish someone would invent a sane religion."

"I'm working on it," he said.

"Go, cat, go."

"But there is more pressing business before the house."

The brandy hit me. "Yeah, I'm coming back up to speed, now. You figure it was Agent Pitt who took out Nika's cousin."

"I can't think of anyone else alive—assuming he's alive—who would both be capable of following a nonexistent link to Nika all the way to your house, *and* interested enough to bother, after all these years. The CIA has been out of the ESP business for over thirty years now."

"Okay. You've been in his head. You know more about how he thinks than I do. What do you think he'll do now?"

"Dig around until he finds a really good handle on Nika or you or both of you. Then squeeze you hard."

"Is that his best move?"

"Yes. Think about it. He wants to capture a telepath. He knows I'm almost as smart as he is. There's no way he's going to sneak up on me, on my home turf, even if he can find out where that is. He needs to get one of you to call me up or email me, and sucker me into a preset trap he can spring from well outside my range. Tricking you into it is too complicated, and how can he be sure he's succeeded? Easier and more reliable to hold some kind of metaphorical gun to your head."

Jesus Christ in a teddy. "And my son is somewhere on the same fucking island with him!" I gulped more brandy. It didn't help enough.

Then I saw the faint smile on Zudie's face.

"I'm almost as smart as Agent Pitt," he said softly. "And I know he's coming for me, and he doesn't know I know."

"You have a plan."

"Well, the beginnings of an outline of one, yes."

"Tell me more," I started to say. But just at that moment, a penny dropped in my head, and I suddenly remembered something. Something horrible. I opened my mouth, tried to speak, failed.

It didn't matter, of course. Zudie went just as pale as I must have done. "Oh God, Russell, that's bad," he breathed. "You really fucked up."

10.

Saturday, June 23, 2007
Heron Island, British Columbia, Canada

When McKinnon woke up the bedside clock said it was 12:13 AM. His watch agreed. He checked: he *had* set the watch for midnight. He always set his watch when he wanted to wake at a particular time—and never needed to, always waking a minute or so before it could go off. So basically he had failed to wake up *twice*. No, three times: the watch alarm repeated after five minutes if he didn't switch it off.

The fake fire was the only light besides the clockface. The room's overhead light had a dimmer switch, he remembered . . . but had recently been supplied with one of the new low-wattage fluorescent bulbs, which do not work with a dimmer. He sat up, turned on the bedside lamp (also flourescent, and therefore of only one wattage: too bright), and looked around at a room furnished in a style he thought of as Quaint Misbehavin', with a 50-inch flatscreen TV above a fireplace so realistic he couldn't stop noticing how realistic it was. It took a whole fifteen seconds for the flame-flicker sequence to repeat, and the accompanying loop of crackle sounds was only ten seconds long. Genius.

He sighed, shut off the fire with a realistic-looking bedside fireplace wall-switch, and tried to recall just how he had come to be here, in this silly room on this silly island in this silly country, on this silly-ass mission. He reviewed the path from birth to here to try and spot just where he had gone wrong—

—realized he was reviewing not his history but that of one of his more memorable cover identities—

—promised himself to be scared by that just as soon as he had the time, and started over.

Born at a rest stop just outside Tampa. Childhood shuttling between warring parents in East Baltimore and Drama City, until he was old enough for acting out to turn into a rap sheet. Very high IQ and reading scores bought him some slack, but two years into state college, he graduated to felonies. Vietnam a way out that didn't involve choices or decisions, until suddenly it did.

Chose to live. Months as a Shadow Company security contractor, with a necklace of ears and a price on his head.

Recruited into CIA's Operation Phoenix by the Major, a Truman appointee. Under his tutelage, traded necklace and rap sheet for a new name, a new personality, a philosophy and a purpose. Morphed from wholesale to retail killer: from a soldier who matched himself against other predators with wolfish joy, to a soldier who accomplished exponentially more by passionless assassination of selected civilians or their loved ones. More important: became politically aware, on a global scale, and for the first time in his life truly pledged allegiance to the flag of the United States of America, and to the republic for which it stood.

Finally too hot to remain in Southeast Asia. Back home to Drama City, which was called Washington when you were wearing a suit and tie and a name with no priors attached to it. Two years of training, indoctrination, grooming and college culminating in a BA in History, then finally he was ready to do real work . . . just in time for him to get in on MK Ultra. A long series of events then that made leaving a village mayor's dead wife outside their hooch seem like a clean way to make a living. All of them were necessary, all in service to an end that justified any means: truth, justice, and the American way. But all of them were hard just the same. They didn't get any easier, and that was the good *news.*

Felt his allegiance begin to waver . . .

*Got himself reassigned to the Funny Farm—the ESP project—as a
kind of vacation that he knew would be temporary. And there, to his
astonishment, he encountered the man who would change the course
of his life even more than the Major had . . .*

His bladder interrupted his life review . . . just as he had
recapitulated himself to the point of remembering why he didn't
have time for this shit. Just as well, probably—the next forty years
would have been dreadful to relive. He shook his head, swung his
legs over the side of the bed, and had a disheartening amount of
difficulty getting up. On his way to the bathroom, he told himself
that perhaps tomorrow would be a little better . . . and realized he had
been doing that for an awful lot of consecutive mornings now. So he
passed the time it took for the "coffee" machine to cycle by working
out. He couldn't do his usual morning routine without waking anyone below him or next door, but he did manage enough to get his
heart pumping and his joints better oiled. When he was done, he felt
fifty again.

Over coffee he started his laptop, confirmed that no one else
was using the B&B's wifi connection, and did some research. The
property owner's name was Russell Walker. Mr. Walker was an
Op-Ed columnist with the more liberal of Canada's two conservative
newspapers. A widower, less than a decade younger than McKinnon
himself. An ex-American—no, he saw on closer inspection: a dual-
citizen, who'd been born in the U.S., and moved to Canada *after*, not
before, Vietnam, subsequently becoming a Canadian citizen without
renouncing U.S. citizenship. Not a lot of those.

Shortly, McKinnon found himself wondering if Mr. Walker actually
existed. The more he searched the more skeptical he became.

One living family member: a grown son living on the opposite
end of the continent, in the U.S. Organizations belonged to: none.
This guy was supposed to be pushing sixty, and belonged to no clubs,
societies, leagues, guilds, associations, religious groups, political
parties, twelve-step groups, boards of directors or porn websites. He
paid for the minimum cable package: no specialty or movie TV channels
at all. The same cable package also provided barely adequate internet
access, slightly better than smoke signals: max download speed 50
Mbps, max upload speed 30 no more than 10 e-mail addresses, and a

data transfer limit of 60 gigs a month that his records showed he rarely approached.

Phone records showed that the man almost never used his phone—save for short flurries of calls over a two- or three- day period, every three weeks, plus a few holiday and birthday calls a year to the distant son, who almost never called back. An odd interval—what actual human activity was on a three-week cycle? It added to the growing impression that this Walker was a phantom. Wait a minute—the comic strip character The Phantom had often used the name Walker as a pseudonym, because the Africans he lived among called him The Ghost Who Walks. *If a Phantom Walks in a forest but isn't really there, do the leaves Russell?*

But the Heron Island Credit Union believed Walker was real enough to give him a mortgage. A mainland bank might have been conned by a Potemkin Man, as long as the checks kept clearing . . . but this rockheap just wasn't *big* enough: everyone on it must know each other.

So: follow the rest of Walker's money.

After the mortgage, his largest expenditures went for, in descending order:

—food delivery, one quarter from the place McKinnon himself had dined earlier that evening, Collinsia Verna's, and three quarters from The Red Bliss, which appeared to be one of those "co-operatives" (how were other businesses structured? Anarchy?) that sold organic fruits and nuts to the organic nuts and fruits.

—prodigious, Voltairean quantities of Tanzanian Peaberry coffee, ordered as beans in bulk by mail from Ontario.

—books and CDs purchased from either amazon.com or one of its associated Used dealers.

—postage apparently used to mail small quantities of discs and books to others, both in Canada and in the U.S.

There were also regular cash withdrawals—at that same irritating interval, every three weeks—strongly suggesting an illegal drug. But the amounts were such that it was unlikely to be anything interesting. Pot, probably, British Columbia being the connoisseur marijuana mecca for the entire planet.

So . . . basically, a guy with no life. Much like McKinnon himself, really, save for the pot addiction.

McKinnon got up from the laptop and made another potlet of coffee-colored fluid. As it dripped, he opened a container of butter chicken and ate from it with his fingers. It was symphonic. When the bubbling sounds ceased he washed his hands in the sink, picked up a cuplet, looked at it, put it down, and took the whole potlet back to the computer with him.

Now . . . where did Walker's money come from? A lot of it, but not all, came from his Op-Ed column, it turned out. He seemed to get paid a lot more per column than the other columnists who appeared on the same page, though his ran only . . . McKinnon smiled suddenly. Walker's column "Past Imperfect, Future Tense" ran every third Friday. The odd three-week interval was explained.

So even at his unusually high word rate, he could not be bringing in enough to cover his nut then. McKinnon kept digging. It was not easy to figure out, but he had special forensic accountancy software designed for that express purpose which was not available to the general or even particular public. Before too long he understood that Walker's late wife had been a very successful painter, who had left enough to cover his needs for the rest of his days if necessary. But that principal was still untouched, because she had also left him an unknown but apparently substantial number of completed paintings. So far, every time his balance began to drop, he had produced one and sold it for enough to keep himself in coffee and CDs for another year or two—a total of four times so far.

McKinnon wanted another potlet of "coffee," but was out of "coffee" pucks, save for the decaf, which he took to be a variant spelling of "defective." He got a canlet of Coke from the room's microbar, took that and the butter chicken container back to the desk. He ate a few bites with his fingers, then wiped them off with Kleenex and resumed netsearching.

Okay. Now for the big question. Why was McKinnon studying this ingrown toenail of a man, this hermit who made his living lecturing an entire country about the events of the day? What was his connection to Zandor Zudenigo?

The obvious approach was to start with the date Zudenigo had dropped off the planet, find out what Walker had been doing at the time, and then wind both their lives backward until they intersected.

Again he had special software for the purpose—but he never even opened it.

Because the very first thing he learned was that on the day Zudenigo had become a Ghost Who Walked, forty years earlier, *Walker had been his college roommate.* McKinnon must have seen his name in the files many times over the years; it had simply been too bland to stick. He said "Yes!" aloud, punched his thigh, sat back and resumed eating chicken without consciously noticing it.

Bingo! It was confirmed, now. *His target was alive . . . and close, too!*

Until now he had not been absolutely sure. The cop *could* have had some innocuous cop-reason to inquire after a man forty years dead over at the far end of another country. But at the first hint of trouble she had made a beeline for the dead man's old roommate, and then both of them had melted into the scenery. There was no reason to be that paranoid about a forty-year-dead guy unless he was not really dead. Case closed. Zudenigo was alive, somewhere in this area.

And his two friends were even now making a beeline for Zudenigo to warn him of danger, with a head start that widened with each passing minute—

Fortunately his thoughts reached that point before he had absent-mindedly finished all the chicken. He wolfed down everything else in the container instead, saving the meat for that damned cat he was going to have to get past. Then he shut his laptop and dressed quickly, pleased that he would be able to keep the beef brisket container sealed and have that for tomorrow's meal. He left in such disciplined haste that he very nearly caught Detective Constable Nika Mandiç loitering outside his B&B, and drove back to Russell Walker's place at exactly the island's maximum legal speed of 40 KPH, or, in his terms, a low idle. The street lights ended within what he would have called a couple of blocks, for good, and there was absolutely no other traffic on the road. After a while he decided he didn't need lights to drive that slowly on empty moonlit roads, and it would be better to approach Walker's home this late with maximum stealth, so pulled over for a moment, reached under the dash and, with the small sense of satisfaction he always got from disabling an unwanted safety feature, removed the fuse for his headlights.

❀ ❀ ❀ ❀

The road leading to Walker's driveway was a slight upgrade. From long habit of caution McKinnon went a couple of driveways past it at the quietest speed he could, then put it in neutral, shut the engine, and let the car drift back downhill. It rolled slowly enough that even by moonlight he had no difficulty backing into Walker's driveway and coasting far enough to be in shadow from the road. He was nearly at rest when his starboard taillight hit the tree—but still going fast enough to produce a miniwhiplash he knew he would feel later, and an absurd amount of crunchy-tinkly noise, with an echo. There must be a damn mountain somewhere out there in the dark, though he didn't recall one.

He sat still and waited for over a minute, listening for barking dogs, people asking one another what the hell that had been, approaching meteorites. He watched his rearview mirror closely enough to finally detect the approaching cat. He located the container of leftover butter chicken on the floor in front of the passenger seat, and got out of the car. He managed to open negotiations with the cat, arrive at mutually agreeable terms, and strike a bargain, but not without diffficulty. He was usually good with cats, but this one seemed to be feral. It displayed zero interest in human touch of any kind, but a lively interest in chicken. He gave it all the meat, sealing the bones back up in the container so it wouldn't choke on them, but the moment it finished the last morsel of bird it made a beeline for the container and announced that it wouldn't mind sampling the gravy too. He wrapped the bones in Kleenex, dropped them in the car's wastebasket, made sure its windows were sealed. As the cat began following the floppy container around the forest like a drunk chasing his hat, McKinnon took two steps and disappeared, moving through the woods beside Walker's driveway like the shadow cast by a suspicion.

Nearly as quietly as the second cat, who materialized in his path about three or four meters ahead and to the right.

No more chicken left. He froze and watched the cat carefully, looking for flattened ears, arched back or rapid tail movement, and listening for growling, or worse, hissing. It blinked at him for a few seconds . . . then put its tail straight in the air and came prancing up to see if McKinnon's hand smelled good enough to be scratched by. It did. He got on one knee and gave the new cat about twenty seconds' worth of scratching. When he heard the other cat moving somewhere in the woods behind him, he struggled to his feet and continued on his way.

He approached the house with extreme care, watchful of alarms, but encountered none. The building was dark, inside and out. He circled it to be sure. Nothing brighter than the inevitable standby lights or digital time displays was visible at any window, not so much as a candle. A small outbuilding briefly held his interest because of faint light from its windows, but it turned out to be only an empty office containing a Powerbook laptop with a gaudy screensaver. He checked the door carefully, found it unlocked, and was tempted to slip inside and examine the computer. But he knew he had to confirm that the house was empty first. His shoes were very muddy from walking through wet woods; he doubled back to a hose he'd seen around the side of the house and was able to tip enough water out of it to clean his shoes, so they would leave no prints inside. He unhooked from his key ring a miniflashlight, the size of the cap on a felt tip marker, and confirmed by touch that it was set for lowest power and smallest aperture.

He was not too surprised to find the front door unlocked—he was beginning to get used to Canada—but he was surprised almost to the point of indignation when he learned that it *had* no lock. Anyone who cared to turn the doorknob could walk in. It made him suspicious enough to dial his miniflash one step brighter and double-check for a silent alarm, but he found none.

He suppressed his irritation, and everything else, and slipped into the house.

He tossed the place slowly, thoroughly, making careful use of his flashlight. Walker clearly lived alone. Every wall of every room except the kitchen and bathrooms seemed to be obscured by tall bookshelves, about a quarter of which held CDs, cassettes or vinyl records. He had four TVs, kitchen, livingroom and both bedrooms, but all of them were cheap crap, no flat screens, no big screens even. Two had attendant VCRs rather than DVD players. Only the set in the master bedroom, a 28-inch tube, had external speakers, and just two of them. Every piece of furniture and appliance in the house was adequate but cheap; all the carpets had acne; all the walls needed paint. The sound system in the dining room contained no components less than ten years old and some much older. Everything he saw was just good enough for its purpose—with a single exception: an absurdly high-tech Swiss unit in the kitchen that produced single cups of fresh ground French-Press-style coffee at the press of a button and cleaned itself afterward. But even that was clearly long past its warrantee.

McKinnon found himself starting to like Walker—the man treated himself well, but did not waste a dime impressing anyone else. The place reeked of marijuana, but otherwise closely resembled McKinnon's own current apartment in Virginia.

He kept up a running search for stashes, hiding places, secret compartments that might conceal clues to Zudenigo's whereabouts. There are a million places to stash something in a house, and he knew them all. But found none in this house. The man's marijuana supply—less than an ounce, but *strong* by the smell of it—was "hidden" in his fridge, in a transparent plastic container.

He found signs of abandonment on a moment's notice. A stereo amplifier left on. Thermostat left on day setting. Crumbs on kitchen counters. Three cups of coffee dregs in the living room.

The master bedroom was comfortable and uncluttered, reason-ably clean and orderly. The kingsize bed was made, and McKinnon confirmed that its sheets and pillowcases had been changed recently. Walker was surprisingly neat and tidy for a widower. This room was where he did most of his TV viewing; it had the largest tube, the only surround speakers in the house, and a fair-sized collection of DVDs and VHS tapes. There was even a tall mirror propped against the far wall at just the right angle to the master bathroom so that Walker could follow a program while sitting on the throne or soaking in the tub.

There was a guest's suitcase in the guest bedroom, open on the bed but not yet unpacked. The cop's? No. Male clothing and ancillaries. Someone who lived and dressed considerably better than Walker. No ID present. The tag on the suitcase handle gave an address in New York City, but no name; the baggage code too indicated that the bag had been checked in at LaGuardia in New York. The bathroom across the hall showed no signs of recent use.

McKinnon thought about that for awhile. Less than an hour after she arrives, Detective Constable Mandiç persuades not only Walker but a newly arrived houseguest to join her in dropping everything and running like hell. How? How many people could possibly share the secret of a telepath who had been hiding successfully—from McKinnon!—for forty years now, and what were the odds of a third one showing up from afar on the very day McKinnon himself finally caught up? He tabled the question and finished his sweep.

The only remaining room was used for storage, of the sorts of items that would have been in an attic or basement if the house had featured either. He gave it a bored but thorough inspection, finding nothing of interest. He was feeling impatient by then, but forced himself to go through the whole house room by room once more. Only then did he go eagerly back outside to toss Walker's office.

It was a glorified shed, perhaps twenty-four feet by twelve, with three windows fitted with venetian blinds. Inside, every inch of wall was obscured by nine-foot-tall bookshelves, all of them full, hand-made by some local artisan to accommodate the windows. An old wooden table covered with a cheap tablecloth served as a desk and held a shiny new Powerbook with cable internet, a big cathode-tube external monitor, and a pair of Lava Lites on either side of it, one blue and one clear. On a small wheeled table beside the desk were both a laserprinter and a color inkjet printer; they and the Powerbook and the seven-speaker surround-sound system connected to it were the most modern and expensive gear McKinnon had seen so far, no more than a year or so old. This was where Walker spent most of his time.

He sat down at the keyboard, killed the hypnotic screensaver, opened a browser, accessed a page that was decidedly *not* part of the World Wide Web, downloaded some software money couldn't buy, and scanned Walker's computer rather more thoroughly than a Vancouver Apple dealer could have. Nothing he turned up was of any use or interest to him, as he had expected going in.

He gave some of Walker's Op Ed columns a hasty scan, and was surprised to find very few stupid opinions. Walker had correctly assessed the significance of 9/11 on September 11, for example, and had seen through the Iraq bullshit from Day One. He had the sense to know and the courage to say in print that Osama had probably been dead for years. The man tended to get his supporting evidence

SOURCES

from sorces like *The Economist* rather than American or Canadian news media. Yet he was *not* a knee-jerk American-basher, like many Canadians and nearly all ex-American Canadians. One paragraph in particular caught McKinnon's eye: "America sometimes fails to live up to its own ideals. If you want to say 'often,' I won't argue. So has every nation since history began. But it must be admitted that so far, the United States of America has the most magnificent set of ideals any nation ever failed to live up to." McKinnon was starting to like the man; he hoped it would not be necessary to end him.

But his hard drive definitely did not contain the text strings "Zandor," "Zudenigo," or "Smelly" with a capital S. Or anything else useful. His e-mail contacts included a few names Homeland Security considered questionable, but no more than was reasonable for a national columnist, and none that were flagged red or even amber. He did not have a website. He did not blog or IM or videochat. He had hardly any real friends—very few of his correspondences produced more than half a dozen exchanges in a year—but he certainly knew some interesting people. His iTunes library ran heavily to jazz, folk, soul and Sixties rock.

McKinnon sighed, put the laptop to sleep, left the office and found himself reentering the main house without knowing why. From long experience he knew that meant he had seen something in the house that was not right, and failed to consciously notice it at the time. So he let his feet go where they would. He found himself approaching the spare room used for storage of obsolete junk.

Five steps before he reached it, he suddenly remembered what he was going to see that was wrong the moment he passed through that door. A laptop. A Mac Powerbook, but several iterations older than the one in Walker's office, a 1400 series. On one that old, all the connections were in a bay in the back, and playing back memory now he was certain the only thing connected to this one was its power cord. He had noticed a tiny light on the laptop's lid blinking at him, announcing that it was sleeping rather than shut off. He remembered seeing a blue cable coming in through the wall that had to be internet, but was sure it had ended in a coil on the floor, nowhere near the computer.

He stopped to think it through. Lots of people kept obsolete old computers around. The new one might break. Maybe a favorite old game would not work with newer operating systems. A Powerbook in sleep mode consumed very little power, so why not keep it plugged in? But even a 1400 could collect and send e-mail, do simple net-surfing, play internet radio—so *why would a man with high speed internet access handy choose not to plug it in?*

Only one answer occurred to McKinnon, and it made him smile. Walker had information on that computer he wanted to be *certain* could not be hacked, not even by people like McKinnon.

It was theoretically possible to incurse a computer through its power cord, but most civilians did not even suspect that, and McKinnon himself could not have done it with the tools at hand—or even had it done on his authorization back when he'd been a Company man. He took a moment to marvel at Walker's peculiar form of paranoia. He had taken precautions sufficient to foil a cyber-antagonist as powerful and capable as the Company itself, or the Mossad, or the late Komitet Gosudarstveno Bezhopaznosti. Yet he'd taken no precautions at all against a man walking in his front door while he was away.

Already grinning as he tried to imagine what lovely information he was about to acquire, McKinnon resumed walking, and within three steps was in the room and staring directly at the spot where the Powerbook 1400—

—had been, half an hour earlier, and was no more.

The window was wide open now. Knickknacks that had been on the sill were scattered on the floor. Someone outside was heading for the trees.

Shit!

He sprang to the window, grabbed it at either side and lifted one foot to the sill—and froze there, in that off-balance position. The unexpected touch of a gun muzzle between the tendons at the back of his neck was shocking. Worse, he felt it only for the second it took him to identify it. Then it was gone . . . and now he had no idea where the gun or the person holding it were anymore. He was up against a pro. And his own gun, though covered by his jacket, was holstered at the small of his back.

"Good evening, Constable Mandiç," he said softly. "May I turn around?"

"Detective Constable," came the reply. "And no. You can put

your leg back down—and then your hands behind your back." He heard handcuffs coming out of a belt holster.

Shit!

He did as directed, and waited.

The first cuff ratcheted closed around his left wrist. The angle and direction told him she was holding the cuffs with her right hand, the gun with her left. Expected form for a right-hander. He made a fist with his cuffed left hand and punched an imaginary fat man in front of him as fast and hard as he could with it. Instinctively she kept her grip on the cuffs, which yanked her right side forward, spinning her left side and gun-hand away from him. He trapped her right elbow and pivoted sharply to his right, whipping her left arm around in a wide arc that ended abruptly when her wrist smacked against the side of the open window frame. The gun sailed out into the darkness.

He was busy then for a while. She was young, strong, fit, and reasonably well trained. But the outcome was never in doubt. He had exponentially more experience.

Once she was unconscious, he searched her, found the handcuff key, unlocked the one on his wrist, and cuffed her right wrist to her left ankle. He found a knife there, and unstrapped that and an empty holdout holster he found on the other ankle. Then, feeling pessimistic, he elbow-crawled to the window and popped up for a quick look.

Good news. The one outside had stopped running away, had come back, was a dark silhouette halfway between the treeline and the house. Both hands were free, he'd left the laptop somewhere. He froze when he saw McKinnon's head briefly appear. Walker? Another cop? A neighbor?

What difference did it make? He spoke loudly enough to be sure he was heard, and no louder. "If you do not bring it back, intact, right now, I will hurt her badly."

Silence. No reply. No footsteps either, either running or slowly approaching.

"Do *not* pretend you don't know what I mean."

Still no response.

He frowned. "At this moment, I have no pressing need to kill either of you. The moment I cripple a cop, that changes fast and for good. Last chance: get the laptop, hand it up through the window, and then go round the house and come in the front door. Hurry. Otherwise I start with an elbow. They're actually harder to replace than knees . . . not that it'll matter."

"Very hard choice."

Oh, really? The voice was surprising, too: definitely not a cop . . . but not a columnist pushing sixty either. And *definitely* bluffing. "Make it quickly."

The sigh was audible. "You win." Footsteps moved away, then came back.

"Come straight to the window," he called, because who knew whether this guy was aware that there was a handgun loose out there somewhere in the shadows to the right of the window.

But the footsteps did come straight to the window, and moments later the laptop appeared in the opening..

"Set it down on the sill," he said. "Good." He raised his hand high enough to be seen from outside, and pointed to his left. "Now go round that way."

"But you *told* me to come in the front door. It's over *that* w—"

"And now I'm telling you to take the long way round!"

Pause. "Whatever." Footsteps moved away, to the left.

He took the Powerbook from the window sill, set it on the floor beside him, located its abandoned power cord, plugged it back in, and stood up. Just as he heard the front door opening at the far end of the house, he saw the open door of the closet in which the cop had hidden to ambush him, and decided it might work twice.

It did. The moment the other had approached closely enough to see the sprawled form of the policewoman on the floor, he raced heedless into the room and knelt by her side. McKinnon pushed open the closet door, took two measured steps, and knelt behind him. He held his knife to the other's throat just long enough for the fingers of his left hand to find the right spot, then was careful to get the blade out of the way as the man fell. He leaned forward and used his miniflashlight to confirm that this was not Russell Walker, or anyone he knew. The guy was about the same age as the cop, but a patdown showed he carried no weapon or handcuffs.

McKinnon sat back on his heels and sighed. A pity the man *hadn't* brought a second set of cuffs. He got to his feet, checked his clothing for damage, and dragged his burden down the hallway to the kitchen by one wrist, hoping for duct tape. He had no trouble locating Walker's tool drawer, but the only tape in it was masking tape, too narrow to be of use. How could a man *live* without duct tape?

But in the adjacent drawer he found a large roll of Saran plastic wrap. Widowers refrigerated a lot of unfinished portions. He took the roll from its box, brought it into the living room, and rolled out as long a sheet of plastic wrap as he could. Then he dumped his newest acquaintance on it and kept rolling him over until his arms were completely pinned to his sides. He cut it with his knife and sealed it in place with masking tape. Then he twisted another length into plastic rope, bound the other's ankles with it, and used what was left over to haul him back to the spare room by, a task made even easier because he offered less friction wrapped in plastic.

When he had them laying side by side, he checked their breathing and pulses carefully, then dismissed them from his mind and eagerly turned his attention to the laptop. It didn't take him any time to find what he was looking for, even though he had no idea what it was. All he needed to do was scan for most-recent-activity: it turned out that these days, Walker used this Powerbook only for a single purpose.

Digging his own grave.

11.
Saturday, June 23, 2007
Coveney Island, Bitish Columbia, Canada

"How could I have been so fucking stupid, Zudie?" My voice sounded like an echo coming back from the far end of a cold dark cave.

His sounded perfectly normal. "You weren't expecting an Agent Pitt to come along out of a past you didn't share."

"I was worried about people a fuck of a lot scarier than Agent Pitt!" My ass hurt. I must have sat down too hard. I didn't recall sitting down.

"And you assumed if they came it would be through the net. How else? The only way you could put yourself or Nika or me in jeopardy, as far as you knew, was to allow any wisp of a traceable connection to occur between you and Allen online, and you took steps to make sure there were none. You tell me: how could God himself have physically followed Allen's trail to your house? Even if that monster e-mailed a friend before he left home to kill us, he himself didn't know where he was going until he got here . . . and when he did, we killed him."

"Still—"

"You reasoned, intelligently, that even if you *did* become the victim of the first burglary in Heron Island history, any reasonable thief would focus on the expensive recent-model computer with high speed internet sitting in your office, and ignore an obsolete old piece of crap worth a hundred bucks tops. At worst, he'd open it and glance through it looking for porn—and get bored decrypting files long before he got near anything of interest. You hid the dangerous file well enough to stymie anyone but a Macintosh power user . . . and they don't tend to become burglars."

"But God damn it—"

"The precautions you took were more than reasonable. This is an unreasonable situation. The sooner you get over blaming yourself the quicker we can get to work on it."

"Work on what? You've convinced me: Agent Pitt is James Bond on steroids. No way in the world is he going to walk past a superfluous laptop with its sleep light blinking. Especially one disconnected from the net, two meters from an internet connection. No way in the world is he going to have the slightest trouble decrypting old Disk Doubler encryption, for Christ's sake. How long will it take him to try the date of Susan's death as my password? Third try, tops."

"You're being—"

"Half an hour later, max, he will have you and me by the balls, and Nika by the ovaries."

"That is not neces—"

"*It's all there, Zudie.* All of it. As close as I could make it to how it actually happened. Every thing we did. Every thing we didn't do. Chock full of verifiable facts. The exact spot we buried the son of a bitch, for example. Put it all together, you've got the single most supernaturally stupid thing anybody could possibly have done. I wrote a detailed confession of murder—"

"You're a *writer*, Russell. It's what you do, it's how you manage to cope with the world—by putting it on paper where it's at arm's length. It's how you coped with the most traumatic thing that ever happened to you."

"—and left it lying around unlocked in a building I knew the CIA would be inspecting soon—"

"—which you were leaving at high speed, scared to death for your son, not to mention yourself."

"A man's supposed to have brains, even when he's scared. *Especially* when he's scared."

"Which man?"

"Huh? OWWW!"

He had grabbed me by the ears, hard. He was at arms' length, on his knees, a big nearly naked pale hairless walrus with a face reminiscent of Tony Soprano as a fat child. "Listen to me. You're absolutely right: the cartoon superheros in the adventure fiction you love to read would all be disgusted with you. At this very moment, Jack Reacher is curling his lip, Hawk is saying something ironic about you to Spenser, and Travis McGee thinks you're as helpless as Meyer. Okay? You're a total failure as Superman. The Saint would be ashamed of you. Parker thinks you're a pussy. Accept that. Deal with it on your own time. Right now, you're in the real world: *work the problem.*"

"Okay."

My voice sounded normal again. The rest of the room was there, once more, and the universe outside. I could feel my lungs filling and emptying.

"What time is it, Zudie? After nine? Okay, obviously the first thing to do is c . . . " I trailed off.

"Oh," Zudie said sadly. "That's too bad."

Well, why would I memorize my son's cell phone number? Christmas and birthday calls I make on a land-line. And why would a Vancouver police officer who wanted only to forget she ever knew me have given me *her* cell? If there was any way to look up a cell phone number, I didn't know it, and if there was, I was sure theirs would both be unlisted.

Wait—Zudie had a laptop and internet, I could . . . oh damn it, that was no good either. Jesse used an e-mail address that was just a random string of letters and numbers, to defeat spammers.

Could I call some friend of Jesse's in New York and get his cell number from them? Not for hours, even if I could think of one; it was after 1:00 AM there now. Could I call the Vancouver cops, and try to use my newpaper credentials to con Nika's cell number out of them? Ha! I remembered how much fun I'd had, a few years ago, just trying to get the cops to tell me over the phone where I could find Police Headquarters.

I could call my own house. If Jesse were within earshot, heard my voice on the answering machine, maybe I could get him to come inside and pick up the phone. Or maybe Agent Pitt would hear me, and I'd have given him a phone number traceable back t—

"Zudie, do you even have a phone out here?" No land-line, obviously, and where the hell would be his cellphone relay? Whatever, he'd stand out like a sore thumb, a single-number cell zone like that.

He pointed across the room to his laptop. "VOIP. Untraceable."

I sighed. "*Boy*, that would be useful, if I could just think of somebody to call. But I can't think of anyone on Heron who'd take a message to a stranger hiding in my neighbor's barn without asking questions. At least, no one I'd feel right sending out in the dark with Agent Pitt on the loose. Of the two RCMP on the island, the good one has slammed car doors shut on his own head three times just that I know of. It's a perfect—" I saw his face, broke off, took a deep breath. "You're right."

"Work the problem."

"Okay. Step one: define parameters. I say Pitt won't make a move until at least one AM. He almost has to have taken a room in one of the B&Bs down in the Cove, and that's the one part of The Rock where there are people walking around on sidewalks under street-lights noticing one another until midnight or so, most nights. So I've got a window of four hours. To get my ass back to my place . . . get Jesse clear . . . grab that damned Powerbook 1400 and physically destroy its internal drive . . . then hook up with Nika and find us all a safe house for the night. Tomorrow, we can cook up a way to get him out here and in your range, so you can figure out how to neutralize him. Zudie, tell me you've got a boat stashed. Something fast and powerful that a child could operate, fully fueled and ready to go."

He hesitated. "Well, I've got a boat."

Just from the way he said it, my heart started sinking. "Show me."

We went outside. The rain had gone, at least for now, and there was a steady warm breeze. Night had fallen. I followed Zudie's pale form through the darkness, and whenever I grew uncertain of my next move, he knew it, and called back directions. Before long we came to a sort of seaside grotto, like a cave open on three sides, easily accessible but concealed from the air.

The boat was a two-man kayak. I looked around frantically without finding anything with an outboard, or fuel cans for one.

"Shit, Zudie—"

"Engines make noise, draw attention. I don't ever need to go anywhere farther or faster than I can paddle. You can't sink one of those."

Just looking at the thing made me tired. I understood perfectly now why he was so incredibly fit for our age: he *had* to be. Well, it was a two-holer, at least. "Can you paddle us to Heron Island?"

"At this time of night? No. Sorry. Too many people awake. No place I know to land where I wouldn't have to come in range of way too many."

I suppressed a groan—a pointless gesture with him.

"I really am sorry, Russell. But you'll be fine. You've got four hours to do a little over an hour's worth of paddling. It won't be anywhere *near* as hard as rowing that big Zodiac you arrived in, and you'll make much better time, and I think the rain will hold off long enough. Keep it slow and steady and you'll be fine. You can afford to stop and rest whenever you need to. The current will be with you, going the other way. The wind direction could be better, but it could be worse, too. Heron's right next door. Try a trip to the mainland, sometime—now *that's* a workout."

I told myself he was right. Heron was a far larger navigational target than Coveney had been, easier to see, easier to hit. I could do this. "Okay, how—"

"Launch straight out and paddle like mad. It'll be nuts for awhile, and then all of a sudden you'll catch a current. It'll let go of you a couple of hundred meters out. When it does, head north. That way. As soon as you're far enough around to see Heron, make straight for it."

I knew if I hesitated I'd never go. Without even looking ahead I jumped into the rear hole of the silly little thing, figured out how to sit, figured out how the paddle wanted to be held, got Zudie to show me how to attach a leash like telephone cord to it so I couldn't lose it. It was wet in there, but not too bad. Zudie showed me where water, flashlight, first-aid kit and flares were stashed, and shoved me off.

He was right: for the first little while it was nuts. Water changed direction and speed unpredictably, spray kept lashing my face, the actions I took sometimes seemed to have no effect at all and other times seemed to have more than I'd expected. More than once I glanced off rock, either seen or unseen, and was glad I was in a kayak instead of a big rubber donut. And then all at once I felt that current Zudie had spoken of take hold of me and start rushing me out into deep water. My speed increased, to the point where I stopped using the paddles to make sure I wouldn't lose them. Distance started to open up between me and the island behind me. I grinned, starting to enjoy myself. I let the magic carpet carry me until I felt it losing steam, and then I put my paddles back in the water and started heading north. It was *enormously* easier than rowing the damn Zodiac had been. I glanced back at the shore and saw Zudie, a pale smudge against the blackness. I waved, but did not see him wave back. I must be invisible to him. And out of telepathy range, too. I resumed rowing, chose a slow, steady pace I knew I'd be able to keep up.

And felt my right lung let go.

Spontaneous pneumothorax is not the scariest thing that's ever happened to me. Not even the very first one, when I was fifteen. The scariest so far was hearing Susan's diagnosis and prognosis. Next scariest would probably be the time, centuries before that, when I watched an angry biker put two slugs through the rear window of my car and then bring the Luger around until it was aimed right between my eyes. I can still remember his.

But it's up in that range.

Even now. Despite all the years of weary familiarity. Despite the fact that it had been years since the last really bad one. Maybe partly *because* of how long it had been: the surgery that had changed my lung collapses from life-threatening to highly unpleasant had been done more than thirty years ago—without warranty or expiry date, in a charity ward. But there isn't even that much rationality to it. Maybe it's just the *intimacy* of the pain. Inside your own personal chest, you feel a giant hand clamp down on one of your lungs and start to squeeze, and it might as well be squeezing your adrenal glands. A state of panic is not improved by entering it with a halved air supply. Every breath reinforces the fear.

And even the fear was less powerful than the dismay I felt.

God damn it, I did not have fucking *time* for this now! My son was in serious danger. My friends were in serious danger. I was in serious danger. This was not the time to be laid up in bed for a few days, living on tea and packaged food and watching all seven seasons of *The West Wing* on DVD again. I had to undo my own monstrous stupidity, or at least warn Jesse and Nika of it—I *had* to. *Fuck* this stupid lung collapse, I didn't have *time* for it, it was just going to have to *wait*. I put the paddle back into the water and took another stroke—

The pain became more powerful than the fear and the dismay put together.

I tried to scream, but lacked the air, and so produced instead a sound remarkably like the one the cartoon animal makes when it realizes it has overrun the edge of the cliff. But I didn't need air to scream with my mind. Just as I had on the way in to Coveney Island, I found myself mentally shrieking, "***HELP ME, ZUDIE!***," on my way out.

And with even less optimism. In the first place, this time I knew for a fact I was outside his range. And in the second place, what the hell could he possibly do if he *did* hear me? *I was in his only boat.* And what the hell difference did it make? If he *could* reach me, on a Jet Ski he'd forgotten to mention, say, the best he could do was bring me back to his Batcave and give me a comfy place to lie down while everything I cared about went to shit outside.

It took me that long to realize what a comparatively happy outcome that would have been. *At best*, I was liable to get that place to lie down a minimum of twelve hours from now, aboard some Coast Guard rescue vessel, and I doubted it would be comfy.

But it seemed at least as likely that I would be getting my rest much sooner than that, at a B&B run by Davey Jones.

I resumed screaming telepathically. Maybe Zudie just hadn't felt like waving back. Maybe he had a windsurfing board stashed somewhere. In my head I bellowed, roared, hollered, whooped, hooted, and produced a better thumb-and-two-finger busdriver's whistle than I actually could aloud.

Meanwhile my body was busy, mindlessly seeking relief, indifferent to any but the most immediate consequences.

When you feel the buildup of pressure in half your chest that means air and blood and other body fluids are moving to a place they're not supposed to be, it becomes essential to be lying down flat on your back on something as soft and supportive as possible, with your head slightly elevated. Only then can you begin to accurately evaluate both the extent and the *rate* of that pressure buildup, which will tell you how much trouble you're in.

The best I could manage in that damn kayak was to bring my arms inside and put them down at my sides and try to breathe as shallowly as possible. The paddle was, sensibly enough, attached to the hull with a leash, so I decided to just let it drift. But its random collisions with the kayak became unbearably irritating. I retrieved it with my left hand and tried to stuff it into the forward passenger compartment, but there was a cover I'd have needed both hands to unzip. I had to stow it in my own cocoon, where there was just barely room for it.

Then my mind and my body had both done everything they could, everything there was for them to do, and sorrow smashed me flat. The only thing you can do to try to ease grief that profound is to burst into tears—and even that small consolation was denied me. I had not cried for longer than ten seconds at a time in over thirty years: it just hurt too much. I cut it off in the first second or two now, from long habit.

I concentrated on slowing my breathing, then, and listening very hard to my lung. After an eternity or two, I began to feel reassured that it was not getting worse. The pressure did not appear to grow, or migrate. I could take in well over half a breath before the pain clamped down. Nothing about pneumothorax is certain, but this seemed to be one of the minor ones.

Just bad enough to make paddling unthinkable.

What I did next embarrasses me a little. It used to drive Susan crazy when she was alive. But if you can't even ease your unbearable grief by sobbing, the only thing left to do is convert it into anger . . . and anger has to have a target . . . and a random and indifferent universe is just not a very satisfying enemy . . . and so I found myself, not for the first time, viciously and bitterly cursing a God I have not believed in since childhood. It always feels wrong even at the time, exactly as hypocritical as suddenly finding faith in a foxhole. But hey, it's the only consolation God has left me—so give me a break, okay? Since I didn't do it out loud, I wasn't even wasting my breath. There *could* be a God, and if so, *somebody* ought to be cursing Her. An Intelligent Designer of *this* mess would have to be a sadist with an infantile sense of humor. I won't attempt to reproduce any of my rhapsody of rage, but I put my heart into it and outdid myself. I mean, I cut the Almighty a new one.

You tell me: what more perfectly, hilariously ironic response could I have hoped to receive to my cursing than a straight-up miracle?

"Cut it out!"

Those had been the very first words Zudie had spoken to me after the thirty-year hiatus in our friendship, exactly. But they weren't coming from my memory. They were coming from about a hundred meters to my left.

Just don't let it happen again, I said to my imaginary God, and stopped believing in Him again. And then I started trying to make myself tranquil, out of politeness to my telepathic friend who had risked death to save my life, and not for the first time.

By the time he reached the kayak I was as calm as I could manage, and he knew how grateful I was. "Let me worry about getting us ashore," was the first thing he said when he could spare breath for talking.

"Fine," I said with relief, for the problem appeared insoluble to me. So did another, more pressing one. "How are you going to—"

He unzipped the cover on the forward seat. "Brace yourself," he said, and I did, and if I told you what I think I saw you wouldn't believe me, and I wouldn't blame you because I don't believe it myself, so all I'm going to say is that one minute he was in the water, and the next minute he was in the kayak. Without, as I'd been expecting, having to roll it over and dunk me. We didn't even rock hard or for long. "Here," he said, and handed me back the wet flotation cushion he'd just sat on. I tucked it between me and my seat back, and it helped.

We sat there together like that without speaking for a while until he got his wind back, him breathing big and fast, me breathing small and slow, rocking on the waves together. Once again I was impressed by his physical conditioning. His upper arms were incredible. He must have swum like a dolphin to catch me. You couldn't get arms like that just rowing back and forth from Coveney to the mainland, not unless you did nothing else with your time—which would draw too much attention, get you photographed or videoed by too many tourists on passing ferries or sailboats. So he must have—

"That's right," he said over his shoulder. "I've never gone as far as George Dyson has . . . but at least once I paddled so far north I was the only living thing bigger than a bacterium."

Sure, it made sense. I could see him doing it. For the exercise. For the trip itself. For the solitude so precious to him.

"And for penance, yes," he said. "It nearly killed me."

—glad to hear it—

"What do you mean, you're glad to hear it?"

—in the four years since we saw each other last, Zudie, I must have rented a boat and come out here half a dozen times . . . okay, God damn it, four times . . . and each time, I pooted round and round your stupid island shouting at the top of my mind for *hours*, and it wasn't so much that no answer ever came back as that I never once got a sense that anybody was even home, listening to me, choosing to ignore me. It was like yelling down a well. I was really afraid you were dead, you big dumb son of—

"I'm sorry. I should have left word that I—"

—you should have left *some* fucking word, Arctic Circle excursion or not. I've been figuring maybe I sent you off to your cave to snuff yourself because I bungled the job you gave me so badly that you had to—

"Chill." The incongruity of the word coming from him helped me do so. "We can swap guilts later, okay? Right now there's paddling to do."

—roger that. Speaking of chilling, you're starting to shiver, you know—

"I know." He reached down into his own body-cast, fumbled around, came up with a hoodie sweatshirt and put it on. "If you raise that seat cushion a little higher, it'll still provide as much support, and you'll be able to lean your head back against it."

—by God, you're right. Thanks, Zudie. You know, this is the first time I've ever had a collapsed lung and been able to have a conversation with someone without sounding like the kid in the wheelchair in *Malcolm in the Middle*—

"Stevie Kenarban. Let me know if the pain starts to get any worse." He began to paddle, and then he paddled, and then he *paddled*, and we were gone gone gone like a cool breeze.

❂ ❂ ❂ ❂

At first I divided my attention between monitoring my right thorax, and trying to think my way out of the hole I'd put us all into. But even with a partial lung collapse and a crisis ahead, skating on black glass through a warm star-spattered night on a kayak being paddled by a man with arms like The Mighty Thor is a magical experience. Distracting. Calming. Soon hypnotic. I knew I had some hard thinking to do. But not just yet. These might be the best moments left in my life. The sun was all the way down, now, and the moon wouldn't be up for hours yet. But the skies had cleared for the moment, and there sure were a lot of stars up there.

Zudie found his rhythm and settled into it, cutting a gigantic silver V through the black water, riding the waves with the effortless ease of a veteran subway straphanger, or, I suppose, a surfer. I entered a mental state deeper than meditation generally took me, but short of a trance. I remained alert and aware of my surroundings and my situation and my predicament. I just stopped having any opinions at all about them for a while.

12.
Saturday, June 23, 2007
Heron Island, British Columbia, Canada

I came out of my fugue without any sense of transition at the point where Heron Island grew close enough for decisions to need to be made. I breathed *just* a bit deeper than I had been, evaluated the pain, and was reassured. It didn't seem any worse.

I needed a spot where Zudie could bring us to shore, but encounter the absolute minimum possible number of people in the process. The prospects were as shitty as could be. It was a warm Saturday night in Paradise. Every good place to land a boat was also a great place to make out. I felt Zudie's paddling rhythm falter momentarily at the thought.

It might almost have made sense to have him head right into Bug Cove. The last ferry of the day had long since left by now: "downtown," such as it was, would be dead. The only place still open would be the Pub, situated at least five hundred meters uphill from the ferry ramp. But immediately to the south of the ferry terminus was the Bug Cove Marina, where about a hundred boat people and their guests were sure to be awake . . .

The best choice of a bad lot was the Yacht Club beach—nearly all the way round the island from where I wanted to end up. Heron Island teenagers all knew it was the only beach on the Rock that the

143

RCMP patrolled effectively, and would roust them from. But there would probably be at least a few tourists or mainlanders. And to reach the shore we'd have to scull past a couple of dozen moored yachts, at least some of which would probably be occupied.

"By some of the richest sons of bitches on the island," Zudie said.

—what can I tell you?—

Short pause. "All right. Which way?"

I visualized it, and he altered course appropriately.

Long before I would have said it aloud he heard me wondering, what's it like, getting too close to another mind?

"Ever know someone who got migraines?"

—a couple of people, one of them real well. That bad?—

"Worse. A migraine plus a couple of abscessed teeth is close."

—Jesus—

"That's for one mind. It gets worse exponentially with each additional one."

—dear God. How is it being this close to *me*?—

He took a breather from paddling. When his breath regularized, he said, "You're different. You always were. Even for a hippie, you were unusually tolerant. Nonjudgmental. I don't know why. I mean, you put up with *me* as a roommate. I've always found that amazing. So did everyone on campus. Excuse me."

He fumbled around in his cockpit, came up with a bottle of water, drank deep. I remembered where he had shown me my own was stowed . . . but it was on my right, too far to reach across myself and get it with my left hand. A whole half liter was way too much weight to risk lifting with my right.

He handed his own water back over his shoulder, angling it so I could reach it easily with my left hand. "Never thirst," he said, sounding as if he were quoting someone. I intended to take a small sip but found myself drinking deep. It was delicious.

"But what amazes me far more," he said, "is that you're still the same, forty years later. You haven't hardened with age, the way most people do. If anything, you're more tolerant than you were in college. You have fewer fixed opinions now than you did then. Even after a lifetime of acquiring the kind of embarrassments and regrets teenage boys can't begin to imagine, you're still okay with the idea of me walking around inside your head."

—You, I trust in there—

"I have—" he began. He was silent then for at least a minute, maybe two. Finally he finished the sentence as if it had never been interrupted. "—only been as flattered once: when Oxy chose to love me. I don't think I've ever been more deeply moved."

—so answer the question you ducked—

"Being this close to you is like having a bad headache."

Even as the sentence was leaving his mouth, we were both regretting it, because it made me laugh as he had meant it to, and you don't want to do that with a partial pneumothorax. But we also both knew the pain was minor, even reassuring in its minorness, and I mentally told him there was no need to apologize. He did anyway.

A great blue heron went by on our right. Okay, to starboard. It was an impressive sight even in the dark. God knows what he was doing out that late. Heron Island gets its name from the fact that it happens to contain one of exactly three great blue heron hatcheries in the lower mainland of British Columbia. There's another in Stanley Park in Vancouver, and I forget where the other one is.

"I really like herons," Zudie said.

"Me, too."

"I mean their minds. They're a lot easier to take than people."

—you can read animals, too?—

"Not all. Some. And not as well, obviously. But I do get something more than just feelings and sensations from some. Several of the smarter bird species. Dolphins. Cats of course, but anybody but a dog can read a cat's mind. Some dogs. Pigs. Pigs are smarter than most people imagine."

—how about whales?—

"Whales are as smart as people. At least."

—Jesus. Can you—

"No. They're are as smart as we are—but they aren't remotely *like* us. We just don't have enough in common to learn each other's thought-language. If I get close enough I can 'hear' them thinking, and be aware that their thoughts are at least as sophisticated and structured and subtle and colored as my own. I just have no idea what any of it means. One of the things I've been doing with my time, since I came to this part of the world, is trying to identify the places where my world-view comes closest to agreeing with theirs, in hopes of one day establishing the basis for a kind of mental pidgin."

—how's it going?—

He shrugged and resumed his paddling.

So I resumed my plotting.

I didn't have much to work with. Way too many unknowns. Almost nothing but. And I was juggling the most precious egg in my world.

Okay, that was a start. Priority number one: keep Jesse alive and out of Guantanamo . . . or worse. Priority two: keep Agent Pitt from getting his hands on Zudie, by whatever means necessary. Priority three: keep Nika and me out of jail for murder . . . or worse. Only priority three was optional.

Zudie was following my tortured thoughts, of course, but kept his mouth shut and let me work the problem at my own speed.

—after you drop me off, Zudie, I want you to paddle back out as far as you need to, and wait there. If you see a flashlight on the beach blink one, two . . . pause . . . three, come in as fast as you can and pick up Jesse. Then get him to the airport as fast as you can. If you don't see any flashlight by first light, take off and get your ass back home and tyle the lodge. Do you still have that cellphone I gave you back then?—

"No. And you can't call my internet phone because it has no number: it's outgoing only. But you can e-mail or instant-message me when I'm home." He gave me the necessary data. And shut up.

I kept thinking. A couple of useful ideas came to me . . . but I had no idea if or how I could put them into effect. Again, just too many unknowns. I was simply going to have to improvise. Against a trained CIA agent. It began to sink all the way in that I might in fact die tonight.

And found myself thinking that everyone dies, and that the "natural" end I could foresee for myself was one of the very bad deaths. Agent Pitt would almost certainly be both quicker and more merciful.

Did that mean I was feeling suicidal?

No. I was just assessing and accepting the stakes before placing my bet. If you want the truth, part of me was looking forward to the challenge of matching wits with a spook. How cool would it be if I actually managed to take him, using nothing but brains? Most of my life, I'd felt like I was the smartest guy in the room. Maybe it was time to find out how smart. If it killed me . . . well, there were worse ways to go, that's all.

A little after 11:30, we finally came in sight of the dozen or two boats moored at the Yacht Club Beach. Zudie paused in his paddling only momentarily. Perhaps he was just sounding the telepathic airwaves to try to pick out the least painful route for him.

I mentally assured him most of those people were probably going to be asleep, but he didn't bother to reply. We both knew it wasn't likely, not before midnight on a warm Saturday night in Paradise.

I could see it first begin to affect him when we were still over five hundred meters from the nearest yacht. His breathing began to speed up. His paddling became less steady. I could see him hunch his shoulders and tense his neck like a man steeling himself against pain. He murmured something, then repeated it louder when I didn't catch it. "Alcohol makes it louder. Some drugs too."

—try focusing on me—

"Good idea," he said.

Three boats were visibly and unmistakably hosting parties, two of them into the raucous stage. Others were occupied but less noisly so. Presumably those would contain the fewest and quietest minds. Zudie aimed that way . . . and from his involuntary physical responses I could tell it wasn't working out as well as he'd hoped. As we approached within fifty meters of a large boat that seemed empty, or at least dark, quiet and buttoned up for the night, he began to moan softly. Then without warning he spun his head to the left, away from the boat, vomited with great force, and changed course to miss it as widely as possible. He was able to close his teeth and lips on the moan, but not to stop it, and his paddling began to falter.

Maybe this will sound stupid, but I tried to be me as hard as I could, to think as loud as possible.

He stopped moaning. "Thanks," he said, just loud enough for me to hear.

The current was strong, this close in, and blindly determined to frustrate him, sweeping him the way he didn't want to go; as his stroke was weakening, each one did him less good. The distance between us and the dark devil boat *was* widening, but just barely—and not fast enough.

I took out my paddle. "No," he groaned, but I ignored him. My right arm was all but useless, but my right hand worked as well as ever. I made it into an oarlock and rowed the paddle like an oar with my left arm. If I timed it just right with my breathing cycle, it didn't hurt a bit. Well, not a byte. It added some velocity. Enough that we finally pulled far enough away for Zudie to start recovering.

—that bad?—

His answer was a shaky whisper. "That man is *vile.*"

—worse than Allen?—

"God, no! No, he's only a man. But as bad as men get."

—who?—

"Never mind. Just . . . thank you, Russell."

That was all I could get out of him on the subject. There were two other boats we had to pass that gave him some trouble, but not as bad, and then we had run the gauntlet. He seemed to regain strength as we reached the shallows, and when we had approached the beach close enough to hear it, he suddenly poured on the coals and then somehow executed a maneuver strikingly like the bootlegger-turn Jim Rockford used to do in his tan Firebird once an episode, so that we hit the sand stern-first.

—showoff—

"Sit tight." He climbed out of his cockpit, and helped me get out of mine without hurting myself too badly. No companion so thoughtful as a telepath. But he was not as much help as I'd expected him to be. Even those stevedore's arms of his had to be tired after nearly two hours of paddling, of course, but it was more than simple fatigue. That last five hundred meters had sapped him.

"Are you sure you can make it back out again?" I asked aloud.

He shrugged. "What if I said no?"

"I'd get back in, help you make it back out, and go to Plan B. I just thought of it. See?"

"You thought of it an hour ago and rejected it. It's terrific for me—and no good at all for you."

He was right of course. The Japanese Buddhist monk Oriyoki Kondo had absolutely no neighbors . . . because his stark little minimalist's sketch of a cabin was in a preposterous location at the base of a rough, near-vertical hillside, accessible only by boat, or by a long and extremely gnarly path that switchbacked its way down the slope from a municipal hiking path that led to paved roads. Best of all, Yoke was sure to be away now, on his annual pilgrimage to a monastery in Osaka. Zudie could land me there in perfect comfort and safety, tie up to Yoke's bare-bones dock, and await further events in peace. Then all I'd have to do was climb a very steep hill without completely collapsing my lung. In the dark, without a flashlight . . . on a path I'd taken a total of maybe five times, all in daylight. And then be left with an even longer walk to my place than the one I was facing now.

"This way is only medium crappy for both of us. I promise I'll get your boy on a plane to New York if he shows up. Good luck, Slim." He shoved the kayak off, boarded it like Hopalong Cassidy, and began paddling like mad.

Slim is not the first nickname I ever had, but it was the first one I ever liked, and Zudie was the one who gave it to me, and kept using it until everyone else did.

—good luck, Zandor—

With no idea whether it helped or not, I stood there at the water's edge, being me as loud as I could, until he had made it safely all the way through the mindfield. I could barely see him wave his paddle. I waved back with my good arm.

Then I turned around, and allowed myself to think about what lay before *me*.

The path that leads up from the Yacht Club beach to the small gravel parking lot isn't *that* steep, but it's long, and sand all the way, hard to walk in. (Trucked-in sand, like the beach itself. Heron Island has no natural sandy beaches.) The road the parking lot leads to is asphalt, a more reasonable walking surface . . . but its first hundred meters or so are way steeper than the path up from the beach, a higher grade than provincial or city codes would have permitted, and it doesn't entirely level off for nearly half a klick. If I had to guess, I'd say that in ideal circumstances—as fit as I ever get, rested, and with two fully inflatable lungs—it would have taken me perhaps two and a half to three minutes to walk from the shore all the way up to level ground, depending on how many times I chose to stop along the way, and I'd have arrived sweaty and breathing aerobically, feeling it in my calves.

It took me about ten minutes, and there were a couple of times I honestly doubted I'd make it, and I arrived soaked with sweat, wishing I could spare the breath to sob, feeling pain riding the sciatic nerves all the way up my legs to my lower back. I wanted, badly, to sit down and rest, but I knew how hard it would be to get back up again. So I picked out a sturdy tree a few meters from the road, leaned back against it very carefully, and let it hold me up until I felt ready to continue. Not soon. Finally I lurched back out onto blacktop and resumed walking home.

Level ground lasted no more than two or three hundred meters. It came back from time to time, but not often for much longer than that.

Every road on Heron Island is a roller coaster to one degree or another for most of its length, and one in particular was clearly designed by God specifically to kill bicyclists and joggers. My route home that night was not that bad, but I feel confident in saying it was the second worst possible, because I gave it a lot of thought, as I walked, replayed each road on The Rock in my mind in detail and compared them. For some reason it seemed important to quantify exactly how bad my luck was running tonight. For some other reason, when the answer came back *almost as shitfully as possible*, rather than minding, I took a weird kind of comfort in it.

Even on Heron Island there are usually at least a few cars on the road at night on a Saturday night. But I was on the least-traveled road, and furthermore I seemed to have precisely hit that golden period during which everybody who wanted to party was already there, and nobody was ready to go home yet.

Ordinarily that walk home would have taken perhaps forty-five minutes. That night it took more than two hours. Each of them composed of longer-than-usual minutes.

I was born with bubbles on the surface of my lungs, called blebs, much like the bubbles on a bald inner tube. Nobody knows why. Every so often, for mysterious reasons or none at all, one of those bubbles pops, and the tire starts to go flat. As the lung collapses, it pulls away from the inner wall of the thorax, leaving a vacuum which promptly begins filling with blood and other bodily fluids. That hurts even more than it sounds like it does, and encourages further collapse.

At worst it stops about halfway . . . but if it gets that bad, you're in for lengthy hospitalization, involving procedures you don't want to hear about and I don't want to think about. Fortunately, thirty years ago a surgeon at Bellevue Hospital in New York did a procedure I also won't describe, and since that time I've never had a collapse worse than five or ten percent . . . which only means a few days in bed and a week or two of feeling frail and moving carefully.

Three decades later I can still vividly remember *exactly* how painful that operation and its aftermath were. Beyond belief—let's leave it at that. I only learned about ten years ago, by accident, that it is considered one of the most painful procedures a human is likely to survive. Nobody at Bellevue thought to tell me that; for twenty years I believed I was just more of a coward than other people. To this day, I can't bear to be touched on or near the scar, which runs from my right nipple almost all the way back to my spine, even though it can hardly be seen any more.

That is why pain in my chest is my worst nightmare. Reason has nothing to do with it. My animal body knows that its lungs once caused it an eternity of unendurable horror, and believes they might again at any time.

My son was at risk. My friend Nika's career and freedom were in great jeopardy. Mine too. Reason had nothing to do with it. I kept on walking through the dark. So my chest hurt; big deal.

Every time I passed a driveway, especially one with light visible through the trees, I fantasized giving up: knocking on the door at the end of it and begging whoever was inside for a ride. I just couldn't come up with a fantasy in which my explanation for why I needed one sounded remotely plausible, even to me.

Keep walking, Russell. Remember to alternate feet.

Because the problem was, I didn't need a ride to my home, or even to my driveway. I needed a ride to no closer than half a kilometer from my home. There was no way of knowing where Agent Pitt was right now—so I had to assume he was in my home right this minute, rummaging through my underwear drawer in search of maps to Zudie's place. If so, I did not want him to hear a vehicle stop at the end of the driveway, make a U-turn, and go away.

Keep walking. Oh, wow—look there: a garbage can as old as I am, metal instead of plastic, *just tall enough to sit on and the lid is flat.* Sit. Rest a minute. Or two.

I needed to connect with my son, one driveway short of mine, just as quietly as possible, and *find out* from him whether my house was still safe to approach . . . and if so, send him to burgle that damned incriminating laptop at once, while I stood watch near the end of the driveway. Armed with, say, a shovel, that I could swing left-handed, maybe two or three times tops.

Back on your feet. Keep walking.

If it was too late, if Pitt had already tossed the place or was there now . . . well, I could ask Jesse to hit *me* with the shovel, and put me out of my misery. He probably wouldn't take much persuading.

Bad upgrade. Throttle back from slow to ultraslow. Listen to chest.

Maybe I would get lucky, and find Nika, too, lurking in my neighbor Doug's barn. Lina might have insisted on waiting around for her, and then if clocking out took Nika less time than she'd feared, Lina could have gotten her back to Heron by about now.

Pause until pain subsides.

And even if Lina had dropped her off and come right home, Nika might have been able to clock out fast and then rent or charter something with enough muscle to beat Lina back here. She might have Agent Pitt in handcuffs right now.

Keep walking.

Or she might have found herself saddled with emergency overtime duty of some sort, and be stuck on the mainland overnight, or worse.

Bad downgrade. Downshift from ultraslow to half that.

Car! Walk backwards, stick out thumb, smile ingratiatingly—

—dive into roadside brush, barely in time, fortunately landing on left side—

Get up. Curse drunken louts. Resume walking.

13.
Outside time and space

It went like that forever.

I can't remember how many times I had to stop altogether, and wait for the pain to recede. At least once on every upgrade. I do remember very clearly giving up, three separate times—just despairing entirely and sitting down somewhere to await the heat death of the universe. I only remember changing my mind the first time; the other two, I simply found myself in motion again with no memory of having decided to be.

At some point I came unstuck from reality, and seemed to be walking through an unedited highlights-reel of my own life. Times and places and especially people from my past came and went randomly, completely out of sequence.

Xerox, for instance.

There was a time when I could have told you what Xerox's real name is, but it's long gone from memory after all these years. Something Hindu and very long and barely pronounceable is all I can recall now. But the man himself I don't think I'll ever forget; for some reason, he made a lasting impression on me. The first thing he said to me was, "Please call me Xerox, my excellent friend. I have renamed myself after one of my greatest heroes." At that time, Xerox Corporation was probably the biggest runaway stock market success story since the Depression; its revenues had risen from chump change to more than half a billion dollars in eight years. I do not know if my friend Xerox thought the company had been founded by someone of that name, or if it was the company itself he admired. But I am quite certain that if he's still alive today, he's doing precisely whatever it is he wants to be doing—successfully, in style, and with huge gusto.

This will sound ridiculous if you're not as old as I am, but trust me: back in the sixties, things got so weird that even genuinely caring parents like the ones I was lucky enough to have could find themselves telling their beloved son he was no longer welcome in their home until he cut his hair short again. So by 1967 I was spending my holidays, semester breaks *and* summer vacations hiding out on campus at William Joseph College, rather than accept symbolic castration. When the administration caught me at it that summer, we worked out a deal where I earned my keep by doing odd jobs, and the first one I got was the weirdest: human fire alarm.

The Marianite Order that ran old Billy Joe had just constructed a small new dormitory that year specifically for foreign students, of whom they'd accepted a large number at inflated rates, and of course the building wasn't ready when the new year approached. Most of the things it lacked (hot water, heat, windows) would merely be vast lingering inconveniences for the new inhabitants, but one lack in particular was really important even in the school's eyes: a fire alarm system. Without one, the building could not legally open—state law forbade it.

So they hired me to walk around the building looking for fires.

Eighteen hours a day, seven days a week, for a total of nearly three months. Even at minimum wage, it added up to a tidy sum, enough to keep me in marijuana for the next two semesters. Minimum wage in 1967 was something like $1.20 an hour . . . but a gallon of gas cost 28 cents, and an average new home went for $40,000. Marijuana was then commonly sold in quarter-ounces called "nickel bags" because they cost five dollars; you could buy a pound of excellent weed for a hundred bucks, or a kilo for two.

I can no longer recall what hashish went for then—I just remember that I got an incredible deal from Xerox.

Most of the international students that first year were dirt-poor, there by the grace of God or scholarship; Xerox seemed, if anything, more affluent than any of the American-born students. When he walked the campus he somehow gave the impression of wearing spats and swinging a walking stick. Girls went crazy for him even though he was short and dark and had a face like a foot and spoke with an accent thicker than that of Apu the Quickie-Mart owner. Guys forgave him for it because of his extraordinary hash, of which he seemed to have an inexhaustible supply.

He shared a bowl with me the night we met, and roared with laughter at my explanation of what I was doing there. It was good stuff; I found myself telling him about my weird roommate Smelly, and my problems with my old lady; he told me about his politics and his mother. And finally we had reached a level of stoned intimacy at which even I, a good American hippie white boy terrified of accidentally saying something racist, felt comfortable asking him what it had been like to grow up well off, while surrounded by so much abject poverty.

He laughed so hard he spilled the pipe, and burned a hole in the one blanket Billy Joe had so far found for him. He had grown up in Bombay (as Mumbai was called back then) poorer than poor: not just broke like everybody else, but without family. He had no idea who his parents were or what might have happened to them; there was nobody to ask. *Nobody* raised him; he did it himself.

How? I naturally asked. He wasn't sure. He said his earliest memories were of running a protection racket that covered three streets, using hired eight-year-olds as muscle. That had brought him to the amused attention of a local crime lord named Yama, who took him under his wing, and bullied him into learning English.

"The big mistake Lord Yama made," Xerox said, passing me the generously refilled pipe, "was to tell me just how great a gift he was giving me: how much people paid for English lessons. Those who tutored the children of the rich, he told me, were paid more than even a good thief could make." He grinned like a hungry hyena. "He was right. I stayed with him for nearly six years, learning many useful things, but only until I could pass for a teenager most excellently. Then I got my first job as a tutor of English . . . and that year earned more money than Yama had paid me in six. The work was also much easier, and *much* safer. In three years, I was lending money to Yama." He stuck out his chin proudly. "Bombay is home to the Bombay Stock Exchange, the National Stock Exchange of India, and the Reserve Bank of India. I am the only person in this international students' building who has paid his tuition and expenses out of his own pocket, every penny. I even offered to pay for four years in advance, but the college was unwilling to gamble so on the American economy."

"I didn't realize they were that smart," I said, and passed him the pipe I now had going well. "But tell me something, Xerox. How did you ever manage to promote yourself that first tutoring gig, without any credentials you could show? I mean, you couldn't put 'graduate of Lord Yama's academy for young men' on a resumé."

"That would not have been prudent, no," he agreed, and took a few hits before continuing. "Instead I went with my greatest strength: bullshit."

"How?"

"I saw a very wealthy person indeed in a park, watching his children being given an English lesson by their tutor, a fat smug fool. I went up to this wealthy man, bowed to him with greatest respect, and said, 'Oh sir, I am normanically gormented by the dumpacity of your genius!' And then I walked away before he could be replying.

"Before long the wealthy person comes after me. 'My children's tutor did not know half those words you used, so I have fired the fool. Will you tell me, please, what means, "I am normanically gormented by," . . . by . . . whatever you said?'

"'Certainly, sir,' I say. 'I will tell you exactly what it means. It means that if you hire *me* to replace that fool, I will teach your children a great deal more than just grammar and vocabulary, all for the same price.'

"For ten seconds I thought I was a dead man. Then his frown became a smile, and I knew I would be attending college in the United States of America."

Thinking of Xerox helped. I'd told Jesse about him more than once while he was growing up. Xerox's was just the kind of insane dogged confidence I needed now, all right. I wondered what he was up to now.

❁ ❁ ❁ ❁

Then the pain got bad enough that I started to replay different memories entirely. Like my first hospitalization for a collapsed right lung.

Spontaneous pneumothorax is not in itself a lethal condition. But being treated for it can be—if you happen to draw dumb enough doctors. They brought me my X-rays, and explained that they were going to have to remove the defective right lung. But, they said, my hippie lifestyle had left me way too anemic to be a good surgical risk, so they were going to spend a week or so fattening me up first.

I know: I'm asking you to believe an American hospital chose to keep an indigent patient in a bed for a week before surgery, merely because he was too weak and in pain to go home. Even Canada's excellent medical care system might balk at that one, today. All I can tell you is, in 1967 Medicaid had only been law for two years, and still actually worked.

Fortunately for me, sometime during that week of high-protein diet, some *competent* doctor (I never got his name) happened to pass through that hospital, glance at my X-rays, and note the proposed treatment. He pointed out to my team that I had just as many blebs on the *left* lung, and gently inquired what they planned to do when *that* one let go?

The operation was scrubbed. The lung had in the meantime rein-flated itself naturally; they said I should go home now, and hope it didn't happen again too often. When I finally bullied them into explaining why, in non-doctorese, I tried to hit the roof—*you almost took my right lung out by mistake?*—but my chest still hurt too much. So I gave up and left quietly, and had *just* slid into the passenger seat of my mother's clapped-out old Buick when I felt my *left* lung go.

None of my doctors ever met my eyes again. But none ever offered a word that even hinted at an apology, either. Two different nurses found occasion to quietly slip me the card of a malpractice lawyer, but I never followed up. It was actually one of my better hos-pitalizations, in that I came out of it no worse off than I'd been when I went in. Modern medicine is mostly guesswork in a white coat. I'm not saying I haven't met excellent doctors; Susan's happened to be exemplary, thank God. I'm just saying the good ones shine like bea-cons in my memory.

I got myself through something like a whole kilometer by fantasizing that I was on my way to punch out all the other ones.

Then that started me thinking about the last time I'd almost been punched out myself, by a guy from Easy Company, and about what had saved me.

"Easy Company" was the chosen name of a group of ultraconservative male engineering majors attending William Joseph College who took it as their patriotic duty to support the Vietnam War by putting on army fatigue blouses and ski masks and beating the crap out of any hippies they caught out of doors after dark. They had the ninja power to become invisible to campus security guards—and if the perpetrators could not be caught in the act and positively identified, what was a poor college administration to do? They couldn't very well search dorm rooms for fatigue blouses with blood on them and ski masks, could they? The periodic searches for alcohol and drugs were already controversial enough . . .

They weren't all that hard to avoid if you were careful. For one thing, they had always been drinking recently. They liked to smoke cigars, because Sergeant Rock, hero of the comic book they'd named themselves after, smoked cigars, and were too dumb not to approach from upwind. And they seemed to find it difficult to resist slapping their bludgeons against their palms as they skulked through the shadows. That they bagged any victims at all was a sort of backwards tribute to the potency of the drugs we used to take back then.

But one night my own luck ran out.

Only one, thank Christ. Easy Company must have just dismissed itself for the night; it was way past curfew, so late this joker felt safe returning to his dorm with his ski mask and army shirt still on. I was just sneaking back on campus after an emergency suicide-prevention run—a successful one that time, I'm happy to say. I came around the corner of Nalligan Hall to find him coming the other way. He'd already been hurrying, to get through the lighted area by the entrance, and had just reached the door when we saw each other. Instant mutual recognition occurred.

I tried to turn and run, corner accelerating, and then bear down: if I could reach and use the dorm's *back* door, alarm bells would go off . . . but disciplinary probation was better than a broken jaw, and perhaps a collapsed lung. But to turn, run or corner, you needed legs made of something stronger than jello, and I didn't seem to have any. So I stood there and waited, trying to remember even one of the dozens of cool hand-to-hand combat moves I'd read about in books. He reached me before I succeeded, slammed me hard against the dorm wall, and began to position me correctly to beat the crap out of me for as long as possible before I fell down.

Just above my head, venetian blinds went up, a window slid open, and a voice said, "Oh wow, man."

"Help," I yelped.

My assailant paused with his fist—no, I saw, his blackjack—raised high, and stared up at the window, *hard*. It was a corner window, easy to remember for anyone who wanted to identify the occupants. It slid shut again, and I heard the blinds drop.

With a chuckle of satisfaction he returned his full attention to me, and chose his first point of impact with some care. "Love it or leave it, asshole," he murmured.

Another window opened above us. Way above us, all the way up on the third floor. Holy shit—*my* window.

"He does, Tom," Zudie called down. His voice was just loud enough to hear.

Looking back on it, I doubt the guy had ever met Zudie; he was just too buzzed on adrenaline and befuddled by bloodlust to realize it. The voice was friendly, absolutely nonconfrontational; PFC Tom let it distract him, when he might have ignored yells of protest. "Huh?"

"He really does love it."

"Huh?" Tom repeated, then added, "Bullshit! *Look* at him, for Chrissake."

"Trust me, Tom-Tom: I know that man. He loves America as much as you do. As much as your brother George. He doesn't even believe we should have stayed out of Vietnam. Do you, Russell?"

"Do you?" Tom asked me, tightening his grip on my shirt.

I cast my fate to the winds and answered truthfully. "No. We gave our word. Maybe we were stupid to, but we gave our word. I salute your brother for doing what the politicians didn't: for putting his ass on the line so we could keep our word." Embellish the truth? "I might be over there myself right now if I weren't a born 4-F." No—don't try to bullshit an angry drunk. "People who piss on soldiers make me crazy. The only thing I hate about the war is the suits and generals who've fucked it all up so badly there's nothing left to do now *but* bail out . . . but prefer to keep sacrificing guys like your brother instead, because it's easier than admitting they blew it."

When arguing with a drunk, give him long sentences to parse. He worked on it for a few seconds, and finally said, "Then you're not one of those fuckin' peace creeps?"

Dodge. "My friend's right: I love America just as much as you and George." It was the truth. I just found America very damn hard to like, sometimes.

Zudie jumped in. "Your father named you Thomas Jefferson and him George Washington, didn't he?"

"Damn right." Back then, I took it for a lucky guess.

"Well, there you go. Russell and I think the Constitution and the Bill of Rights are worth fighting for, too. He said to me just the other day, our system may not be perfect . . . but it's ten times better than anything else anybody's ever dreamed up."

It nearly worked. But saying my name a second time had been a mistake. "Russell? Russell *Walker*? The folksinger faggot?" He leaned closer. "Yeah. You *are* a fuckin' peace creep! I heard you sing at that peace rally."

"No, you must have misunderstood what I was—" I stopped talking as his hands closed around my throat. Tom was so mad, he'd forgotten he held a blackjack in one of them, and it really hurt digging into my neck.

"You *mock* me? You mock *my brother's sacrifice*? You cocksucker, I'm gonna tear your head off and piss down the hole, you—"

Something hit the ground right beside us with a loud wet *splat!*

"Speaking of piss . . . " Zudie said.

We both looked up to see Zudie balancing a large jar on the window sill. Something sloshed over its sides. A few more little splats landed all around us, like ordnance taking our range and bearing, and one of them, maybe a quarter cup, got me square on my head and splashed Tom in the face. "Hey," he yelled indignantly, "what are you doing? What the hell is that?"

"This," Zudie called softly, tapping the can, "is exactly what it smells like. Piss."

Tom let go of my neck. "What the *fuck* are you—"

Zudie raised his volume for the first time, overriding him." I promise you this, Thomas Jefferson Mitchell: if you do not immediately let go of him and go home, I will empty this whole thing on your head, so help me God. Russell's a hippie; he won't give a damn. But you'll never live it down. The story will follow you even after you graduate; it'll be too good not to tell."

Tom was gone from there so fast, the vacuum of his departure tugged at my hair.

Better yet, when I got upstairs, the jar turned out to be full of water from the shower. He'd even had the sense to make it just a bit warmer than room temperature.

Thinking about it now, I laughed so hard the pain brought me back to myself again, and I had to stop walking altogether for the dozenth time. Laughter is supposed to be *good* for pain. I guess nothing is true always.

Reliving pleasant moments in my past was clearly better than letting the pain remind me of times of terror, though. By the time I was ready to continue again, I'd managed to come up with one more inspiring memory of unexpected good fortune to recall as I plodded: the morning I was led into a judge's chambers and informed that the felony charges pending against me had been dismissed by the county. That I was not only free to go, right now, but was legally entitled to answer "no" any time I was asked if I'd ever been arrested.

The news was so stunning, it didn't really hit me until an hour later, just as I was walking in the door of my friend Bill Doane's place. Bill was as happy as he'd ever been himself, that morning, and not a little distracted: he'd just gotten married—by the very same judge who'd turned me loose an hour ago, weirdly enough. But he also knew what day this was for me, and saw the grin on my face as I came in the door, and correctly worked out what it must mean. He came over with a grin bigger than my own, and took both my hands, and spoke the memorable words, "My brother, I perceive that a great express train has been lifted from your testicles."

Susan and Jesse heard the story enough that it became another of our family in-jokes, a catch-phrase that could produce a laugh all by itself, like being normanically gormented by someone's dumpacity.

It sure would be nice, I thought, if I could somehow uncouple myself from the express train I seemed to be scrotally dragging behind me now . . .

Let's see now. Happy memories. Happy memories.

Hell, that's easy. I'll just replay every day I got to spend with Susan. Start with that first day, when she met me as I was sneaking off campus, going down the hill to Wanda's to get in line to Bang the Bunny (a campus legend), and she politely pretended not to know where I was going, and I completely forgot where I had been going, and followed her to an art exhibit in town. She said later she felt rather as though she was being tailed by a dreamily smiling pink zeppelin, that kept its distance but could not be shooed away. I just remember her eyes being remarkably large and bright.

Then there was the next day—the first time in my life that I ever literally sprang out of bed, laughing with joy. Over breakfast, I had—

I think I actually came pretty close to doing that comprehensive a review. Everybody has days that are just unmemorable, in which nothing of real interest occurs. There've been periods in my life when I've had *weeks* like that, and I'm sure the same went for Susan. But she and I as a couple had fewer than average empty days: we found each other genuinely interesting on a day-to-day basis. Even the parts that baffled or repelled or irritated us. And somehow we kept it up for years and years without interruption. We took annual vacations from one another for the express purpose of inner refreshment, but in the nearly thirty years we were granted, neither of us was ever unfaithful to the other, or more than healthily tempted to be. In the last years, I'm convinced we came very close to something like the telepathy I had with Zudie—but it must have been different, because it hardly ever hurt, and it always flowed both ways.

It had pissed Jesse off a little. No sensible boy finds his parents genuinely interesting, but he could sense that our fascination with each other created something that excluded him, that had nothing to do with love or being loved, but did have something to do with intimacy, with closeness, with surrender—things for which young men are counterprogrammed. Some of them, unfortunately, for life.

Susan said that only meant that his competititive streak would one day cause him to love someone even more and harder and more totally than I had—a concept I had serious trouble imagining. So far, her prophecy had failed rather spectacularly to come true: so far—as far as I knew—Jesse had never been in love. Even after he grew old enough to start looking outward and ahead, Jesse had just never seemed interested in any relationship deeper than fuck-buddies. Like so many young people nowadays.

But there was time. And anyway, it was his life. Maybe being raised by two happy loving parents had made him grow up so strong, he had less of that desperate need to touch and be touched by another that had driven both of us. If so, was he better off, or worse? It seemed to me he was worse off . . . but perhaps every junkie feels the same sense of superiority over all those poor fools who've never known what a joy it is to be enslaved, to ease an unbearable need.

All I know is, casting my mind back over all the many times and many ways Susan and I had eased each other's unbearable needs gave me a large number of happy thoughts to sustain me as I trekked through that eternity in hell. I hope Jesse is banking *something* that will help him the same way when he needs it.

Combing my memory for happier times helped, some. For perhaps as much as two thirds of the total distance. After that, all I could do was suffer, and keep alternating feet.

Longest night of my life, no question.

14.

Saturday, June 23, 2007
Heron Island, British Columbia, Canada

So much of my energy was going into just staying upright and moving slowly forward that it wasn't until I spotted my mailbox-bank coming, five or six hundred meters up ahead on the left, that I realized I not only was going to make it, but had nearly done so. I lit my watch and saw it was after 1:00 AM. I'd done a twenty-minute walk in a little over three hours.

Much too late, I put my attention on the question of how I was going to approach Jesse's hiding place in Doug's barn without scaring the mortal shit out of him.

Then I changed my mind. Reuniting with my son was second priority. First, I needed to know if he was busy, just now.

For all I knew, Agent Pitt was even now inside my house or my office, tossing the place, and Jesse was watching from a place of concealment. Or, knowing him, skulking along outside the house, ducking when he came to windows, following the sound of Pitt's footsteps.

Or Pitt might be sound asleep in a B&B down in the cove, and Jesse catnapping in the drafty barn just ahead.

Or Pitt might have come, and with the instincts of a feral creature felt or smelt the presence of an observer on the next door property.

If so, he'd have emulated a hunted tiger: doubled back on his own tracks, circled around, and come up behind Jesse. Dawn would find the boy either dead or cuffed and ready for delivery to the CIA. Or worse, to the oxymoronic and moronic as an ox, massively overfunded and underbrained Department of Homeland Security.

The latter wouldn't even be a first: not long before, the American DEA had invaded Canada (with the craven clandestine cooperation of the government and RCMP), kidnapped a well-known Canadian citizen in Vancouver, dragged him back across the border in chains to the States . . . and there charged him, in America, with committing—on Canadian soil, only—an act which is barely a misdemeanour in Canada, but happens to be a felony in America. (Selling high-grade marijuana seeds by mail.)

Try that from a different angle. Imagine you sell beer wholesale for a living. You'll ship cases of beer to anyone anywhere in the world who meets your price. One day two Saudi Arabian cops break down your door, drag you off in chains to the airport, put you in a small jet and fly you directly to Riyadh, where a mullah explains that you're going to have your head cut off for violating a Saudi law that forbids importing beer. Wait a minute, you cry, I never heard of this cockamamie law! I'm an American, I was in America: I'm only subject to your law if I'm in your country, and I never was until you enslaved me and dragged me here against my will. I demand to see my ambassador! Certainly sir, and in the meantime, would you kneel right here and rest your face in the little face-shaped depression in the top of this tree stump? This won't take long . . .

Would you feel fairly treated? Or mistreated by savages for violating a taboo that doesn't apply to you?

The DEA had little choice, of course. The fiend in question, Mark Emery, had been in effect exporting B.C. marijuana—the undisputed best in the world—to anyone in the world who was bright enough to plant a seed. Joe Blow in New York, happily paying more than US$300 an ounce for B.C. Bud, could suddenly grow himself an endless supply of grass just as good for a couple of dollars, including postage—of which not one cent would flow as payoffs to the DEA, the FBI, the federal, state or local drug enforcement agencies . . . or to the mob that did the actual heavy lifting. Emery had to be stopped, or members of the many branches and layers of the drug war forces might have to start living on their salaries—

Damn it, Russell—no more woolgathering! Focus.

I hadn't considered Nika, yet. Where was she now, and what was she doing? It was not out of the realm of possibility that she could be somewhere on The Rock now. Lina might have decided after all to wait around for her, or she might have found some way to lay her hands on a rocket-boat and beat Lina back here. Either way, the timing would suggest that she might very well arrive any minute. Now what was the best way to—

In the far distance, coming toward me, the sound of a car.

For a few moments, I thought about waving down whoever it was when they reached me, and persuading them to turn around and take me a couple of hundred meters. I knew I must look desperate enough to pull it off—and at that point, even that short a ride would have been a godsend

But fortunately, it dawned on me in time that I heard a car coming, but I didn't *see* a car coming. And then I did—a car moving slow, with its headlights off.

I hadn't realized that could be done with a modern car. And I couldn't think of a legit reason to go to the trouble. So I left the road, found a spot where the drainage ditch alongside it wasn't too steep for me, and crouched down in it to await developments.

The dark car, a Camry, went past my driveway. Two curb cuts later, a little ways short of me, it slowed to a stop in the road and shut its engine. Then the driver put it in neutral and let it slide backward on the slight downgrade. When he reached my driveway again he backed into it. A few minutes later a small musical sound announced that he'd failed to completely miss the tree that's too close to the driveway on the left. Still, he'd done rather well without power steering to help.

If I'd had the energy or the air, I'd have burst into tears of frustrated rage. All that effort, all that pain, all that determination . . . and I'd arrived only minutes too late! It was monstrous.

No, God damn it, all was not yet lost. I beat back the despair—or maybe just lost the strength for that too. Perhaps he would decide to toss my office first—I would have, in his shoes—and would get hung up examining the hard drives and internet history of the new

Powerbook there, long enough for me to slip into the spare bedroom and grab the old one. If I entered and left the house on the side opposite from the office, through the washer-dryer room, I might just pull it off.

I gave him a little time to get out, check his surroundings, take a pee, and skulk off down my driveway to creep my place. But as I started to climb up out of the ditch, I froze. Another car was coming,

Another car with no lights! Here it came now, even slower than its predecessor had.

It did almost the exact same maneuver the Camry had. But it waited until it was well past me to shut its motor and drift back—I ducked my head—and then it went one driveway farther downhill. The one it chose to back into was that of Doug, my neighbor, and it was either better or luckier than the first, for there were no crunch sounds.

For a moment I didn't know what to think. Which car was Pitt? Or did he have backup? What the hell was my move?

Then I realized the second car had been an Echo, just like my own. Nika was back on the island! And on her way to back up Jesse. At last, some good news.

As I climbed up out of the ditch, Nika walked back out to the road to see if her arrival had drawn any attention; we saw each other simultaneously. I waved *hello*. She waved *get your ass down here*. So I did.

She must have noticed the way I was moving, and met me well short of my own driveway. "Jesus Christ," she whispered, "what the hell happened to you? You look like—"

"Partial right lung collapse," I answered parsimoniously.

She didn't need a diagram. "How bad?"

"It only hurts when I'm conscious."

"I'll get the car."

"No! Just give me your shoulder."

It felt like she carried half my body weight. Even so, I was breathing a lot louder than she was the whole way.

Finally, my million-year-marathon was over—at least for a few minutes—and I found myself sitting on an actual cushioned surface, with a cushioned back that included neck support. It was a reward that put Paradise to shame. I bathed in it, basted myself with it, orgasmed behind it. At least ten seconds.

"That was Agent Pitt in the Camry?" I asked with my first pain-free breath.

She was fast. "Is that his name? Yeah, Jesse has him staked out from the barn up ahead like you said. And he scoped out a good spot for me around the other side of your house."

"How do you know all that? You just got here too."

She blinked at me, and showed me her cellphone, and I felt like an idiot. There's just no way around it; I really *am* an old fart.

She didn't stop to rub it in. "The plan is to wait until he splits, go in and deactivate whatever boobytraps and bugs he left, and then try and figure out our next—"

"No good."

"What's the problem?"

"The worst problem is I'm a moron. In my spare bedroom is a laptop so old the next time it needs parts it's a paperweight. Uses an OS nobody else has in years. Uses fucking MacWrite for a word processor; nobody else has in decades. It's just barely possible to connect it to the net, and I never—"

Like I said, Nika was very fast. "Oh *fuck* me, tell me you didn't write down—"

"Only thing I was afraid of was one of Allen Campbell's cybergenius monster friends hacking me. Figured if there was ever one inside my house, decoding and reading what look like twenty-year-old files in a junk computer, I was already fucked."

"Christ, Russell, didn't you—"

"Damn it, Nika, it's how I process, okay? Keyboard's always been my confidante. Only one I've *had* since Susan. It's my shrink. My bartender. My stranger on a train. You cops get training. How to handle this shit, where to put it. You can just kill a man and keep going, but I—"

"I wrote mine longhand," she interrupted.

"Really?"

She nodded, embarrassed. "In Herzegovinian."

"What's that, some kind of shorthand?"

"A dialect of Croatian. My grandmother made me learn it."

"Wow. That beats my MacWrite 2.2 with DiskDoubler."

"Not for the CIA. But mine's in a safe deposit box nobody else knows about. Still, what are the odds this guy is going to even glance at an obsolete computer?"

"Zudie says Pitt is really smart. Zudie knows smart, and he was in Pitt's head once, forty years ago. He's been hiding from him ever since."

"Still—"

"I left the damn thing connected to wall current, but not the internet. He'd notice things like that."

"What . . . oh, I see. Whatever you use the thing for, why wouldn't you want e-mail and net access while you were doing it? Why have to go all the way out to your office to Google something? So you can't be hacked."

"Exactly."

"Hell. Where is Zudie now?"

"Waiting offshore in a kayak for us to bring him Jesse. Zudie's going to get him out of the country and then dive in his hole and pull it in after him, and I won't blame him. It's the safest place I know in this part of the world. I don't want him anywhere *near* a guy like Pitt. Let's go tell Jesse." I started the painful process of getting up.

"Sit," Nika said, and gave me her cellphone.

I squinted at it in the dark. "I can't find the redial button."

She looked at me like I was from Mars. "There isn't one. You push 'send,'"

Feeling silly, I did. Jesse's number appeared onscreen. I put the phone to my ear.

"And push it again," she prompted.

Feeling sillier, I did. The word "dialing" appeared. She took it from me and turned on the speakerphone somehow.

I *will* enter the twenty first century, yes I will. At my own pace.

"Yah."

"Jesse, I'm at the end of Doug's driveway with Nika."

"Hi, Pop," he said very softly. "How are you?"

The only thing to do with that question was fail to hear it. "He's a CIA agent named Pitt, Zudie says. Very smart. Very scary. So scary I'm speaking as softly as you are, and I'm a couple of hundred meters away. Where is he now?"

"Just now coming up on the house through the woods. He spent some time making friends with your cats. He moves slow, like he's tired."

"Don't bet on it. Listen carefully. This is important. If Pitt goes into the office shed first, slip in my back door. I left it ajar so the cats could get in to eat and out to shit. Go to the spare bedroom, the one at the far end of the hall. There's an ancient Powerbook, black. Plugged into the wall but not the net. Grab it and bug out. You hear him leaving the office, go out the window. Short drop and the office itself will cover you from his angle. We'll meet you at the barn."

He was as fast as Nika. "Understood. Something on that laptop Pitt mustn't see."

"A diary I forgot," I confessed miserably. "I'm sorry."

To my surprise, all he said was, "Can he see any house windows from the office?" It had been a long time since my son had passed up a chance to break my balls, and this was a real good one.

"Only the bathroom, and it's frosted anyway."

"Good. Shit."

"What?"

"He circled the office and looked in the window, but now it looks like . . . yes, he's going in the house."

"Damn."

"He has to," Nika said. She was crouching by the open car door, close enough to me for the speakerphone to pick her up even at very low volume. "He can't trap himself in that office until he's absolutely sure we all really bugged out. Your car and mine are still parked in front of the house."

"And after he's been through your house, he can ask your computer more intelligent questions," Jesse added. "While he goes about it, I've got two questions. First, are you having one of your lung collapses?"

I nearly dropped the phone. "Jesus Christ, how could you possibly—?"

"It's the only time you ever speak in short sentences. How bad?"

For some reason my eyes stung. "Extremely minor. Little short of breath is all. Not much help to you guys. But I'm okay, and I'll be fine after a night's sleep. Second question?"

"I'm glad it's not worse. Once I've got this laptop back here to the barn where I can pulverize it without him hearing—then what? What's the plan? I mean, Pitt searches your house, your office, your computer, then he'll probably go back to his B&B and work on locating you and Nika and squeezing one or both of you for Zudie. What do we do then?"

"First thing we do is get you to the Yacht Club Beach. West end of the island. Zudie's waiting for you offshore. Two-man kayak. He'll take you to the mainland and you can get a bus to the airport. You need to be out of the country. You have your passport on you, right? I saw you grab it as we left the house." God, that seemed like days ago!

"Yes.

"A kayak's close quarters," he said dubiously. "I don't think he's going to find my mind as endurable as he does yours."

"He knows that. He still volunteered. Trust me, he's endured *much* worse than you already, tonight."

"What does he do after he drops me off?"

"He disappears. He has a Fortress of Solitude, if you get the reference."

"No, but I can figure it out. He has a safe house."

"And you guys will meet him there and figure out what to do?"

Nika and I looked at each other. Our eyes met. We had not discussed this. She had a very hard choice to make, and no time to make it. How far was she prepared to go, to keep Zudie out of the hands of a CIA agent he'd been running from his whole life?

She was a police officer, a detective constable, with a career and a future to lose. She only had those things because a few years ago, Zandor Zudenigo had risked his life and sanity to save her—and me—from rape, torture and death at the hands of a sadistic super-genius with extensive experience. But now she had those things, and they were all she had.

"Just a second," she said, and did something that apparently muted the phone. Because her next words were, "Damn it, Walker, just *once* I would like to visit you out here and not end up hiding a corpse."

I was shocked speechless. And not just by her decision. As near as I could recall, it was the very first time Nika had ever said anything funny. I wanted to salute it by giving her the funny comeback I knew she wanted, but for the first time in my life I could not think of one. I settled for "Me too. Thank you." She understood everything I meant by that, I could see it in her eyes, and she nodded.

She unmuted the phone. Jesse said, "He's in the kitchen now, I can see his flashlight through the window. I said, you guys have your own transportation to Zudie's, right?"

I didn't seem to have *any* choices. I opened my mouth and lied. "Probably not right away. We need to decoy him in the wrong direction first while you're getting out of the country. Forget your luggage. It'll be here for your next visit. Turns out this isn't a good time for houseguests after all."

"Don't be silly, Pop. You can't undo me. I boarded a plane, crossed a border, used my passport. I'll have to do it all again to go home. I'm *documented.* Agent Pitt has my voice on tape, for Christ's sake."

"I want you documented off the board, very soon."

"Why?"

"Because bad things are about to happen."

"Russell, do I have to remind you how many years I've been an adult?" His voice was still low and quiet—but he only used my first name when he was thinking of punching me. "Or what I do for a living? Burston-Marseller may not be more powerful than the CIA . . . but we've had more than one client who *is.* I've met the current assistant director socially. There are two guys in my address book right now I'm sure are CIA, and one or two others I suspect. But I also have the private numbers or e-mail addresses of six senators, a couple of congresscritters, a Supreme Court Justice and an ex-president. If you're planning on mixing it up with the CIA, I could be an—"

"Pitt's not CIA," Nika interrupted.

"He's not?" Jesse asked.

"Ex-CIA, I'll buy. But he is definitely off the reservation on this. He's on his own time."

"Why, because he has no partner?" I said.

She shook her head. "The FBI always travel in pairs—so there'll be a witness. CIA prefers to go solo, so there won't be."

"Then why—"

"I've seen him. Just glimpses—but up close and in decent light, three times now. I'm the only one of us who has. The most recent time I saw him open a door, walk, get into a small car."

"So?"

"So I'm telling you: Pitt is pushing seventy, hard. A vigorous seventy; I wouldn't be surprised if he can take me. But the CIA has mandatory retirement at sixty-five, and they pull in field agents younger than that."

"Oh."

"Just a second." Nika took the phone from me again, did something that brought up a photo of the man, and then another. They were awfully tiny photos, but he did look too old to be on active duty. Then she did something else, and Jesse said, "Got 'em. Huh. You're right, he looks seventy."

"If he had the seniority or the weight to override mandatory retirement, we'd have agents coming out of our ears. Which would be in Guantanamo."

"I agree," Jesse said. "If he were still active CIA, Pitt could just make your chief order you to go see him, and then demand you give him everything you know about Zudenigo. Naturally you'd refuse, and a little while later you'd wake up at home with a slight headache and that would be that. *This* asshole is acting like he doesn't want to show up on *anybody's* radar."

"The car he's driving is not American, it's Canadian," Nika said. "So he stole it after he got here, and swapped plates with something in long-term parking at the airport. They do hot-plate searches out there now, not fast but steady. That car's got a shelf-life of about two or three more days. He's on a budget, improvising. He's probably already used three identities since he crossed the border."

"Okay, you've both convinced me," I said. "He's a rogue elephant. That makes him *more* dangerous. Nobody at Burston-Marseller can tell you who he answers to, Jesse, because Pitt answers to nobody. *I want you the fuck out of here.* Out of the country, on your home turf surrounded by the most powerful friends you have. You're the only leverage Pitt could possibly use to squeeze Zudie out of me—"

"But if—"

"You're all I've got left, Jesse."

"That doesn't—"

"God damn it, *you're all I've got left of her,* don't you get it? I can't risk you."

Nobody said anything for awhile. Nika's eyes were close to mine, little more than a cellphone's width away. They were studying mine intently. I studied hers back. We became aware of each other as male and female.

"Okay, he finally finished casing the house, and he just went in your office."

I yanked my eyes back to the woods ahead of me. "How the hell can you tell that from Doug's place? There's a *house* in the way, Have you—"

"Chill, Pop: it was open and shut. I heard the front door open and shut. Then I heard the office door open and shut."

"Oh. Sorry. So you are still in the barn, then?"

"Not any more. Didn't you hear me? He's in the office. It's show-time. Time to see if your laptop diary's still in the house, and snatch it if it is."

"Wait for me," Nika said urgently.

"Why do I need you?"

"Are you armed?"

"Come around the right side of the barn, not the left. I'll wait for you by the back door."

She stuck the phone in my shirt pocket. "Do you know how to text?"

My face answered for me.

"Never mind. If that vibrates, bug out. Keys are in the dashboard bay. The fuse for the lights is in the ashtray if you want 'em; your call, but make it now." She stood up and walked away, reaching behind her to unsnap the holster she wore at the small of her back. A few steps later she stopped, dropped to one knee, and took a second, much smaller gun from an ankle holster. She came back and handed it to me butt-first, shocking me speechless for the second time that night. It was a little snubnosed revolver, resembling a child's toy in everything but weight. "In case bugging out doesn't work. No safety. Point and click."

"Nika, I—"

"If you use it, lose it." She was gone.

I blinked stupidly at my new gun. Five slugs, not six. If I had to fire it at all, I'd be lucky to live long enough to squeeze off all five. I had no idea what caliber they were, whether they were hollow points or anything. I'd read enough mysteries to know its accuracy was pathetic beyond about two meters, but maybe that and my lousy aim would cancel each other out. Especially left-handed; I could support its weight with my right arm, but it hurt.

I got the car keys out of the little hollow in the center of the dashboard where people keep sunglasses, replaced them with the gun, and got out of the car. One of the many improvements they've made to cars: you can close the door with hardly any sound at all now. The driver's-side door opened and closed just as quietly. I had to rack the seat back; Jesse's shorter than I am. I replaced the fuse for the headlights with difficulty and acceptable pain. I fastened my seatbelt and put the key in the ignition and sat back to wait.

I was confused and worried and bone weary. But it did feel wonderful to be sitting down, not walking, with the chair supporting the back of my chest. Now that I had my breath back and my pulse normal, the pain began to ease off a little. This one really wasn't all that bad, as pneumothoraces go, and wasn't getting any worse with time. I could take in nearly three-quarters of a normal breath before it started to hurt. More, if I sat very still, and did it very slowly . . .

Distant voices shouting in the woods.

I was standing beside the car with no memory of having gotten out of it. A billion billion stars weaved around overhead, inviting me to come dance with them. I wished I had the time. The wind had picked up, enough to make it hard to hear the voices. But nobody sounded happy.

I turned and hurried up the road. I wanted to approach the house through the trees, and I knew the woods alongside my own driveway *much* better than I did the woods between Doug's driveway and my place. With no flashlight, that would be important. Call me Hawkeye.

I was twenty meters up my drive and ten steps into the trees before I remembered the revolver sitting back in the dashboard slot. Call me Asshole.

Voices far ahead. Gun not far behind. I seemed to stand there forever, a jackass between two piles of hay.

A trick of the wind brought me Jesse's voice, saying, "Very hard choice." I couldn't make out the reply he got, but the tone was that of a man giving orders.

I moved forward.

Maddeningly conflicting imperatives: go very quickly, and don't make a sound. Extremely difficult. Feet want to make noise in the forest. But no point in arriving if I was expected.

I think I did a pretty good job. But the sound of my breathing and my pulse thundering in my ears were enough to keep me from making out what they were saying. I arrived at the closest safe vantage point, a little less than a hundred meters from the house, just in time to hear Pitt finish a sentence with " . . . long way round."

I could see Jesse outside, his back to me, not far from the open window of the spare bedroom. I saw his shoulders slump, then shrug. "Whatever," he agreed dully. He walked to his right, the long way round to the front door, and disappeared around the corner.

I gave Pitt five seconds to turn away from the window, and then broke cover, moving as fast as I could without making noise, thinking faster. Pitt wanted Jesse to go to the right for some reason. If he was looking out any window it was on the right side of the house. I went left, headed for the narrow passageway between the house and the office, made very good time until I stepped wrong on something hidden in the grass and sprained my ankle falling down and landed on my bad side.

I couldn't believe it. It seemed most unfair of all that I couldn't even curse. That open window was just too close, and for all I knew Pitt was still right beside it. I lay there clenching my teeth until the chest pain backed off enough to let me sit up. I'm not sure why I groped in the grass for whatever I'd stepped on; maybe I was planning to beat my brains out with it.

It was a handgun.

Nika's gun. A big mother.It wasn't the Berreta I remembered her carrying, and I recalled reading in the Vancouver Sun that the VPD had recently switched to the Sig Sauer P 266. That would mean I had 15 rounds, 9mm Parabellums. Now it seemed most unfair of all that I couldn't laugh out loud. That damned open window—

Faint, hard-to-interpret sounds came out that damned window, and I stopped wanting to laugh. If Pitt chose to stick his head out he could hardly miss me. I drew a bead on the window, holding the gun the way I'd seen in a million movies, and waited.

After ten seconds or so of that I remembered to wonder what those odd sounds had been. Like . . . well, as if someone in the same shape I was had tried a few pushups, and then groaned, given up and let himself fall to the mat. Just then I heard another odd noise, like a soft hissing, that faded out. Like . . . like something heavy being dragged.

Up on your feet. Places to be. *Expect* the ankle to hurt like flaming Jesus fuck when you put weight on it, so you won't yelp. Hey there, you see? It only hurts like fuck. Now walk like Kwai Chang Caine, leaving no trace on the rice paper—but haul ass. Your son might still be alive.

15.

McKinnon closed the laptop, smiling.

Detective Constable Mandić was awake now, sitting up against a stack of cardboard boxes much like the one McKinnon sat on himself, as comfortably as she could with a wrist cuffed to the opposite ankle. She had nothing to say, and he was not surprised.

"Cheer up, Nika," he said. "You don't know it, but you're very lucky I found this computer."

Her face gave back nothing. "Am I?"

"I'm not being ironic. You won the lottery. And not just you. *All* of us did. Really. I can't tell you how much better I'm feeling than I was a few minutes ago."

"All who of us?"

"You, me, Russell and Zudie." Maybe everybody, he thought almost giddily. "We've all hit the jackpot."

"Why is that, Agent Pitt?" she returned the serve. He smiled fondly; that had been one of his favorite names and he hadn't thought of it in years. She sounded exactly like a computer shrink program. He was liking her more by the minute.

"It's McKinnon today." He gestured toward the laptop beside him. "Because if this account is remotely accurate—and I know it is, I know an honest report when I read it—then all three of you are unusually ethical people."

"Are we?"

He got up, turned on the overhead light, closed the window and blinds. The plastic-wrapped man on the floor stirred, groaned, turned over and began to wake up. "*Hell,* yes. Zudie, coming out to Russell, jeopardizing a cover he'd worked on really hard, to save people he'd never meet, who'd never know he'd done it. Russell, risking his life for the same strangers and for a friend he hadn't seen in over thirty years and remembered as a flake. You, risking your job in order to serve and protect . . . prepared to lose your life, career, freedom and good opinion of yourself if the situation called for it. Any of you could have just walked away, and no one would ever have known. Instead all three of you went up against one of the scariest freaks I ever heard of—just because he was. I hope you won't be offended if I say all three of you have balls of steel. But that I've seen before, often. Ethics of that order, however, I have found to be about as common as albino Negroes. I salute you."

She was studying his face carefully. After a few moments of silence, she said, "You know, I have to say I agree with you. Why is that lucky for me?"

"It means there's an excellent chance I won't have to bury you beside Allen Campbell tonight. Or your friends either."

She didn't blink. "What would clinch the deal?"

It had been a long time since McKinnon had been asked smart questions. "I would need to be convinced that you don't oppose what I plan to do."

With help from Nika, the man he didn't know had struggled to a sitting position now. McKinnon knew his head hurt badly but he didn't let it show. "We would all like very much to know exactly what you plan to do, Mr. Pitt," he said quietly.

"It's Mr. McKinnon today," I said. "Tom. Am I correct in guessing you're Walker's son? Jason . . . no, Jesse Walker?"

"I am," he said, carefully not nodding.

"That headache will be gone in just a minute," McKinnon promised. "Do I have it right that you're in public relations?"

"You didn't go through my wallet?"

"I've been busy. Reading."

"I'm a junior associate at Burston-Marseller. New York office. I did a couple of years overseas."

"Interesting. Which of the current directors do you like best there, Jesse?"

"In what sense, Tom?"

"Who's the most ethical human being in the firm, in your opinion?"

Jesse allowed his surprise to show through his poker face for a moment. "Thank you—for presuming both that I like ethical men, and that there are any in public relations. Neither of those is a gimme. As for your question, I'd have to say it's a toss-up." He named two names.

McKinnon grunted. "Very good answer. Thank you. What do you honestly think of your father's columns? I'm sure you read them."

"What's it to you?"

He lived in New York, alright. "Indulge me."

"If you ever tell him a word of this I'll kill you. I think they are well-informed and well-reasoned, smart and wise both, one hundred percent honest and utterly fearless. I can't believe he gets published in a national paper."

"Nobody cares about anything that happens in Canada," McKinnon explained gently.

Nika was frowning. "McKinnon, what does—"

"I like his ethics too, now," he interrupted. "Here," he added, and tossed her the handcuff key, and then her own ankle-knife in its sheath.

She stared at them, then at him, then at them.

"There are scissors in that open box in the corner. They'll probably work better than your knife for cutting Jesse loose."

She and Jesse exchanged a dubious glance. Neither moved.

"I'm extending trust," he said. "This conversation is going to take awhile, and you'll both listen better if you're comfortable and less pissed off."

Nika picked up the key, freed herself, strapped her knife back on, and took his advice about the scissors. "Extending trust to a point," she said as she was cutting Jesse loose. "I bet you still have that gun in your spine holster."

"Of course I do. We just met. But if this goes as well as I hope, in a little while we'll go outside and you can find your own in the weeds."

"Really?"

He nodded. "You're a good cop. I *know* that you won't try to shoot me unless I force you to. You don't know it yet, but I feel the same. I quit killing people who didn't need killing a long time ago, and for good."

The new voice behind him in the doorway was soft, hoarse, and shockingly close. "Me, I only started killing guys a few years ago. Haven't really started making . . . distinctions like that yet. So don't move."

McKinnon never flinched, because he always expected sudden assaults. He kept his voice calm. "Hello, Russell. I was hoping you'd show up. Congratulations: you're the first man to sneak up on me in thirty years."

"My turf."

The voice had moved back, out of reach. "Of course. You know every floorboard, every hinge. Still nice work. If you didn't hear, I'm Tom McKinnon tonight, not John Pitt. Are you pointing Nika's service weapon at the back of my head?"

"Center mass. I can see you're not wearing a vest. But in a casual, purely precautionary way. And only because I'm scared shitless."

"Sensible." McKinnon sighed. "All right. I am going to stand up in slow motion, with my hands in sight. I will reach into the open carton of stationery items right here. Very carefully I will take out a magic marker I saw in there."

"A Sharpie, you mean?" Nika asked.

"Probably. Here I go. Russell, don't shoot me."

He rose with great care and did as he'd said, keeping his back to Russell. "Now I take four slow steps forward." They brought him to the room's far wall. He uncapped the marker—sure enough, they were called Sharpies now—and used it to write on the wall, large, but in script, the name "Zandor Zudenigo." The capital zed isn't easy to do in script, but he managed a pretty fair hand.

"What does that tell me?" Russell asked behind him.

The cop got it. "It tells us he's right-handed."

"So?"

McKinnon capped the Sharpie and dropped it to the floor. "Next, I'm going to lose my jacket, revealing my own weapon." He shrugged it off his shoulders, and held his arms out wide as the jacket slid down them to the floor.

"Now I will very slowly use only the thumb and pinky of my *left* hand to unsnap the gun, lift it from the holster, and extend it behind me at arm's length for Nika to take. Beginning."

Shortly he was lighter by nearly three pounds of polymer, lead, and a little bit of metal.

"Now I will resume my seat and you will find one of your own and we will all talk for awhile." He turned around and saw Russell Walker for the first time. He looked older than McKinnon had expected, and in some sort of pain.

"What about?" he asked.

Russell was right-handed too, but held Nika's gun in his left hand. Perhaps he was having one of his lung incidents. He talked in shorter sentences than McKinnon had expected from a columnist. McKinnon pretended not to notice; it would only make Russell more insecure if his weakness were exposed. His left arm was certainly strong enough; Nika's weapon looked like a Sig Sauer 9mm, and it wasn't wavering a bit in his grip.

Nika and Jesse were both on their feet now. Nika had taken a good position, probably without thinking about it, and had McKinnon's Glock pointed at him, also at center mass. Jesse was rubbing the back of his neck.

"Excuse me, Russell," McKinnon said. "I'm not dodging your question. I just haven't had this much fun in years. I'm going to talk about my plans and how important they are, and when you've heard me out, you'll give me your opinions of them."

"What for?"

He liked Russell's questions as much as Nika's. "It is my hope that when we're done talking, all three of you will agree that Russell ought to take me to meet Zudie. If that happens, we all walk away from this."

Russell shook his head. "Zudie would rather cut his throat than come within a thousand meters of you.

"I know," he agreed. "I don't blame him. His fiancée's death was on me, and what he must have found in my mind back then would have scared anyone shitless. We'll have to come up with a way to fix it so I'm immobilized and he gets to decide how close he comes to me. That's all I ask. If he's still as powerful as he was forty years ago, it won't take him long to know whether to stay afraid of me or not.

If you kept any damned duct tape in your house, all we'd need is a tree in the middle of some wild part of the island."

"I have plenty in my trunk," Nika said. "Unless your GPS snitch ate it by now."

"Excellent." He sat back on his carton, brought up both legs and crossed them with some difficulty, then leaned forward on his elbows. The position left him about as harmless as possible, and made him look sincere and intense. "Okay, let's take the first hurdle. Jesse, awhile ago you thanked me for being willing to entertain the concept of an ethical public relations man."

"Many would call it oxymoronic," he agreed.

"I've known a few. The two you named among them. I'm going to propose an even bigger stretch to you. Can you conceive of an ethical CIA agent?"

"You're too old to still be CIA," Nika said.

McKinnon felt his voice harden involuntarily. "On this laptop here, I found the secret that could destroy Russell, and you, and Zudie. Now I am going to tell you the secret that could destroy me, the one I've been protecting all my life. Here it is: I love the United States of America, and always have. I have great difficulty *liking* it, but I can't help loving it. If my former employers had the slightest idea I do, or how much I do, they'd have taken me out long ago. The book I could write would bring them all down. Unfortunately, it would bring the whole country down with them. We as a nation simply could not survive the disclosure of the secrets I know, and there is no way to tell only part of them.

"I *never* was a Company man at heart. I worked against them as often and as hard as I worked for them. I've always been in the Saving America business for myself; I just do it on my own dime, now. There used to be some of us like that in the Company: we never once met as a group or even had a conversation about it, but we knew each other and abetted one other in screwing things up. But there are only a very few left there, now, and all but a few of *them* are approaching retirement age too.

"The man who brought me in was one of the last holdovers from the original, Truman-administration CIA. No one remembers it now, but back then nearly everyone in the Agency was a liberal intellectual Democrat: the parking lot was a sea of Adlai Stevenson bumper stickers. The Major was one of the left from those days who managed to stay low enough to escape the purges that followed when the Dulles Brothers arrived with Eisenhower. And he taught me to do the same, to be his replacement. I tried to train my own replacements, but of the four I chose and mentored, two are dead, one slipped up and was canned, and one lost the faith. There's just me now. And Zudie is all I have left."

After a short silence, Nika said, "You really aren't CIA."

"Take back 'old,' too," Russell advised. "Look at his body language. He's perfectly at ease facing two guns and a knife in a small room, barehanded. He can probably take us all if he needs to."

McKinnon stepped over that. "I don't need to be told the U.S. has deep flaws, important ones. I know more than all of you put together, more than almost everybody alive, about its flaws, its mistakes, its deep shames. I was there at the time, doing what I could to minimize the horror, and I'll be the first to admit I didn't do enough. But the Constitution and Bill of Rights are among the most enlightened political documents the human race has produced so far, and its people are, God help us, some of the kindest who have yet walked the earth."

Nika reacted as most Canadians probably would have. "Are you serious?" she asked. "Who thought up the War on Drugs? Who else lets people die of poor credit? *Kindest*?"

"As empires go. I know you Canadians are kinder, but there are hardly any of you—not enough to populate California. Ask anyone who lived under Pol Pot, or Idi Amin, or Hitler, what I mean by 'kind.' We may have an occasional McCarthy era, but we don't have Cultural Revolutions or intentional famines or ethnic cleansing as policy. We took Europe, and we gave it back, helped it get back on its feet. The same with Japan. The same with the Evil Empire itself. We're the country that *didn't* set up apartheid. We're as racist as any other nation in history—including kinder Canada, as you must know—but so far nobody's ever been as *ashamed* of their own racism as we are. O'Rourke wrote that all nations are basically parliaments of whores . . . but at least we've always *wanted* to have hearts of gold.

"I do not deny we are also sometimes total utter bastards. If I start giving examples we'll be here all night, and I'm sure you have your own list. America has done shameful things, lots of them. I did some of them myself. But it's *unusual* for our soldiers to rape, for our cops to be fences and pimps, for our judges to be for sale. Yes, too many of us are bumpkins, drones and corner boys fooled by even the most childish tricks, ready to believe any nonsense we hear on TV, chasing the wax carrot while being whacked from behind by the credit stick. But we try. Tell me you wish the Soviet Union had won the Cold War."

Russell and Nika were silent, frowning. "I don't disagree with what you say in general terms," Jesse said finally. "But I'm sorry, Tom, America really needs to get its head out of its ass. And soon."

He nodded vigorous assent. "*Yes.* Exactly. Look . . . can I assume all of us here agree that America has been stampeding blindly toward a cliff at least since the towers fell, acting almost as irrationally as possible?"

All three said "Yes," in near unison, and Russell added, "If not long before."

McKinnon declined to quibble. "And do we all share a sense that people of good will and good sense seem helpless to do anything about it, even once they get the facts? That no matter how many voters want us out of Afghanistan and Iraq, or how loud they shout, there somehow doesn't seem to be anybody in Washington, even a Democrat, who's willing or able to bring that any closer to happening?"

"They just broke ground on fourteen new permanent U.S. military bases in Iraq, half a billion dollars worth, *and* the largest embassy building in the world, bigger than the Vatican," Russell said. "A hundred and four acres, over a thousand employees, and a guard for every two of them. We'll definitely be leaving any day now."

"Perhaps you've noticed that no matter how many Americans are finally growing ashamed of Guantanamo and Abu Ghraib, the best we seem able to do is get them relocated or outsourced? That no matter how many of us write our senators and congressmen demanding action for New Orleans, nothing gets done? That no matter how many of us cry out for a decent health-care system like every other industrialized nation on the planet has, we can't seem to find one politician interested enough to come up with a halfway sensible plan, even with all the excellent examples available for study and improvement?"

"I never did get why a government can't possibly care for its people more efficiently than corporations legally required to show their stockholders a profit," Nika admitted. "Some things government just *should* do. Prisons. Firefighting. Disaster relief. Defense."

"What are you telling us?" Jesse asked.

"I'm saying that the kind of decay I'm talking about didn't just *happen*, all because nineteen psychopaths had a lucky morning one September. The United States of America I've lived in for seventy years didn't suddenly change its mind and decide monopolies were good and small business and poor immigrants were bad again on its own. It didn't dismantle its own Constitution and Bill of Rights and the Geneva Convention and its own image of itself in less than ten years without help."

Russell's weapon was no longer pointed at him. "What do you mean, 'image of itself'?"

"All my life, if there was anything everyone in America knew for sure, without even thinking about it, it was that *John Wayne would never beat up a little guy*. We've done it *twice*, now—and the latest one turned out to an innocent bystander. We used to know that Americans were the ones who *didn't* torture people, *ever*, and that it *hadn't* made us weaker than the Nazis or the Japanese. A man I greatly admired, one of my teachers, solemnly assured me there were no imaginable circumstances in which the United States would *ever* fight a preventive war. He told me that in 1965, and he said it again in 1980, and he still believed it when he died in '87. Twenty years later, the America he knew is gone.

"That process of change didn't just happen. It had help."

"From whom?" Russell asked. "Are you talking about the extreme religious right wing? A political elite? White Power fascists? The Illuminati? The fucking DaVinci Code? Who are we talking about, here?"

McKinnon shook his head. "The kind of people I'm talking about are not politicians or religious nuts or even gangsters. They're just very very rich. So rich, in some cases, that not many people *know* just how rich they are. They're not impressed by political power, popularity, or viciousness. They use people like those as chess-pieces—pawns. They've got handles on them all. They themselves are off the radar. They don't think of themselves as Americans. They don't even think in terms of nations or ideologies or the improvement of mankind; they are fundamentally indifferent to *all* suffering and death except insofar as it affects their game."

"Getting richer."

"What's new about that?" Jesse asked.

McKinnon shook his head. "Too much."

"I don't get you."

"Look, the history of the U.S., like that of all countries, is basically a story about the battle between the very rich and everybody else. Since 1776, those two groups have struggled for power, and democracy leveled the playing field just enough to make it a standoff, a continually revised working compromise. But at least once a century, the very rich get sick of having limits placed on them by their inferiors, and make a grab for total power. So far, every time somethng has screwed them up. When the J.P. Morgans came along, the rest of the country invented antitrust legislation and unions . . . and so on.

"But what's going on now is an historic joint push for real power by some *really stupid* rich people, some of the dumbest the world has ever seen . . . and the tools they have now are finally good enough to completely subvert democracy. It doesn't matter how many people want their country to supply free fair health-care, like every other civilized country. No politician in America will even offer it to them, and if one tried she'd be bought off or put out of business."

"The internet will save America," Jesse said, and then repeated it. Like a mantra.

"Maybe. I hope so. I really do. But they're already working on controlling that, too. For months, Google Earth was forced to show us all *fake* pictures of New Orleans, taken before Katrina happened. That not only shows you how powerful they are, it shows you how *stupid* they are, like cats trying to pretend there isn't a turd on the floor.

"Good luck with the internet underground. But be real careful what sites you visit, and look carefully to see who's watching."

Jesse started to reply, and thought better of it.

"I think of them as the Vandals," McKinnon went on. "They are both ignorant *and* stupid, extremely powerful, absolutely selfish, utterly contemptuous of all morality and ethics. They believe in no god, do not hope for an afterlife or rebirth, are certain life is pointless and death is extinction. So they want to have fun while they're here, and things like the War on Drugs and the War on Terrorism are their idea of a joke. The Cold War was fun, but it's done. The new one with their opposite numbers in China has been under way for more than five years now, but almost nobody has noticed, or will for a while yet. So they're working on toughening America up for the struggle."

"Another McCarthy era," Russell said, "but subtler and with better technology. Another fucking Cold War."

Nika lowered her weapon for the first time. "Who *are* these people?" she exclaimed. "How many of them are there?"

McKinnon shook his head. "I won't discuss that with anyone but Zandor Zudenigo. If he'll let me."

"Why not?"

He sighed. "It took me almost half a lifetime of unusual access to identify these bastards—some of them, anyway—and I've spent every day since doing my very best to conceal that awareness from them. They scare me more than the fires of Hell. They're like the monster you two buried down by the stream, capable of *anything*. I cannot risk letting them learn I know about them . . . and forgive me, but I just met you people. No names. It's one of the movie clichés I hate most of all, but I'm afraid this is one time it really applies. If I told you, I'd have to kill you."

"Why tell Zudie, then?" Russell asked.

"Because he's the only man I know who can help me stop them. I need more information to fight them, but I don't dare look for it. They're too careful. Zudie is my only hope of learning more about the bastards without getting caught looking. My unsuspected Enigma code-breaker. My only way to sneak up on their blind side, penetrate their security. That's why I've kept hunting him for so long."

"Jesus Christ," Russell said softly.

"Forgive me for bringing this up," Jesse said, "but you are in your seventies. What could you possibly hope to accomplish in the limited time you have left to live?"

"How much difference did Osama make in one morning? I don't even know what I would have to do to whom, to have that big an impact. I haven't dared to find out yet. But I know there *is* something, and I know if I had a telepath I could find out what that is, and do it. All I'm asking is that you put Zudie and me together, in circumstances where he'll feel safe approaching me close enough to read me. I believe if he does, once he sees my mind and knows what's in my true heart, he will agree to help me. Give me that chance."

"What if Zudie doesn't agree?" Russell asked.

McKinnon's shoulders slumped. "Then he's of no use to me. If he doesn't want to help me, I can't imagine a way to coerce him. I admit I've thought about it, as a mental exercise, but the idea is ridiculous. I doubt I could manage to keep him in custody."

Russell held his eyes. "You know it tears him up to be close to other people? That his so-called gift *hurts*?"

McKinnon nodded. "When I knew him, he had to keep everyone at least fifty meters away, just to stay sane and conscious. Hence the whole 'Smelly' business. Ingenious."

"Well, it's gotten worse with time. *Much* worse. He says it makes migraine look good. He couldn't walk across a college campus today without having a meltdown and passing out. And then being trapped in a hospital, surrounded by minds full of fear, agony and sorrow, would probably finish him off. He's a pretty limited secret weapon."

"I expected that," McKinnon said. "I can work with it. Think of the way he found out about Allen Campbell: a plane went by overhead unusually low. Imagine Zudie a few hundred yards beyond the end of a runway, miles from anybody except the targets who sail over his head and never notice him. There are a dozen other ways I could use him effectively without hurting or endangering him. If he wants to. And no way I can think of if he doesn't.

"For Christ's sake, let me ask him. And then one way or another, at least all of us can go home and get some sleep."

Seconds ticked by.

Russell cleared his throat. He went to where his boy was sitting, bent and handed him the gun, "Hold onto this for me, son."

"Sure, Pop."

He straightened and turned back to face McKinnon. "Let's go in the kitchen, Tom. I'll make us coffee before we go. And then I'll introduce you to my friend Zandor."

McKinnon exhaled a breath he hadn't realized he was holding. "Thank you, sir."

"Hold on a minute," Nika said, and got to her feet with an ease McKinnon envied. She held her weapon at her side, but did not holster it. "I have a question I want answered before I sign off on any of this."

"Ask."

"What the hell did you do to my cousin?"

McKinnon grimaced at the memory. "I pressured Vasco hard. Scared the living shit out of him. Made him believe he was two steps from Guantanamo. And had him transferred as far away as I could. I had to. He's really tough, and he really cares about you, and he was the best lead I'd had on Zudie in more than twenty years. I know that doesn't excuse it."

"Did you hurt him?"

"Yes, I put a crimp in his career, and another in his self-image."

"Did you lay hands on him?"

"No." He hesitated. "But I might have made him believe I would, if nothing else had worked. I was desperate."

"Jack Bauer wouldn't have hesitated to torture under those circumstances."

He shrugged. "I don't care about cartoon characters. I was taught you don't become a Nazi even to beat Nazis. I went further than I should have. I'm going to have to make it up to Vasco somehow."

"See that you do," she said. She holstered her weapon. "Let's get that coffee."

McKinnon said, "I'll be with you in a minute. I have to do something first." He stood, picked up the Powerbook, and saw everyone in the room tense up. He left the room with it, and they all followed him.

To the guest bathroom just outside. Where he set the laptop in the bathtub, plugged the drain, and turned on the water.

16.

There had been lively discussion over coffee in my kitchen. I had envisioned a two-man party: Tom and me. Keep the minds to a minimum, for Zudie's sake. But Nika and Jesse were adamant about accompanying us. "We'll stay back well out of range. Zudie's range. No offense, Tom," Nika said, "but for all I know you could be a really great con man, and I've been taken by a few just good ones. When you're within a hundred meters of Zudie and he tells me everything is alright, that's when I'll really start to relax."

He nodded. "See why I need him? He's the only touchstone in a world without trust."

Then more chatter about how many vehicles to take. Nika and Jesse both wanted to ride with us, protective of me, which I found warming and annoying in equal measure. This time I put my foot down. Tom and I were going in my car; they could follow in the vehicle or vehicles of *their* choice. Reluctantly they agreed to ride together.

I assumed they would pick Jesse's Echo or Tom's Camry, but when we left Nika made straight for her ancient piece-of-crap Honda. She called "I'll back it out of your way," over the ghastly noise of it starting up, and that did make sense; I could have just backed around it, but not without difficulty. Jesse got in the passenger side, and that made sense, too: she could take them both to his car, up at the end of Doug's driveway next-door. Tom's Camry was safe enough for now where it was, out on the road next to the big green mailbox-box.

As we reached my car, I handed Tom the keys.

"Really?" he said.

"I shouldn't drive with a pneumothorax. I've only got one good arm."

He nodded. "Is it bad?"

"As these things go, no. So far."

We got in, and did the seat-adjusting and seat-belt dances. He adjusted the rear view to his satisfaction, gave the dash and controls a quick inspection, and turned the key. Nika and Jesse had opted to remain in her heap, waiting for us out on the road. Tom backed out in front of them, put it in drive, and they fell in behind.

Once we were on the road I said, "I'm going to get something from the glove compartment."

He nodded. His eyebrows rose when he saw it was a joint.

"I hope you don't expect me to ask if you mind in my own damn car," I said mildly, and pushed in one of the last car cigarette lighters in captivity. "The windows are open."

"I didn't object," he said. "A guy once said to me, "'I'll live by your rules in your house. You can live by your rules in my house. But if you ask *me* to live by your rules in my own house, then you go too damn far.'"

"It helps Zudie for me to be a little buzzed when we're together. Not too much. Take the right fork here, and slow down by about a third."

"Got it. I can see how that would be," he agreed. A few moments of silence went by while I lit up, and took a few tokes. They helped. Then he sighed audibly, and said, "What the hell. It's been more than twenty-five years. Give me a toke."

"When we're almost there," I said, pinching it out. "I had you slow down because suicidally stupid deer hang out on this road. And if you haven't smoked anything in that long, this will be much stronger than anything you remember."

"Okay."

We only saw one deer and he missed it easily. After a while he made a snorting sound.

"What?"

"I was just thinking about the drive up here, how the drivers changed as soon as I crossed the border. At the time, I felt contempt for them, found their odd habits irritating, made fun of them in my mind. Thinking back on it, all they were doing was treating each other with courtesy and common sense. Merging without cheating. Not tailgating. That kind of thing. The kindness I was talking about earlier, that Canadians do so well."

I waited.

"I see now that what made me mad was, people used to treat each other that way in America when I was a boy."

"It has a lot to do with why I moved up here," I said.

"Maybe I've lived there too long," he said softly.

In no time we reached the Yacht Club. Instead of parking in the lot, I had him drive past it all the way downhill to the beach access for boat trailers. I'd climbed that damn hill already tonight; once was plenty. He parked just short of the sand, lit the joint, and took a single deep hit, then put it out again and gave it back to me. Nika's Honda pulled into the parking lot and parked facing out. Then they walked down to us. She and Jesse must have smelled the weed, but neither commented, even with their expressions.

By mutual unspoken agreement we had all given up the idea of immobilizing Tom with duct tape; the thought seemed grotesque. "Okay," I said. "You two are going to stay at least five hundred meters back. That should keep you completely out of Zudie's range, and he's got enough on his plate." They both nodded agreement, but Jesse said, "Let me hang a cellphone on your belt, Pop"

"No," I said at the same time Tom shook his head. "We're going to keep this conversation as simple as we can."

"Don't put it on speakerphone then. We'll only be able to listen."

"Please do as he asks, Russell," Nika said stiffly.

I gave in. Jesse fixed his cell to my belt, made sure I knew the buttons to start and stop a call. "Give her your number," I reminded him.

"I have it," Nika said, and they both looked embarrassed.

"Let's go," I said.

Tom turned to Nika. "Wouldn't you like to pat me down first?" She hesitated.

"I'd rather you would," he said.

She nodded. She did a professional job, which is more thorough than they show in the movies, then stepped back and said, "Thank you, Tom."

"We'll both feel easier now," he said. "I'm ready, Russell."

"Let's do it."

We crossed the beach without difficulty. The moon was just setting, which made it somewhere around 3:00 AM, but there was more than enough starlight to pick our way through the driftwood and mossy spots. The temperature was perfect, just warm enough for the gentle breeze to be welcome.

"Why do you both feel easier now?" I asked as we walked.

"Nika's more confident than she was that I'm unarmed, so she feels better. That makes her less likely to shoot me through the spine, so I feel better."

I glanced over my shoulder, made out their silhouettes. "From that range?"

"She took her car because she has a long gun in the trunk. I bet she's good with it. She's a very good cop."

I felt an urge to walk farther away from him. Instead I moved closer and put my left arm around his shoulder. He made no comment. We walked that way all the way to the water's edge together. Then I stood closest to the surf, directly in front of him, where a through-and-through would get me too. He squeezed my left shoulder briefly and said, "Thank you. What now?"

The phone buzzed at my belt, startling hell out of me. I brought it up where I could see it, hit start, put it to my ear and said, "I'm here, Jess."

"What now?" he said.

"Now we both wait here at the shore, for a long silent interval, both of trying to think as loud as we can, 'Come closer, Zudie, it's safe, I promise.'"

"How long do you think that might take?"

"I have absolutely no idea. Somewhere between ten minutes and eternity. He has forty years of paranoia to overcome. I'm going to put this back on my belt again. You'll hear us if he comes close enough to talk. Over and out."

As I was pulling the phone away from my ear, I just made out his voice saying, "I love you, Pop." It startled me so badly I nearly dropped the phone. Then I just looked at it. Finally I brought it back near my mouth and said, "I'm very glad, son. I love you too," and hooked it to my belt.

Fifteen minutes later I spotted Zudie, way out. A few minutes after that Tom did too. "I see him," he murmured.

"I think he'll be in range, soon."

He came forward and stood next to me on my left, making himself a viable target for Nika. I had my eyes shut for concentration, but I could hear him straighten to his full height, square his shoulders, rotate his head on his neck once, and stand facing the sea, taking long slow deep breaths I wished I could emulate. But I didn't need them to bellow in my head.

—I BELIEVE HIM, ZUDIE—

—I DON'T THINK YOU NEED TO BE AFRAID OF HIM—

No result. I could practically feel Zudie's skepticism.

—NIKA CAN DROP HIM WHERE HE STANDS IF SHE WANTS TO—

—HE SURRENDERED HIS WEAPONS, PUT HIMSELF IN OUR HANDS, TO TALK TO YOU—

Minutes went by. Tom waited in silence.

—I BELIEVE HIM, ZUDIE—

—I THINK YOU SHOULD GIVE HIM A CHANCE—

Tom had taken Oxy from him. Tom had made him spend the rest of his life hiding as a hermit. This was never going to . . .

—DO YOU REMEMBER THE DAY WE MET? THE FIRST THING I NOTICED ABOUT YOUR EYES? WHAT THEY TOLD ME YOU WERE VERY GOOD AT?

The voice came from so far away I could barely hear it.

"Forgiving. I remember, Slim,"

Tom filled his lungs to shout a reply.

"Don't!" I said urgently. "Unless you want to meet the RCMP. A lot of those boats moored out there are full of sleeping rich guys. You don't need to speak out loud with Zudie either."

He emptied his lungs reluctantly. "I want to."

"Don't worry. He'll be here soon."

He subsided.

About five minutes later we could hear Zudie's paddle. I opened my eyes and saw him. In another few minutes he braked to a stop about a hundred to a hundred and fifty meters out, and waited. So did I.

"Zandor Zudenigo," Tom said aloud, but probably too softly for Zudie to hear him with his ears, "I humbly apologize to you. Your Oksana's death was my responsibilty: I chose the security system that killed her. It is my fault you've spent the past four decades running for your life, hiding from me. I took your love and I took your life and I have no excuse.

"The man I was the first time you touched my mind was gravely damaged. I was better than Allen Campbell only in that I wasn't enjoying my work, but I'm sure we both used some of the same techniques. I think I only started to get better when I learned that you existed. I had begun to believe that the hijacking and corruption of the United States I already saw going on behind the scenes was inevitable, unstoppable, that they were just too smart, strong and well dug-in . . . and you were the first hint I'd ever gotten that it might be possible to fight the sons of bitches. I'd have sold my mother to get my hands on you. It was only after I lost you that I began to realize I didn't deserve you, that I wasn't a whole lot better than the people I was fighting. I'd been thinking of myself all along as a Good Guy, who'd been placed in a position where he had to do bad things."

"You kept screaming that after me with your mind, as I ran through the forest that night," Zudie called back. "'Stop! I'm a Good Guy!' I remember."

"And you didn't buy it for a second," Tom agreed. "After you were gone, I had to resolve that. There were only two possibilities. Either you were a lousy telepath, and no help to me—or I was some-one who didn't deserve your help." He was silent for maybe half a minute, and then said, a bit louder than anything before, "I've been working on that ever since."

Zudie let the waves take him in a little closer to shore before sculling to hold position again. He stayed there in silence for a minute.

His first words were, "God, you look like hell, Billy," followed by, "You too, Russell."

He was right. I know what I must look like, and Tom/Billy looked for the first time typical of his calendar age or maybe a little worse. But Zudie made us both look good. I saw a painting in a comparative religions book once that was supposed to be the Buddha in Hell Realm. Zudie looked like that.

Billy made a noise in his throat. "Nobody's called me that in over fifty years," he called back.

"You're still him, though."

Zudie's voice sounded strained. All that time drifting near yachts had taken a lot out of him. "I'm going to back off a ways," I said. Neither objected. I took the cellphone from my belt, handed it to Billy. He nodded and hung it from his open shirt collar, and I backed away about thirty meters, at an angle, so I ended up the same distance from them both. I sat down on a driftwood log. I could still hear them speak, and I took a second to confirm that Nika and Jesse could too.

"Here's what I need to do, Zandor," Billy said then. "Here's what I want from you." And then there was silence for two minutes, maybe three.

Zudie let the current take him even closer in, until he was no more than fifty meters away. I could just make out his face now, and I was shaken by the awesome total overwhelming *sadness* on it. I'd seen it only once before. In Susan's eyes, as she was telling me the doctor's prognosis. Wishing she didn't have to, even more than I was wishing I wasn't hearing it.

"This is a good news, bad news thing," he said.

Billy seemed to turn to stone. "Bad first."

"I cannot help you. Not 'will not.' I can not. What you want is not doable."

Billy gasped as if he'd been knifed, and rocked slightly. He took a long slow breath so deep it hurt me just to watch it, filled his chest, held it until he must have been seeing spots, and then released it as slowly as he had taken it in. "Why not? What did I get wrong?"

Zudie sighed. "Several things, but chiefly a flawed premise. You've been assuming I'm the only telepath in the world, and that you are the only player in this game who knows there are any."

That hit Billy even harder. "*No!*" he gasped.

"How the hell did you *think* they became so strong—so fast—so surreptitiously? Enough to take us from the America of the sixties to the America of today, from Flower Power to Guantanamo, in a lousy few decades?

Holy shit! I felt my stomach lurch. I had been making the same assumption for years, ever since I'd first learned Zudie's secret: that he was unique, a one-of-a-kind mutation. Most mutations that radical just *die*, before or shortly after birth. I'd always thought of him as being sort of like a two-headed baby that had miraculously survived, a once-a-generation freak. Now I felt stupid. Did *anything* ever happen *once*?

"It *can't* be," Billy insisted. "If they have telepaths, why am I still alive?"

"I hate to say it, but they must not have thought of you as a significant threat. There are too few of us, and we're all too fragile, for them to have *everyone* vetted. You just never scared any of them enough for them to run you past their telepath."

If it shook me, it shattered Billy. He seemed to age before my eyes, like Dorian Grey, to shrink five percent. He sat down heavily on the sand, and it seemed surprising not to hear an accompanying crack of forearms or hip breaking.

Zudie shocked me, then. He paddled to shore, beached the kayak, got out of it, tugged it farther up on the sand, and sat down equidistant from Billy and me. No more than ten or fifteen meters from either of us. I could see that it hurt him terribly, and that he didn't give a shit. Billy sat too.

"Your ace in the hole is worthless, Billy," he said softly. "They know how to protect themselves from people like me; I'd never get near them. And they know how to use people like me. You and I together would be *easier* for them to hunt than you alone."

"How many?" Billy asked hoarsely. "Worldwide."

"I can't tell you for certain. I'm sure of three, pretty sure about another, and there must be others. But I have almost no facts."

"How many are working for or with the Vandals?"

"At least three."

"What are they like? Can they be reached?"

Zudie shook his head. "I can't really say. Everything I know about them is based on inference. I spend two hours a day monitoring news, worldwide from multiple sources. I'm a mathematician by trade, and when I look at the planetary news flow and think of it as an enormous equation, I can intuitively spot anomalies, apparent errors that resist analysis. Until I include the assumption that people like me exist in the world, and then the anomalies make perfect sense."

"Haven't you tried to investi—"

Zudie cut him off. "No. I have not directly touched another mind like my own since I was fourteen years old. I hope I never will again. It was . . . horrible in a way I can't explain. I'm sorry, Billy: I will not be your telepath-detector. Not at gunpoint. Not even if you threaten to send my friends to jail for being heroes. And even if you could drug or con me into it, the second I detected one, he'd know everything I knew. You'd be dead within the hour, and I'd be waiting for you in Hell. The secret weapon you've had your hopes pinned on is a dud. That's the truth."

Billy sat up straight, folded his hands in his lap, raised his eyes to take in the murmuring surf nearby, the far horizon, and the unthinkably distant stars overhead. He started some sort of measured breathing exercise, yoga for all I know. We all left him alone with it, doing our own processing in our own ways.

"You said there was good news," he said finally.

"You've been overestimating the power of the Vandals to manipulate the country. There aren't as many as you think there are, and they aren't nearly as smart as you think they are, their influence isn't half as strong as you think it is."

"*Then why are they so fucking effective at fucking up my country?*"

Zudie flinched and winced, but stayed where he was. He shook his head. The sadness was back in his eyes. "I'm sorry, but that's on the country."

"What?"

"Face it. No secret cabal can corrupt a country that doesn't want to be corrupted, no matter how slick they are. If American does self destruct, it will be because in the end it chose to. It *is* possible to sit in front of a widescreen surround-sound HDTV and listen to a professional liar try his best to terrify you out of your wits with transparent nonsense and CGI effects . . . and to reject him, decline to take the exhilarating adrenalin high he's offering. Americans don't *have* to eat bullshit, and they're learning more about how to spot the taste every day. Vandals or their minions can manipulate news and entertainment on paper, on radio and on TV, but as your son said, there's not a lot they can do about the internet yet. America can still wise up and turn itself around. But only if it wants to enough. If it doesn't, no secret weapon will help."

"So what am I supposed to *do*?"

Again Zudie flinched, but took it. "What people of good will have been doing for millennia. Wait, watch for chances to nudge things the other way, and hope. Take the long view, and be content with small victories."

"That's not good enough any more."

"Why not?"

"If the Vandals get their way, all the ethical progress of the last two hundred years will reverse itself. It could take centuries for the pendulum to swing back. My guess is they'll end up establishing a religious tyranny that will take an ocean of blood to bring down, because those offer the maximum control."

"That's happened before in history," Zudie called. "It can be recovered from. The wheel keeps turning."

"*Not forever,*" Billy said sharply.

"What do you mean?" I said.

"Time's running out—for the whole human race. We *have* to start acting globally; there's no choice anymore. We have a century or so, tops, to get this stupid planet organized, to build the kind of wise benign compassionate Terran Federation you see in so many science fiction movies, to start making the world fair, and get it self-sustaining. If we haven't gotten at least that far by then, the resources necessary to develop and build and maintain the necessary space-based technology will be gone, pissed away in pointless squabbles. Then everything falls to shit, and the future holds only tribal anarchy and progressive decay."

"You're losing me," I said.

"On the evening of September 10, 2001, the United States was closer than any other nation in history has ever come to being widely trusted. That's not very close, granted. Many people despised us. Quite a few just disliked us. But deep down, most people trusted us, on that day, at least a little. No other nation ever had a better shot at persuading and cajoling all the nations of the world to come together and work together to save ourselves before it's too late.

"And ever since the next morning, we've been blowing it. Setting fire to a century of built-up good will, frightening half the planet and offending the rest. We needed to be telling the world that had just seen us win the Cold War, *you can trust us; we are just and fair . . .* and instead we told them, *murder two thousand of us, and we'll murder six hundred thousand people who had nothing to do with it, even if we have to kill another three thousand of our own and wound twenty-five thousand more in the process.*

"We need to get our heads straight, and we don't have forever to do it. Not anymore. This is our very last chance to get it together."

Zudie rose to his feet, brushed sand from his legs, walked right up to Billy and gave him his hand, helped him to his own feet. I couldn't recall the last time Zudie had physically touched me.

"Then let's hope we do," Zudie told him, so softly I barely heard.

"That's not good enough."

"I know. It's just all we have. I promise you, in the end it isn't about you and me, or the Vandals, or which political party hired the best PR firm this term. It's about the American people. They've been freer than any humans before them for centuries now. If they do decide they'd rather be sheep, it'll be their choice. If they really are determined to turn off their brains and entertain themselves to death, we can't stop them.

"But I'm much less sure that will happen than you are. Again and again in its history, America has gone through love affairs with ignorance and superstition and meanness and conformity, like recurring attacks of a bad fever. But so far, it has always recovered, rediscovered that knowledge and reason and kindness and personal liberty really are worth all the dreadful effort they cost.

"We tend to start out each new century by going crazy for awhile, usually with fear, and behaving like idiots for the first thirty or forty years. But each time we seem to start returning to sanity around the fifties or sixties, and by the close of the century we've reached a new plateau of ethical awareness, higher than any before it. *There's no reason to think it can't happen again.*"

"And no reason to think it *has to,* just because it always has," Billy cried. "What if it *doesn't* happen this time?"

"Then it won't, and America will join the British Empire and

Rome and a whole bunch of other pinnacles of ethical achievement. And perhaps in time, it will be replaced by an improved version of them all, that will learn from past mistakes better. It is *never* safe to say that new technologies won't be discovered before all the oil and metals run out. If that *doesn't* happen, then you're right: the human race will die before long. On the bright side, you'll never live long enough to know the answer for sure either way."

"What if it isn't replaced? What if we never do get to the stars, and everything ends here, in the mud?"

Zudie shrugged. "Then life is a pointless joke, suffering followed by extinction. Deal with it."

"What am I supposed to do in the meantime?"

Zudie's hand settled on his shoulder. "You've done enough."

"No."

"Yes. Remember, I know everything you've ever done in the last half century. I'm the only one but you who does. I'm telling you Thomas Jefferson didn't love America as much as you do, or give as much to it." He pulled Billy's face closer to his own, even though it obviously killed him to do it. "Go home now. You're off duty. Enjoy your retirement."

"I don't know how!" Billy cried desperately.

"I know. I'll help you."

"You will?"

"As much as I can."

"How?"

"You've done internet videoconferencing?"

"Yes,"

"I have a videoconferencing address Skype doesn't know about, off the web. I'll leave the URL for you in Vasco's cousin's dead-drop account. I will accept a call from you any time day or night. I can help. I know more about you than you realize you do. Ask Slim; I cured his depression once."

"Lifted it," I said. "It's been back since."

"And I haven't been taking your calls," he said sadly. "I am sorry, Russell. I was in bad shape for a long time."

"You had a lot to process."

"Well, I have. And I'm going to be a better friend to you, and to Nika, and to your boy. And to you too, Billy, if you want."

Pitt/McKinnon/Billy backed five or ten meters away from him. His expression was indescribable. "*I killed her*," he cried out.

Zudie shook his head. "Very bad luck killed Oksana. Even back then, you didn't kill without cause if you could possibly help it."

"How can you know that?"

"Because you do. You really do."

Billy tried to look away from his eyes, and could not. "Will you at least keep thinking about this problem, Zudie?"

"Of course I will. We all will. How could we help it? If you acquire any new relevant data, use the message-drop gimmick Nika's cousin did. We'll do the same." He named an e-mail address and a password.

Billy blinked and opened his mouth. "I—my—"

"I already *know* your own address and password," Zudie reminded him gently.

Nothing at all showed on the former CIA man's face; it might as well have been a deathmask. But something titanic must have happened in his head or his heart. All at once Zudie lost it, turned on his heel and sprinted to his kayak. "That's it," he called over his shoulder. He ran it into the water, mounting the kyak the way Hopalong Cassidy used to mount a speeding horse, and was rowing before he settled into his cockpit. He took off like a rocket, leaving an impressive wake.

Billy and I looked at each other across the sand.

"He held out as long as he could," I said.

He just nodded. We watched Zudie's progress for a while, long after he was out of sight. Then Billy turned without a word and headed back to the car, and I followed.

17.

As we approached the car, we saw that Nika had already walked uphill to the parking lot. To give us room, I guess.

But Jesse was still waiting. "I need to talk to you," he said to me as we reached him.

"Can it wait, Jess? At least until we get home and get some more coffee in us? I'm sorry, but it's been a *long* day. I'm just fried."

He shook his head. "No."

"Five minutes?"

"No, Dad. This can't wait another minute. We could both crash and die in that five minute drive."

I stared at him.

"I'll be in the car," Billy said, and left us.

"Okay. Go ahead, Jess."

He said, "I need you to know this. That guy—Pitt, McKinnon, whatever the hell his name is? What he says he spent his life doing in the CIA? Working undercover to try and nudge it in more humane directions?"

"Yeah. Hell of a job for man to assign himself. I think he's—"

He cut me off. "*That's what I'm doing at Burston-Marsellar.*"

"*What?*"

"That's why I went into public relations. The Vandals he talked about: public relations is their best weapon. That's what wags the dog. That's what changes people's most basic attitudes and beliefs over time without them noticing. That's what cons a nation. That's how they sold the War On Terror. That's how they got forty percent of Americans believing Saddam was directly involved in 9/11. It's about the only place left where a man can actually do some good, find ways to sabotage those bastards effectively—going into politics or journalism just doesn't *work*, anymore."

There was a loud buzzing in my ears. I could feel my knees threatening to give way. "Why . . . why the hell didn't you tell me this, Jesse?"

"*When*? You wouldn't, wouldn't, wouldn't come to New York no matter how much I begged you—and surely to God you must see I couldn't trust the phones to say something like that. Besides, you and I . . . " He looked down. "Well, we haven't been talking." He met my eyes again. "I was too fucking mad at you."

I swallowed something. My pride, maybe. "Are you still, Son?"

"I came to you. What do *you* think?" He reached out and took my hand in his. "I needed time, okay?"

I opened my mouth to answer, and instead burst into tears. It was probably the first time I had cried since the night Susan died, and I hope it's the last because it hurt more than anything else that had happened to me all that day, but I simply did not give a shit. My son embraced me and held me, squeezing my chest with his strong arms while I cried, and that helped some. He cried with me, and that helped even more. I knew we were crying for his mother, together, and I had wanted that more than anything else for years, now.

Billy started my car as as we reached it. As soon as I was belted in, he backed uphill at startling speed without looking over his shoulder, using mirrors alone. He turned at just the right instant, skidded to a stop on parking lot gravel, and waited while Jesse walked up the hill and got into the other vehicle, idling ahead of us out on the road. Then Billy put her in drive, and cornered *hard* on the way out of the lot. Nika drives like a lunatic, but he had no trouble keeping her taillights in sight.

After a few miles of silence, I asked him, "Are you okay? You're welcome to crash with me and Jesse. There's a foldout couch that's actually comfortable."

He didn't answer.

✿ ✿ ✿ ✿

In fact, I never heard him speak another word. When we got back to my place, he ignored anything any of us said to him. He accepted his gun back from Jesse, and shook his hand. He went to the back of Nika's car, recovered the GPS snitch from the bumper, and shook her hand. He shook my hand with both of his, and nodded once. It felt as if I'd been saluted. Then he got in his Camry and drove away, blinking his taillights once in farewell. I presume he returned to his B&B for his things, and perhaps a nap and a shower, and took one of the early ferries back to the mainland. I never saw him again, never heard from or of him. If he's still alive in the world I have no idea where or what he's doing. I hope he is alive, and enjoying his retirement in whatever way pleases him, but I don't know. Zudie probably knows, but he's never said, and somehow I don't feel I have the right to inquire.

The three of us all stayed at my house that night and most of the following day. We talked together in the kitchen until dawn, and then I folded, left Nika sheets and blankets for the foldout, and tottered off to my bedroom. It felt inexpressibly good to finally rest my chest. I was asleep at once, and slept like a stone.

For three hours, and then I had to get up to pee. One more of the many joys of aging. My bathroom is just a thin wall away from the guestroom bathroom. As I entered it I clearly heard a giggle from next door. A female giggle. The lewd kind. A kind I had never expected to hear from Detective Constable Nika Mandiç. After a moment of thought I tiptoed back to my bedroom, closing the door silently behind me, and peed out my open window, narrowly missing Fraidy the Cat.

I took half a Zopoclone before I laid back down, and this time I was out for a solid seven hours. I woke feeling terrific, except for a *really* full bladder, to find that my house was empty, and only the guestroom bed showed signs of having been slept in. A note on the stove said only, "Back later, Pop," and when Jesse did return just after dark, alone, he did not mention Nika and I didn't raise the subject.

Where, if anywhere, they've taken it from there, I couldn't say. Jesse has been back in New York for a couple of months, now . . . trying to make some very hard choices, I think. We did—finally—get stoned together on Kootenay Thunderfuck before he left, and it was as nice as I'd hoped. Nika is still on the force, serving and protecting Vancouver; how well she's doing at it, I don't really know for sure. I called her a couple of times . . . but we don't really have a lot in common to talk about, and hardly any of what we do is safe to talk about on the phone. She doesn't seem eager to come back out to Heron Island any time soon, and I can't say that I blame her.

Zudie and I did two of those videoconferences, for over an hour apiece, but then he e-mailed me that he had to make a trip to an unspecified destination, and would be gone for a few months, so I can't tell you with any assurance where he is, or what he's doing there or how it's going. And like I said, Agent Pitt/Tom/Billy could be anywhere, or nowhere.

When you come down to it, I don't really know a hell of a lot about much at all, I guess.

But some things I do know. My emotionally damaged friend Zandor Zudenigo is finally on the mend, starting to forgive himself for what he did to Allen Campbell four years ago in my living room. Thanks in large part I think to the sincere praise of a fellow professional she respected, my seriously-uptight friend Nika Mandiç has begun to lighten up a little and forgive herself for condoning and abetting what Zudie did. My son Jesse never really did stop loving me, and, for whatever miraculous reasons I care not, has finally started to forgive me for not making his mother stay longer than she wanted.

And after all these years, my Susan has finally started coming to me in my dreams, happy and proud of both of us, and it helps. It really helps.

That's enough to know for now. I've got a column to write.

—30—